Destined

To

Change

By Lisa M. Harley

Published by Lisa M. Harley

Copyright 2013 © Lisa M. Harley

All Rights Reserved.

This is a work of fiction. All characters, organizations, and events portrayed in this novel are either products of the author's imagination or are used fictitiously. Any resemblance to actual persons, living or dead, events, or locales is entirely coincidental.

All rights reserved. This book or any portion thereof may not be reproduced or used in any manner whatsoever without the express written permission of the author, except for the use of brief quotations in a book review.

This ebook is licensed for your personal enjoyment only. This ebook may not be re-sold or given away to other people. If you would like to share this book with another person, please purchase an additional copy for each person. If you're reading this book and did not purchase it, or it was not purchased for your use only, then please return to Amazon.com and purchase your own copy. Thank you for respecting the hard work of this author.

The author acknowledges the trademarked status and trademark owners of various products referenced in this work of fiction, which have been used without permission. The publication/use of these trademarks is not authorized, associated with, or sponsored by the trademark owners.

Dedication

First and foremost, I would like to thank my family. They have supported me in making my dream of writing a novel, become a reality. I have to give a special thank you to my mom, who I really hope never reads this book...love you, mom.

I would like to thank my Destiny Darlin's: Alison Gaskin Bailey, America Matthew, Ana Duarte Zaun, Ciara Martinez, Crysti Perry, Drita Dusovic Kinic, Kimberly Shackleford, MaryBeth Provence, Megan Hand, Michelle Tranberg Finkle, Rachael McClusky, Shannon Nemsi, Shawnte Borris, Stacy Bailey Darnell, Susan Pauloz Sunderlin, Virginia Tesi Carey, and Yvette Holguin Huerta. Without ya'll this book would've been a mess. You made me smile every day. And your fighting over Jaxon and Cade was truly awesome.

Cade would like to send a shout out to his Facebook group - Cade's Cuties: Alison, America, Ana, Drita, Kimberly, Megan, Shannon, Stacy (Even though Jaxon is hers.), Virginia, and Yvette. I couldn't believe Cade got his own Facebook group before the book even came out. Thank you so much Alison Gaskin Bailey for creating the group. And thank you America Matthew for finding the perfect pic of Cade. He really wishes he could push all of you up against the wall.

Jaxon would like to send a shout out to Rachael McClusky who loved him since his picture was posted on BDHM, and Stacy

Bailey Darnell (SBD) who staked her claim on him from the moment she read about him. STACY WILL CUT YOU!

This book wouldn't have happened without these ladies: R.L. Mathewson and Molly McAdams. Ya'll are the entire reason why I decided to write this book. I hope I made you proud.

I want to give a shout out to my buddies in: BDHM, Kindle Buddies, Book Broads, Book Lovers and More, and Write With Me.

Special thanks to Stacy Darnell (DSD) for keeping my Facebook page up and running, Shawnte' Borris - you should start a phone sex company – seriously, and Lynda Ybarra for answering all of my annoying questions.

I also have to thank the amazing Robin Harper from Wicked By Design for her amazing (and speedy) work on my cover. You are amazeballs!

Last but not least, I want to thank everyone who has liked my Facebook page. And to the Harley's Angels. Ya'll ROCK!

Don't forget your history, know your destiny - Bob Marley

Table of Contents

Prologue

Chapter 1

Chapter 2

Chapter 3

Chapter 4

Chapter 5

Chapter 6

Chapter 7

Chapter 8

Chapter 9

Chapter 10

Chapter 11

Chapter 12

Chapter 13

Chapter 14

Chapter 15

Chapter 16

Chapter 17

Epilogue

Destined to Succeed Prologue

About the Author

Prologue

Destiny...it's really an interesting thought isn't it? Destiny...

Mine was determined before birth. It was very simple. I was expected to graduate from high school, marry Declan Sharp, and have two kids. I would stay at home with them, while my husband worked on our family farm.

But wait, I'm getting ahead of myself...here is how my destiny started:

My parents, Samuel and Margaret Harper, known by everyone as Sam and Maggie, were best friends with Max and Louise Sharp. My dad met Uncle Max when they were kids. They grew up just down the road from each other and had always been best friends. My mom and Aunt Louise became fast friends when my mom moved to town from Los Angeles, California in the seventh grade. My mom said Aunt Louise made the culture shock less severe by always making her feel like she belonged.

The population of Kipton, Missouri is three hundred and seventeen. There is a diner, a gas station, and a post office. That's it. When I say it's a small town, I really mean it.

Now my dad would tell you the moment he saw my mom walk into the school with her bleach blonde hair and tight blue jeans, he fell head over heels in love with her. For mom, it took a bit more time. She admits she didn't completely fall in love with him until their freshman year when they were paired up in the

Homecoming court. My mom would never admit it, but I believed the fact that he was on a date with someone else was what did it. Although, she said it was the way he looked at her while they danced. Those big golden brown eyes danced with love for her and only her. Yep, that was what did it...

My Uncle Max joked that he and Aunt Louise had been together since Noah built the Ark. In actuality, they became a couple in fifth grade and had never been apart since.

Really the only sensible thing for these two couples to do was graduate high school, have a double wedding on New Year's Eve, and live on the family farms that my Dad and Uncle Max grew up on. So that was exactly what they did. They always dreamed of having children and they also dreamed about what those children would mean to each other.

My destiny was born on July first at midnight. His name was Declan Samuel Sharp. Yep, Uncle Max insisted his son be named after his best friend, my dad, Samuel. Declan was a beautiful baby. He had tons of dark hair and big crystal blue eyes that had a mischievous sparkle to them from birth. My Aunt Louise could definitely confirm that. Like clockwork my mom and dad welcomed a little blonde haired, brown eyed girl into the world on, July first the following year. I was born in the morning though, if we had been born at the same time that would have just been weird. My name is Lorelei Maxine Harper. You guessed it, my dad had to name me after my Uncle Max.

I honestly don't remember a time that Declan and I weren't together. Every picture of me from when I was little had Declan in it. He was my destiny and I was his. We spent all of our time together at school and after school. We loved to go to the pond on my family's farm and just play. He loved to tease me with frogs, snakes, or whatever he could find to make me scream. That was actually how I got my first kiss.

I was ten years old, so Declan was eleven. He had just caused me to release a blood curdling scream when he *threw* a huge frog at me! I was freaking out and he came over and that's when he did it. He hugged me. It wasn't like he hadn't before, but this time was different. When he pulled away he gave me a little peck on the lips, and then, I was pretty sure he was going to start screaming. The look on his face was horrific. He looked scared to death. I didn't know what to do, so I did what any good country girl would do…I stomped on his foot and ran all the way back to my house.

I didn't see Declan again until the next day at school and, thank goodness, everything was back to normal. I didn't know what I would do if things changed between us…if only I had known how much things would change in the next few years.

Declan and I became an official couple on my fifteenth birthday. My mom and Aunt Louise held our normal joint birthday bash at the American Legion Building on Main Street. After the party, my best friend, Emma, and her boyfriend, who happened to be Declan's best friend, Eric, took us to the diner to meet up with some other kids from school.

"Emma, what's wrong with Declan today?" I asked.

"I don't know, but he is acting like a total nut job!" she said.

He had been staring at me all day, as if I had something on my face. It made me so self-conscious that I kept checking myself in the mirror all night.

"Hey, Dec, what's up with you today?" I heard Eric whisper to Declan.

"Nothin' man, I'm just thinkin."

I wondered what he could be thinking about that would get him so upset. I was a little worried. I thought maybe he was mad at me, but I couldn't think of anything I had done to make him angry.

When it was time to go home, I climbed into the cab of his old black pick-up truck and hoped that he would tell me what was wrong. We started driving back toward my house when I asked, "Declan, is everything okay?"

With that question, he pulled off onto the next dirt road and slammed on his brakes. I didn't know what to think. Was he mad at me? Had I done something to upset him?

When I looked over at him he was staring at me again, but his face looked different. His expression was soft and he reached over and ran his knuckles down my jaw. "Loralei, do you like me?"

"Of course I like you, Declan. You're my best friend."

His eyes looked so sad. It was like I had punched him or something. "No Loralei, do you *like* me? Because all I've been able to think about all day is kissing you."

I could only imagine what the look on my face told him. I was shocked, but not nearly as shocked as when he started to lean toward me and then softly pressed his lips to mine.

I couldn't close my eyes. What was happening? This would change everything forever. He pulled me closer and ran his fingers down my back and that was when it happened. I closed my eyes and let my best friend kiss me. And boy could he kiss! Where did he learn how to do *that*? The kiss became more intense and all of a sudden he licked my bottom lip and slid his tongue into my mouth! *Oh my God* Declan's tongue was in my mouth and well, I liked it. No, I *loved* it. It felt amazing. When he finally pulled away my heart was racing and we were both practically panting.

"That was some kiss, Dec," I said with a chuckle.

Then he added with his, what I just realized was sexy as hell, southern drawl, "It wasn't quite as scary as when I kissed ya the first time, sweetheart." He grabbed my hand and ran his thumb over my wrist.

"Lor, do you hate me now? Is this gonna mess everything up?"

"I couldn't ever hate you, Declan. You're my best friend. I can't imagine not having you in my life."

"I feel the same way, Lor. I just don't want things to change between us. I want us to stay best friends, but I can't quit thinking about you. Now that I've kissed ya, I don't think I'll ever be able to get that thought out of my mind. You are the most beautiful girl

I've ever seen and it's been killing me to watch the boys at school drool all over you. You don't even realize how amazing you are."

"You're crazy! Nobody drools all over me. I'm just the Plain Jane best friend of the school's star basketball player. I don't know what you've seen, but I think you might need glasses!"

Declan was beautiful. He was very athletic, with lots of muscles, shaggy black hair, and those amazing bright crystal blue eyes...they really were amazing. Nobody looked at me, and if they did it was only because there weren't that many girls in our school.

Declan pressed his forehead against mine and laughed. "I have something for you." He handed me a little purple box with a silver bow on it. When I opened it a tear came to my eye. It was a silver charm bracelet with 3 charms on it – an "L", a "D", and a silver frog, to remind me of our first kiss out by the pond. I couldn't help myself, I threw my arms around his neck and held him while I cried at his heartfelt gift. "If ya don't like it, Lor, I can take it back and you can pick something else out."

"No Declan I LOVE it. It's beautiful and..." I couldn't help myself, I kissed him. Hard.

From that moment on we were completely inseparable. We always knew we would end up together, but when it happened it was scary and amazing all wrapped up into one.

One Year Later

I was so excited to be turning sixteen years old. I was practically an adult now. Not only was it Declan and my birthday, it was also our one year anniversary. My mom and Aunt Louise held our annual joint birthday bash at the American Legion building last night. Tonight was also planned, Emma and Eric were throwing a huge bonfire party for me and Declan at the pond where we had our first kiss.

"This party is going to be *insane!*" Eric screamed at us when we pulled up. Declan had his arm around me and was squeezing me tight. I loved this gorgeous guy. He was my world and I was his and tonight was *the* night. Declan didn't know yet and he had never pressured me but I planned on giving myself to him tonight. I couldn't think of a better way to celebrate our birthday.

The party had been going on for hours and the beer was flowing. We'd seen a couple of fights and at least one girl threw up out by the pond. *Good times*. I had been trying all night to get the courage up to pull Declan aside and ask him to take me to his house. His parents were out of town at the big annual cattle sale that weekend and we would have the whole house to ourselves. I told my parents that I would be spending the night with Emma, and of course, she corroborated my story.

I walked up behind Declan and placed my arms around his neck and started kissing him below his ear. Then I whispered, "Are you about ready to get out of here?"

And with that my gorgeous boyfriend said in his sexy southern drawl, "Yes, ma'am." We hopped into his truck and started driving toward his house.

When we pulled onto the dirt road that lead to his house, I reached over and ran my hand along his jaw.

"Everything okay, sweetheart?" he asked.

"Yeah, baby, everything's fine. I just can't believe how lucky I am to have you for my boyfriend. I love you, Dec."

I thought that might scare him, I had never said it out loud before. Instead, he looked at me with those beautiful blue eyes shining in the moonlight and said, "I love you too, with all of my heart, Lor, forever." Those words did it. They literally melted my heart. This was it. He was mine, and I was his. After tonight, we would be even more connected to one another.

That long winding, tree lined drive back to his house had never seemed so long. Uncle Max and Aunt Louise had a beautiful home. It was a little more contemporary than my parent's house. It was grey brick and there was a huge porch all along the front of the house. They had built this house when Declan was a baby, after a fire took the old farmhouse. They lost most of their possessions, but everyone walked away without incident. Uncle Max always said he was just happy they hadn't been home at the time and that no one had been hurt.

When we walked into his house, we immediately started upstairs to Declan's room. As we walked upstairs, Declan held my hand. I was so engrossed with the pictures of us that lined the stairway. Aunt Louise loved to take pictures of us. Tons of them were displayed in that stairway. We were smiling in every picture. They made me realize how happy Declan and I were going to be for the rest of our lives. I was going to marry this man, have babies with him, and someday we would sit out on that big front porch and hold hands as we rocked in our rocking chairs and watched our grandkids play. All of these thoughts just solidified my decision to give myself to Declan tonight.

Declan and I had spent lots of time in his room alone. His parents totally trusted us. Besides that, they expected us to spend the rest of our lives together, so they didn't think a few stolen kisses in his bedroom were inappropriate. I honestly didn't think Declan had any idea of what I had planned tonight.

When we got upstairs, all of that confidence I felt in the stairway about our future disappeared, as the nerves kicked in. As we stood beside the bed looking at each other, I was almost shaking. Then I mumbled to myself, "I don't know if I can do this."

Declan said, "Do what, sweetheart?" I then realized I had made that comment out loud. "You know I don't expect us to do anything but sleep, Lor. I may steal a few kisses. I mean, I am a guy, but I would never ask you to do anything else, unless...? Do you want to do something *else*, Lor?"

I was so embarrassed I couldn't even look up at him. I thought to myself *come on Loralei...pull it together! This gorgeous, amazing guy loves you and you are going to spend forever with him. This is just one night...you can do this!* My personal pep talk made me a little more confident. I slowly took a step toward Declan, placed my arms around his neck and pressed my lips to his. I was so scared...I was surprised I didn't miss his mouth.

Our tongues were dancing and our hands were exploring each other. The kiss was amazing. It was like we both knew tonight was going to be different. We had made out every day, sometimes several times a day, for a year. This just felt different. The kiss seemed to last forever.

Before I knew it, I was unbuttoning his shirt and pushing it down his arms. When I finally got it off of him, I was pretty nervous. I threw it on the floor near the foot of the bed. Then, I grabbed the hem of my shirt and started to pull it over my head when Declan grabbed my hands and stopped me. I didn't know what to think. I didn't think I had done anything wrong. I was pretty new to this, but so was he. I couldn't understand why he was stopping.

Declan looked down at where our hands were intertwined along the hem of my shirt. He lifted my left hand in his right and rubbed it over my jaw. He let go of my other hand and used his to tuck a strand of hair behind my ear. Then, he released my hands and very slowly pulled my shirt over my head. I instinctively crossed my arms over my chest to cover my breasts when I realized they were barely covered by my white lacey bra.

Now, I had been nervous, but at this moment, I realized I was plum scared to death. This was really happening, and I had started it. What if I disappointed him? What if I didn't do it right? What if he decided after we did it that he didn't want to be with me anymore? All of these thoughts were completely freaking me out, but then I looked up. Declan was looking at me with this look. His eyes were sparkling and he was smiling. His look said everything I needed to hear. It told me that he loved me, it told me that this was going to perfect, and most importantly it told me that this was just the beginning of us.

All of my fear went away as I unhooked his belt buckle and started to unzip his jeans. He grabbed my hand to stop me, leaned down to my ear, and whispered, "Slow down, sweetheart. I'm not in any hurry."

He placed his hands high on my hips and slid my skirt down to the floor. When it hit the floor, I kicked it, and it landed on top of our shirts at the foot of the bed. Without taking his eyes off of mine, he leaned in, reached behind me and unclasped my bra. Then he slid it down my arms and tossed it into our ever growing pile of clothes.

Declan had felt me up before, but we had never been like this. He may have felt my breasts before, but he had never really seen them up close and personal. And my breasts were really large...DD's. I hated them, but judging by the look on his face, Declan was impressed. He took a step toward me and closed the gap between us. He kissed me and pressed his body against mine. I could feel how excited he was and the fear of disappointing him crept back up.

I had no idea what I was doing, but at least I wasn't the only virgin here. Declan didn't know what he was doing either, so we would just have to figure it out together.

We climbed into bed, and Declan laid down next to me. I had to giggle, because he was rather mesmerized by my breasts. I looked over, and he was just staring at them. "Do you like what you see, sweetheart?" I asked sarcastically. He just nodded and then looked at me and his eyes were so full of love, a little bit of lust too.

He held my gaze, "Are you sure about this, Lor?"

"Yes, Declan. I have never been more sure of anything in my life." After I said that, Declan took off his jeans and boxers.

He leaned over and kissed my neck. He ran his hand over my stomach and then gently squeezed my left breast. I heard a moan escape his lips. He nervously massaged my breasts and then he took my nipple into his mouth. He kept looking up at me, I assume to make sure he was doing okay. *Oh my god*, he was doing great.

I could feel something building. I wasn't sure what was happening, but the ache between my legs was getting pretty intense. Then he released my nipple. He reached down and ran his hand across the front of my white lace panties to pull them off. When his hand grazed me *there*, that intense ache turned into the most amazing thing I had ever felt. My back arched and I swear my eyes rolled back into my head. I had never felt anything like that before. I felt like I was floating.

Declan climbed up and lowered himself down onto me. He put his knee between my legs and pushed them apart so he could position himself where he needed to be. He pressed himself against me. *Oh my God*, he was so big. I think he could tell by the look on my face that I was scared. I blushed with what I was sure was a very deep shade of red, "Declan, I don't think that will fit. You know, *inside* me."

He laughed, "Sweetheart, I don't remember Mrs. Edgeller mentioning anything like that in health class."

I knew he was trying to act cool, but he was scared too. He caught my gaze and started to press himself into me. Once he started pressing into me, all of our fear went away. We were ready for this. This was how it was supposed to be. Declan and I were meant to be together.

Emma had told me how horrible it was when she had sex with Eric for the first time. She told me it hurt so bad that it wasn't even enjoyable. I was so afraid that it would be painful or scary. There was a little pain when he pushed through my virginity, but after we got past that, it was perfect. I really didn't think Emma and Eric did it right, because when Declan and I made love it felt truly magical. I know that sounds really cheesy, but we were so in sync with each other.

When we finished, Declan and I laid in each other's arms, knowing that life could never get better than this.

I heard a really annoying buzzing sound, but I was so comfortable lying in Declan's arms that I tried to ignore the noise I heard. Finally, I realized it was my phone. I crawled out of bed, grabbed my skirt from the pile of clothes at the foot of the bed, and pulled my cellphone out of the skirt pocket.

"Why are you bothering me, Ems? You know *I am busy* right now?" I said in my most hateful tone.

"Lor, Eric is so damn drunk. He's puking in the pond and I can't get him to leave. Can you guys come take him home? You know he always listens to Dec," Emma said nervously. She made a good point. Eric and Declan had been best friends their entire lives and if anyone could get him home safely, it was Declan.

"Sure, Ems. I just have to wake Declan up. Then, we'll get dressed and head back that way."

"Thanks, Lor...love ya lots," Emma said.

Declan had been awake and heard the entire conversation. "Let's go get his sorry ass and take him home so we can crawl back into this warm bed." He kissed my bare shoulder. "And if you aren't too sore, maybe we could do *that* again?" I just giggled and shook my head at him.

As much as we didn't want to leave the bed, we threw on our clothes and headed back to the bonfire party.

When we pulled up, the lights from the truck shone down on the pond. We could see Eric puking in the pond. Emma was standing behind him, yelling at him about how stupid he was. Declan ran over to help Eric. I walked over to Emma and tried to calm her down.

"Ems, breathe," I said as I wrapped my arm around her shoulders.

"I can't believe he did this tonight! Lor, sometimes he's such a jerk."

"Yeah, but you love that big jerk," I said with a little smile.

"Damn it, I do love that jerk." I could tell she was upset, but she was trying really hard not to be.

"Go on home. I don't want your parents to freak out. We'll get him home safe."

She got in her little purple Ford Escort and drove off toward her house. When Declan was sure that Eric was done puking, he threw him into the truck, and we headed toward his house.

Declan was holding on to Eric to make sure he didn't get sick inside the truck. About the time we got in the truck it had started raining. It was coming down so hard that I could barely see the road in front of me.

"Dec, it's really raining hard. I can't even see the road."

"Oh, it's not that bad, sweetheart. You're doing great. Just speed up a little, so we can get back to what we were doin' earlier," he said with a wink.

I knew it wasn't a good idea, but I listened to Declan and sped up. It was so dark and the rain was coming down hard. I couldn't see even two feet in front of the truck. All of a sudden the cattle were in front of us. The last thing I remember doing was slamming on the brakes. But I heard so much after that, breaking glass, crunching metal, and screams, so many screams. Then I must've lost consciousness, because the next thing I remembered was Eric standing over me crying. I sat up slowly and screamed, "DECLAN!" Then Eric cried even harder.

That was the moment my destiny was changed forever.

Chapter 1

Ten Years Later

To celebrate my twenty-sixth birthday, Emma forced me to go into town last night to a dance club. That was so not my idea of a fun time. Ems was always harping on me about not getting out enough. I finally caved and went with her.

Emma and I were so much more than best friends, we were like sisters. Eric and Emma have been in love since we were kids. They finally got married about five years ago. They very rarely fought, but last night Eric didn't want us to go out. He was worried about us going to a dance club alone. He hadn't been there before, and he just didn't think it was safe for us to go.

When he told Emma she couldn't go, of course, she was pissed, which made her even more bound and determined to go. That anger only fueled her fire to say the least, we closed the place down. They actually had to make us leave. We danced, we drank, and actually I kinda enjoyed myself. Sometimes, I forgot that I was only twenty-six. I was much too young to feel so damn old.

My birthday had always been a difficult time for me, it always took me back to that night…the night when everything changed.

I really didn't remember much about what happened right after the accident. I knew there was a lot of crying and people saying, "I'm sorry." I couldn't understand why everyone was saying that. It wasn't their fault. Why were they sorry? I was the one to blame - I was the one who killed my destiny. I was the one that put the man of my dreams in his grave. It was all my fault. I had caused the accident, I wrecked the truck, and everyone should hate me. Why did they keep hugging me and telling me it would be okay? Didn't they know this could never be okay? Didn't they understand what I had done?

The entire funeral was just a blur. The thing I remembered most was the smell of the funeral home. It permeated throughout my entire being and I would never forget it as long as I lived.

I remembered sitting on the pew, looking up at the steel grey casket with the baby-blue lining, and thinking to myself that this was like watching a really bad movie. I just kept thinking Declan would sit up and look at me and say, with that sexy southern drawl, "I'm sorry, Lor, this was just a really bad joke."

But of course, that never happened. I had to watch them put Declan in the ground as I listened to his favorite hymn being sung by his cousin Joan. *Amazing Grace*...God, I used to love that song, and even now when I heard it, I sobbed uncontrollably. Ten years had not lessened the blow of what happened that night.

"I really need to get out of this bed and get down to the barn," I said to myself. When I got to the barn, I saw our farmhand, Jake Marshall. Jake was a sweetheart. He had worked for my family for many years. He was just a good ole country boy. He was in his late fifties with graying hair and a little bit of a beer gut. But really what old cowboy doesn't have one of those.

Jake said in his deep, southern drawl, "Good morning ma'am, how are you feelin' this mornin'?"

"How do I look like I feel, Jake?" I muttered back at him.

He laughed and started filling me in on everything that had been going on overnight. I managed the Harper farm now, just like my parents had always planned. My dad loved to spend his time down at the pond, or playing with the little ones, Sammy and Mags. I was so glad that I could do this for my parents.

The farm had been self-sustaining for years and it really made me proud that I had a hand in that. We had 20,000 acres and more cattle than I could count. We raised only the best and our reputation had spread across the state.

I could feel my phone vibrating in my pocket. I answered and heard Emma say in her normal high pitched squeal, "How are you feeling this morning?"

"Not as good as you, apparently."

"Aww, don't be that way Lor, ya know you had a good time."

"Yeah, I did. Thanks for making me go. We really oughta do that more often."

"Hallelujah!" Emma said as she hung up the phone. She thought she had finally gotten through to me. My parents and Emma could not understand how I could possibly live without a husband.

My dad was always saying, "You need someone to take care of you, Lor. You do such a good job taking care of everyone else, but you deserve that too." I know that's true, but no man could ever live up to my Declan. I had never even looked at another man and felt anything remotely like what I felt for him.

So many things changed that night ten years ago. I couldn't go back to school. I just couldn't. I couldn't face the other kids or all of the memories of Declan that lived in those halls.

My mom and I decided that instead of just quitting school and working on the farm, she would home-school me until I felt like I could go back and graduate. I didn't want to tell Mom, but I was pretty sure that day would never come.

When it was time for my home-schooling to start that September, I felt like I was ready. My mom had gone to the school and got all my books and information. The first day of school had always been so exciting. Declan and I got to reconnect with all of our friends, and we could find new hidden places in our little school to sneak away for a make-out session. But that year was going to be so different.

On the morning I was supposed to start my homeschooling, I woke up feeling really crappy. It was like I had the flu or something. Mom came into my room and held a cold cloth on my head. She tried to bring me some breakfast, but when she walked in my room with the scrambled eggs she had made, I barely made it to the bathroom before the puking started. It was awful. I was so sick! Mom called Dr. Hudson's office and made an appointment for me for that afternoon.

I have always hated going to the doctor. I can't explain it, I just always had. We walked into the clinic and my stomach immediately flip-flopped. Just seeing all of the horrible, old paintings on the walls, the old green shag carpet, and the chairs in the lobby that probably hadn't been cleaned since before I was born, made me want to run away screaming.

Before we left the house, I had been feeling a little bit better. I had actually been able to keep down some toast, and my stomach hadn't felt quite as upset.

Dr. Hudson came in and started his normal exam. He took my temperature, checked my blood pressure, listened to my lungs, and pressed on my stomach to check for tenderness. When he pressed on my belly, it hurt. I gasped, and he looked at me funny, and then continued his exam.

He asked me all the normal doctor questions. I just wanted this to be over so I could go home. I just wanted him to give me a prescription and make me feel better. While I was thinking about what I was going to watch on TV as I laid in bed and recuperated from the bug, Dr. Hudson grabbed my knee and asked the question that made me get really nauseous again. "When was your last menstrual cycle, Loralei?"

Oh my god! I hadn't even realized it. I had been so upset over what happened to Declan I hadn't even thought about myself.

My mouth was so dry. I could barely get out a response, but I finally said, "I'm not really sure."

Then Dr. Hudson asked a question that made me even sicker. "Is it possible? I mean, is there any way you could be pregnant, Loralei?"

Oh my god! At that point my mom was looking at me with tears in her eyes. I think she already knew what I was trying so hard not to answer.

After what seemed like forever, I responded, "Yes, I could be."

When we had sex, Declan and I hadn't used protection. Everyone told me you couldn't get pregnant the first time, and I was so naïve, I believed them. So, after a simple blood test Dr. Hudson informed me that I was pregnant. He guessed my due date would be around the end of March. That would be about right.

"*Mom*!" Mags screamed at me from across the field.

"What's wrong, sweetie?"

"Sammy hit me and then he hid my iPod!"

"*Sammy*!" I screamed. "Give your sister back her iPod right now!"

"But, mom, she bit me."

"LIAR! I nipped you. I didn't bite you. You little wuss."

"Don't talk to your brother like that, Mags." Oh my goodness, these kids were going to be the death of me, but I really didn't know what I would do without them. I had fulfilled my destiny, well almost. It had been done just a little out of order though.

I had my babies on March first, exactly eight months to the day of the accident. They were preemies, and they were so tiny.

Margaret (Mags) Louise Sharp weighed 3 pounds and 9 ounces, and her brother Declan Samuel Sharp Jr. (Sammy) weighed in at a whopping 4 pounds 8 ounces.

Mags was born with blonde hair like me, and Sammy had black hair like Declan, but both babies got Declan's amazing blue eyes. My dad told me at the hospital right after they were born, "I know I'm prejudiced, but those are the most beautiful babies I've ever seen."

"Well, Gramps, I would have to agree with you. My babies are the most beautiful babies ever born!" They really were the most beautiful little creatures. I couldn't believe Declan and I had made these two little perfect pieces of us.

Sammy looked just like Declan. Mags had his eyes, but she looked more like me. Sammy was a little Declan. He was a mischievous little brat, but he was my brat.

I graduated high school in May, a year early but my mom had homeschooled me all through the pregnancy, and I was ready to be done with that part of my life. I was a new mom of twins, and I just needed to be done with school, so I worked my butt off and got it done. My parents decided I should just spend time with the babies for the first year.

I continued to live with my mom and dad, and my babies made everything better. After I lost Declan, I could hardly get out of bed, but once the twins came and I saw those crystal blue mischievous eyes looking back at me, I just melted. They were ours. We made them. And now I would always have a part of Declan with me.

I had been managing the family farm since I was eighteen years old. When my dad told me I was ready, I didn't believe him, but apparently he was right. The farm had always made a living for our family, but once I took over we bought a couple of the surrounding farms and started to really do well for ourselves.

The twins and I moved into one of the old farmhouses we bought when we added on to the farm. It was a big two story white farmhouse with a porch that wrapped all the way around it. My dad and Uncle Max helped me remodel it, and now it is the home I always dreamed of having. The kids had plenty of space to run and play, and they definitely made good use of the over 20,000 acres we owned. Grandpa Max had built a huge playhouse in our backyard with a castle on one side for Mags and a fort on the other for Sammy.

Grandpa Max and Granny Louise loved the twins so much. I had caught Granny Louise crying while watching Sammy play on more than one occasion. It was such a blessing to have them so close to us. The kids got to spend a ton of time with them, and I think that really helped them not miss Declan so much. The twins were that last remaining piece of their son, and they couldn't have loved them anymore than they did. My kids were blessed with two amazing sets of grandparents.

Mags was a little shy and quiet around strangers, but I thought she would come into herself soon. Sammy was already a star basketball player, and he was only nine years old. He had played since pre-school and he was a natural, just like his dad.

Emma and Eric had been great friends to me. Eric had taken on so many of the duties that a father would normally handle. He helped me teach the kids how to ride a bike, he taught Sammy how to play basketball, and he was always there to have a tea party with Mags. The kids adored their Aunt Emma and Uncle Eric. Emma was always more than just a friend to me...she was like my sister. And when she and Eric got married that didn't change, like we worried it would, it actually intensified.

Eric was always very protective of me and the kids. On the very few dates I ever went on, Eric always got to know the guy first, and I am pretty sure he had a discussion with him before and after our date. Maybe even during on a couple of occasions.

Once, I had gone on a date with a guy we had gone to high school with, and this guy tried to get more than a little fresh with me. Eric never mentioned it, but the next day, I received a huge bouquet of flowers from the guy with an apology and a promise to never to call again. When I saw him a few days later, he was sporting one hell of a black eye. I didn't have to ask and he didn't have to tell me, I knew Eric had handled it for me. He was like the big brother I never had.

After my night out with Emma, I was really feeling old. I did have a good time though, and my parent's loved watching the twins. I knew that I needed to get out more, and I needed to meet someone. If not for me, for my kids. They needed a dad, and they needed me to be happy. I don't know who I was trying to kid, but I knew that I would never be happy with any other man besides Declan. He was it for me, and now, I had two great kids to remind me of him.

I rubbed my fingers over the charms on the bracelet Declan gave me. It now included two baby carriage charms, one with a pink stone and one with a blue stone. I never took it off, even when I was working out on the farm.

Chapter 2

I hopped on a four-wheeler and headed out to the back edge of the property to check on Jake who was mending fence. The ride out there was invigorating. I always loved riding across the property and surveying our land. It brought me great joy.

Our property was huge. This time of year it was always so pretty and green with the rolling hills and the beautiful red maple trees decorating the property. Autumn on the farm was my favorite time of the year. When the leaves started to change colors, it made our property look like a picture perfect postcard.

When I got closer to where Jake was working, I noticed there was another man out there working with him. I was still pretty far away, but I could already tell he was built, and when I say "built" I mean, he was *huge*. He had muscles on his muscles. As I got closer, I also noticed his ass, his gorgeous "you could bounce a quarter off of that" ass.

When he heard me riding up, he turned toward me. My lady parts did a little dance they hadn't done in ten long years. This man was gorgeous, really beautiful. He had kinda shaggy dark brown hair, huge deep brown eyes. He was wearing skin tight blue jeans, not Wranglers, but "fancy pants", which is what my dad called any jeans that weren't Wranglers, and a black Metallica t-shirt. His arms were covered in tattoos and his eyebrow was pierced. I had to chuckle, because he looked so out of place standing out there in the middle of the herd mending fence with Jake.

I climbed off of the four-wheeler and walked up to Jake and this sexy stranger. He couldn't take his eyes off of me. He just kept staring. I mean what the hell, I knew I looked a little rough after my night out with Emma, but it wasn't like I was gross or anything. His eyes seemed to be glued to me. It actually weirded me out a little bit.

"Loralei, come here. I want to introduce you to my nephew, Jaxon Daniels. He just got into town from California." Jake said. Jaxon made a grunting sound and then turned around and walked back toward the fence. "He's having a hard time right now kid, sorry, about that."

I wasn't sure what to think of this guy, so I asked curiously, "What's he doing here, Jake? Is he staying with you?"

"It's a long story hon, but he's gonna be working with me for a bit. Your dad said it was okay as long as he stayed out of trouble."

I shrugged my shoulders. "If it's fine with ya'll, I guess it's fine with me too."

Jaxon

Shoveling shit at six o'clock in the morning had not been my idea of getting away from everything, but apparently, Uncle Jake had other ideas.

"I got no problem with ya staying here, son. But you gotta earn your keep."

"Sorry, sir. I shouldn't be complaining. I really appreciate you letting me stay here. I needed to get my ass out of Richmond."

"You can stay as long as you need. But we'll work some of that city right outta ya." He laughed, and then threw me a pair of gloves. "These will help with the blisters."

I sure never thought my life would come to this. Living in podunk Missouri on a fucking farm. This wasn't part of my plan. But my plan had been totally screwed.

I had just finished my shoveling when Uncle Jake yelled at me from outside. I walked out and he threw me the keys to a four-wheeler. "Let's go. I'll take ya on a tour."

We started riding out through the field. Harper Farms was huge. I didn't realize how big twenty-thousand acres really was. I mean it sounded big, but this was crazy. And, so many cows. I had never seen this many cows in my entire life. I didn't think the entire state of California had as many cows as the Harper's had. They had a ton of horses too, but they were mostly up by the horse barn.

I had to admit it, this place was beautiful. It was so serene. Didn't I need that now? After everything that happened before I left home. Yes - the answer was yes. This was exactly what I needed. I needed to get away and not think about anything for a while.

Uncle Jake stopped and motioned for me to come over his way. "We're gonna have to fix this up. The herd could get out." He was pointing at a piece of fence that had been knocked down.

"Just tell me what I need to do," I told him as he grabbed some tools and wire and we started fixing it up.

Soon, I heard another four-wheeler coming up behind us. I figured it was one of the farmhands, so I didn't turn around. Uncle Jake turned to me and said, "Be on your best behavior. The boss is here."

When I turned around, and saw her, I immediately thought, *Oh shit*! This couldn't be happening. I was trying to get away from stuff. I couldn't be starting anything up, but damn, she was beautiful. Long blonde hair pulled up in a ponytail, tight blue jeans, and a red Waylon Jennings t-shirt. *Shit.*

Uncle Jake tried to introduce me to her, but that was the last thing I wanted to do. I walked over to her. She said something to me and I grunted at her, and then headed back to the fence. I knew I was rude. I came off as a total ass. But that was the way it had to be. A hot ass country woman was the last thing I needed right now.

Loralei

After my run-in with Jaxon and Jake, I headed back to my parent's house. All I could think about was the way Jaxon had looked at me. I didn't know what was wrong with me. I had never had thoughts about another man like that. All I could think about were those tattoos on Jaxon's arms. I blushed and bit my lower lip, holding back my smile, as I thought about bouncing a quarter of his ass.

What in the world had come over me? I was becoming one of those sex crazed women. That was so unlike me. There was just something about Jaxon that made me well, want to lick his face. *Oh my god!* I wanted to lick his face. Something was definitely not right with me.

Thank goodness, I wouldn't have to spend much time with him. I didn't think I could stand being close to him, when I was having all of these thoughts about him. The only other man I had ever thought about like that was Declan. Sigh, Declan. How could I think about another man like that?

Yep, something wasn't right. I needed to talk to Emma about this.

I picked up the phone and dialed her number. "Ems, something's wrong with me."

"What's going on, Lor?"

"I just met Jake's nephew, Jaxon. He's going to be working here for a bit." I described him to her, and then said, "I want to lick his face." I immediately regretted saying those words. That was Emma's catch phrase.

Every time she saw a hot guy, she would scream, "I wanna lick his face!" I didn't say things like that, though. Jaxon was making me think and say all kinds of things I didn't normally do. There was just something about him that made me feel tingly. His tattoos and piercings were so different to me. We didn't see things like that in Kipton. And those muscles - *wow!*

Emma started screaming at the top of her lungs, "Oh my god, finally! I have never been so happy, Lor! You're having feelings for a man! Finally, you wanna lick someone's face and hopefully other body parts too."

That last statement embarrassed me to death. I could feel my cheeks warming up and I knew they were turning a dark crimson. "Ems, I do, but I'm not going to do anything about it. You know I can't be with someone like that." *Or someone at all.*

Emma spent the next fifteen minutes explaining the benefits of sex to me. She informed me that I didn't have to marry him; I could just have a fling and get it out of my system. Then, I could marry some nice, safe local guy. She was sure there were tons of men around who wanted to marry me. I was pretty sure she was crazy, but I let her keep her delusions.

Of course, I had been asked out before, but every time I went out with someone, it always ended the same way, with me thinking about Declan. My feelings for him were so strong, that I wasn't able to move past them.

I hadn't really even kissed any other man, but Declan. Honestly, I never thought I could. Now that I had met Jaxon maybe I could. Something about him made me want to know what his lips would feel like against mine.

I couldn't think about him anymore. I just wanted to enjoy my afternoon in peace. It was so nice to have the house to myself. Uncle Max and Aunt Louise had taken the kids into town for their weekly movie and ice cream outing, so I had the whole afternoon to myself. What to do? A bath...that sounded heavenly.

I started the water and decided to add a little of the lilac scented bubble bath Ems gave me for my birthday. The water was warm and causing the mirror to steam up. The entire room smelled of lilacs...*heavenly.*

I took off my clothes and slid down into the warm water. It felt so good. I could feel the tension slipping out of my shoulders. I was becoming so relaxed. I really needed this, especially after my run-in with Jaxon today. I also needed the large glass of wine I had brought with me. Not to mention the glass I had before I had the wonderful idea to take this bath.

As I was soaking my mind started wandering. I started thinking about Declan. Thinking about that night we spent together. How it felt when he made love to me. I closed my eyes and gently caressed my breasts. I could feel him touching me. I could feel his lips kissing my neck. His fingers were massaging my breasts. He was kissing me lower and lower...this was new. Declan hadn't done this when we made love.

In my fantasy I could hear Declan whisper, "It's okay, sweetheart. I love you." I was touching myself, imagining Declan. My breathing was labored, little moans were escaping my lips, and just as I was about to explode with pleasure, the face in my fantasy changed. It was no longer Declan, it was Jaxon. He was touching me. His mouth was kissing me. His fingers were on my breasts. I screamed and jumped up so fast that I slipped and just barely caught myself before I fell out of the tub.

I wrapped myself in a towel and ran into my bedroom. I sat down on the bed and tried to figure out why that happened. What was wrong with me? Why was I thinking about him like that? I had always only thought of Declan in that way. I didn't even know this man. He was making me feel something. Something that I hadn't even thought about feeling in years. I didn't know what I was going to do, but I knew that I needed to stay away from Jaxon.

On Sundays, my whole family attended the First Baptist Church of Kipton. Church day was the day we dressed up in our Sunday best and listened to the pastor preach. Afterwards, we would eat a big hearty lunch made by mom and Aunt Louise, while the kids played outside, weather permitting of course. Sunday was also a day of rest. That was a big rule in our family and we always abided by it.

When the kids and I walked into church, I was immediately drawn to the back pew on the left side. Jaxon and Jake were sitting there whispering when Jaxon looked over at me. Our eyes met and he quickly looked down. He looked agitated. He was fidgeting with his tie. With his white dress shirt on, all of his tattoos were covered - *damn it*. I shouldn't be thinking about this man's tattoos, especially not while I was at church. I had never even liked tattoos. I didn't understand why his were turning my mind to mush.

I kept telling myself that I could do this. I just couldn't look back at him. *I couldn't turn around.* I suddenly started having flashbacks to the incident in the tub. *I should not be thinking about stuff like that in church.* I told myself. I could feel the red creep up my cheeks.

We took our place on the second row with my and Declan's parents. I swore I could feel his eyes on me. My body was reacting to his stare. My cheeks were flushed and I started sweating. I had to fan myself with the church bulletin.

My plan was a solid one. I would stay away from Jaxon. I needed to keep enough distance between us so that I wouldn't feel the need to lick his face or any other parts of his body. I slid down in the pew. I was so embarrassed. *Oh my God* - I was going to go to hell. I was having thoughts of licking a man while sitting in church sandwiched between my kids and their grandparents - yep, definitely going to hell.

Jaxon

I hadn't been to church in years. Uncle Jake insisted that not only I go, but I wear a damn tie. I felt like a freak. I had on my black jeans, a white dress shirt, and the fucking tie I borrowed from Uncle Jake. We walked in the church and I shuddered. Half the shit I'd done, I was surprised it didn't burst into flames when I walked in. But I was working on that. I didn't want to be a bad ass anymore. I wanted to be normal, or as normal as a fucked up guy like me could be.

"Mornin' Jake, this must be your nephew, Jaxon was it?" an older gentlemen asked Uncle Jake, while reaching his hand out to mine.

"Jaxon Daniels, nice to meet you," I said, as I shook his hand.

"Sam Harper, and this is my wife Maggie." He said as he gestured to a beautiful, blond woman standing next to him.

"Pleasure to meet you, Jaxon. What brings you to our little town?" Maggie asked.

I started to answer, but Uncle Jake interrupted, "Just needed to get this boy out of the big city for a little while. Ain't that right, son?" I nodded.

"Well, Jake, I expect you and Jaxon to come over for lunch after church." Uncle Jake started to say something and Maggie stopped him, "I won't take no for an answer. We'll see ya'll right after church."

"Yes, ma'am," Uncle Jake said as he motioned for me to sit down on the back row with him.

The fucking tie was still driving me crazy. "Leave it alone, son. You're in the house of the Lord. You can take it off in a few minutes," Uncle Jake whispered.

I nodded, but I couldn't quit messing with it. That's when I saw her walk in. Damn, she looked amazing. Our eyes met for just a minute. She was blushing and I smiled, thinking, *I did that.* I watched her and her kids walk up and sit down with her parents and another older couple. I wasn't sure who they were, but they were spoiling the hell out of those kids, so I assumed they were they're grandparents too.

I couldn't quit staring at her. If I wasn't going to hell before, I sure was now. I shouldn't be thinking about the things I was thinking about doing to her, while we were in church. I noticed she was sweating a little and still blushing. I thought maybe she was having some of the same thoughts about me.

She finally kinda slid down in the pew. Wasn't she cute? She actually thought she could hide from me. When I wanted something, I got it. I could see right now that I was in trouble.

After church, we went to the Harper's house for lunch. I was pretty excited about it. I had been really nervous this morning. I had never been much of a people person. So, the thought of spending an afternoon with a bunch of people I didn't really know, had not appealed to me until…well, it wouldn't be so bad to spend the afternoon around Loralei.

Trying really hard not to make eye contact with anyone, I walked through the front door. She was standing in the kitchen looking even sexier than she had earlier. I couldn't tear my eyes away from her.

I started at her toes, which were painted light pink, and headed up, and up, until I got to her breasts. Then my eyes stopped. *Wow!* I was in so much trouble with this one. Finally, I made it to her eyes. *Shit!* She'd caught me staring. She blushed again. I was beginning to really love that blush.

Uncle Jake grabbed me by the arm and started walking me toward the living room. "I don't think that's a good idea, son." He whispered, once we were out of earshot.

"I don't know what you're talking about." I couldn't even look him in the eye. He knew, that I knew, exactly what he meant.

"That girl's had a hell of a time. She don't need any shit. If you ain't serious, you stay away, kay?"

That was that. I needed to stop this shit right now. I had enough baggage without taking on someone else's.

<u>Loralei</u>

Sunday dinner at my parent's house after church was our weekly tradition. Their home was the largest and oldest on the property. The house was a two-story farmhouse. They had completely remodeled it a few years ago. It was similar to mine, only much bigger. It was painted a beautiful buttercup yellow with white shutters. Each window had a flower box filled with bright flowers, mostly purple tulips, because that was mine and my mom's favorite color. The long winding drive was lined with apple trees. The kids loved to pick those apples, and the trees always smelled so good. I had many amazing memories of this house. It would always be my home.

I didn't know why I was surprised when Jake and Jaxon walked in today. Of course my mom invited them. She was too nice sometimes. She couldn't have Jaxon and Jake sitting at home while we were eating a good ole home-cooked meal.

Jaxon had removed his tie and rolled his sleeves up, and I finally got a closer look at his tattoos. They were so intricate; all I could think about was running my hands over his arms. I wanted to look at them up close and personal, but I could never do that. So, I decided I would just admire them from across the room.

I was standing in the kitchen when I caught Jaxon as his eyes looked me up and down, lingering just a little bit longer than they should have on my breasts. When our eyes met, the stare lingered, before I broke it by looking away. I may not have been the most beautiful woman, but I had to admit my body wasn't bad.

Jaxon's eyes lingered on my DD's, and it took me back to the night Declan died. The way he was so enamored with them when we made love. I chuckled out loud as I remembered him lying beside me and just staring at them. My chuckle was quickly followed by a tear. I still couldn't think about that night without crying. I hoped no one noticed, but I saw Jaxon's face, and I knew he did. He must've thought I was crazy. Maybe he only thought I was a normal hormonal crazy woman. I could only hope.

We had sat down at the table when Sammy walked over to Jaxon and said, "Mister, what's that thing on your face?" He pointed at his eyebrow piercing. I immediately cringed. Why, oh why, did my little man always feel the need to play twenty questions with strangers? I would never forget the time he asked the gentleman selling Shih Tzu puppies on the square downtown if their name meant they "shit" all the time. I tried so hard not to laugh at that one. He definitely had inherited his dad's sense of humor.

Jaxon looked a little startled by my son. "It's a ring. I have my eyebrow pierced."

Sammy countered with, "Why would you do a thing like that?"

"Because I wanted to have my eyebrow pierced, kid."

Sammy looked like he was really thinking hard about something. "Do you have your penis pierced too?" *Holy hell*, my son had not just asked that question. I was just praying that someone would wake me up from this horrible nightmare, but no, no they didn't. It happened, and I needed to fix it, but all I really wanted to do was crawl under the dining room table and die of embarrassment. I was trying really hard to pick my jaw up off of the floor.

All of the conversations around the room ended. Everyone was staring at me as if to say "do something now."

Jaxon looked over at me with a sexy grin. He winked and told my son, "I don't really think we should talk about penises at the dinner table, little man."

That wasn't really an answer, but it was good enough to make Sammy move over to my mom, "Do we have any chocolate pie, Granny?"

My mom grabbed him and took him into the kitchen to get a piece of pie. I couldn't look up. I could feel Jaxon staring at me again. My cheeks were on fire. I really thought I would die of embarrassment right there at the dinner table. I looked over at Jaxon, who was still grinning, and said, "Sorry about that. He's kinda inquisitive."

"No problem. I probably look a little a different than the guys he's used to seeing."

I didn't know what to say to that, so I just shrugged my shoulders and got up to go see what Sammy was getting into in the kitchen. After that embarrassing ordeal, the rest of lunch was pretty uneventful.

After lunch, we headed out to the pond and fished for a bit. It had always been one of my favorite places to be. Going there always brought my stress level down several notches. I loved to go to the pond in the evening. To see the moonlight glistening on the water, hear the crickets chirp, and see the fireflies sparkling. It was so soothing and serene. It was a rather large pond with a little white dock that my dad and Uncle Max built for the kids to fish off of.

The kids had a blast, and I think Jaxon did too. Nobody caught anything, but that didn't matter, we always just threw them back anyway. Everyone was standing around, chatting, and having fun.

Jaxon helped Mags when her line got stuck in a tree. She looked like she was scared of him. I didn't know if it was the tattoos or the piercings or just the fact that he was a stranger. Finally, he leaned over and whispered something in her ear and she smiled. Then she didn't look so scared of him anymore. She smiled every time she looked at him.

When she came over to get a drink of iced tea from me, I asked, "Honey, you looked like you were a little scared of Jaxon. Do you think he's scary?"

"I did, mommy, but he's really not. He told me that Jake was his uncle, you know, like Uncle Eric is my uncle? Then he told me he was really glad he was here to help me get my line out of the tree. He's so tall, mommy. He didn't even hardly have to jump! Jaxon said he was sorry if his tattoos scared me." She leaned in and whispered, "They really aren't scary at all, mommy, they're kinda cool. Oh, and he told me I was really pretty just like you mommy." Then Mags looked up at me with her beautiful blue eyes sparkling and said, "I think he likes you, mommy."

Holy hell. He told my daughter I was pretty, and now she thinks he likes me. There was no way that was true. I was sure he just told Mags that so she wouldn't be scared of him. There was no way he thought I was pretty, but he did stare at me a lot.

Watching Jaxon play with my kids was not making my thoughts about him go away. Even Sammy really liked him. And it was hard to get into Sammy's good graces sometimes. He had a huge heart, but he loved to give people grief.

I thought I might be starting to like him a little bit too. But I couldn't stop the feeling of guilt from rearing up. Sammy and Mags were Declan's kids. How could I enjoy watching them have a good time with Jaxon? It felt like I was betraying Declan just by thinking about Jaxon. But to think about him being around the kids felt like I was completely betraying him.

Chapter 3

Loralei

It had been exactly two weeks since that day at the pond. I had only seen Jaxon once, and it was just in passing. I hadn't made it to Sunday dinner last week because the kids had a stomach bug, but Mom told me I hadn't missed anything.

Today we went straight to my parents' house after church for lunch. This time Jaxon went home and changed into jeans and a green Aerosmith t-shirt before lunch.

I heard Jaxon tell my mom, "Mrs. Harper, I apologize for my appearance, but I couldn't stand to wear that damn tie a minute longer."

My mom chuckled, "It's okay, hon. That thing looked like it was strangling you to death anyway!"

Of course, Mom didn't have a problem with his appearance. She raised me to believe that it didn't matter what someone wore or how they looked on the outside; what really mattered was what was inside. She definitely saw something in Jaxon, but for the life of me I didn't know what it was. He was really sexy, but that better not have been what my mom liked about him...*ewww*.

She had called me last night and told me to wear a pretty dress to church today. I always dressed up for church, but usually I would wear slacks and a blouse. She insisted I wear a dress. I relented and wore a white lacey dress with little pink flowers around the hem. I felt so girly - I hadn't felt that way in a long time.

I even spent a little extra time curling my hair, which now lays all the way down my back, and I wore a little eye shadow – I actually looked like a girl, instead of a farmer. It was almost like I was dressing up for someone. Subconsciously, I probably was. I knew Jaxon would be at church, and I enjoyed the thought of him liking what he saw.

Lunch went by with no awkward questions from my children, which was really nice. Unexpected, but nice. I believed they were still a little weak from their stomach bug and didn't have the energy to cause a scene. After lunch, my mom informed me that Jaxon and Jake were driving into town to pick up some supplies, and she wanted me to go with them.

"Why do I need to go? They're grown men who are perfectly capable of getting supplies without me."

"Honey, just go and have a good time. Maybe you and Jaxon can get to know each other a little bit better. Jake says great things about him. He's had some problems, but he seems to be doing better here. Jake thinks he just needed to get out of the big city and relax for a bit."

"Mom, I don't want to get to know him. And what problems? Is he in trouble or something? And besides that, I have a million things to do today, and I have to take care of the little monsters."

My mom gave me her best "I am your mother, stop arguing with me face." "Lor, I'll keep the kids, and there's nothing that you need to do that can't be put off until tomorrow. I don't know what's going on with him, but Jake seems to think staying here will be good for him. Honey, I just want you to be happy. I see the way Jaxon looks at you. It wouldn't hurt anything to get to know him a little better. Declan wouldn't want you to be alone."

That last statement made my breath hitch. "Mom I'm not alone. I have Mags and Sammy and I just don't want to complicate things."

Mom huffed, exasperated. "I'm not taking no for an answer, honey, you're going into town with them. Now go get prettied up, and they'll pick you up after lunch."

Great. I was twenty-six years old, and my mommy still told me what to do. The worst part about it was, I normally listened.

I tried to come up with a reason why I couldn't go into town. But as hard as I tried, I couldn't think of anything. So, I pouted to my mom, went home, and got ready. Then I patiently waited for Jake and Jaxon to pick me up. *Get prettied up?* Uh, no. We were going shopping, not to a party. I put on a pair of blue jeans, my brown cowboy boots, and a light tan sweater. My hair was still curled from this morning, so I piled it loosely on my head in a bun, with some tendrils hanging down on both sides.

I heard the old pick-up truck roaring down my drive, and I went out the front door. Much to my surprise, Jaxon was alone in the truck. It was not Jake and Jaxon, nope. It was just Jaxon and Loralei. *Shit!*

My mom had totally set me up.

Jaxon flashed that sexy smile, "Ready to go?"

"Um, isn't Jake coming with us?"

Jaxon looked a little confused. "Uh, no your mom said you wanted me to drive you to town to pick up some supplies. Don't you still need a ride?"

I couldn't believe her. I decided I would exact my revenge on her soon. For now I needed to figure out how to handle this situation.

"Nope, mom told me that you and Jake were going into town to get supplies, and I should go with you."

Jaxon laughed, shooting me the sexiest damn look I had seen in a long time. "Sounds to me like your mom wants us to have some alone time. Why do you think that is?"

Holy hell.

I didn't know what to say to that, so I just climbed in the cab of the truck and pretended his sexy little grin wasn't affecting me. Because it wasn't - it couldn't be, right? Oh hell, I didn't know what to think. This man was seriously hot and sexy. So – damn - sexy. I thought to myself *my lady parts deserve to be happy, don't they*? I decided to get through this trip without any embarrassing experiences, and we would be home before I knew it.

The forty-five minute trip into town seemed like it took hours. We barely spoke. If it hadn't been for the classic rock playing on the radio, the entire trip would have been silent. Jaxon and I didn't make eye contact. He looked straight ahead with his hands perfectly at ten and two on the steering wheel.

As much as I tried to not think about him, I couldn't help myself. He was so close and he smelled so amazingly good. His scent was hard to describe. It just screamed *man*.

I started fantasizing about what it would be like for him to kiss me - to press those beautiful lips against mine. And what it would feel like when he slipped his tongue into my mouth, or how amazing it would feel to have him touch my breast, or for him to unzip my jeans and slide his hand down...

Finally, from the corner of my eye, I caught him sneaking a peek at me. I wondered what he was thinking. I was so embarrassed. My cheeks were bright red and my heart was about to beat out of my chest. I was worried that he somehow knew what I had been thinking about. But apparently that wasn't the case.

Jaxon asked me the one question I had hoped I wouldn't have to answer, "So, where's the twins' dad?" That question completely squashed all of the amazing fantasies I had been having about Jaxon and brought me back to the real world, real quick.

I couldn't believe he was asking me this question. Didn't Jake or my mom or anybody in this little town tell him? I said the only thing that came to mind, "Dead," I deadpanned as I fixed my eyes straight ahead of me. That was it. That was all I had to say about it. Jaxon looked baffled. He didn't mutter another word all the way into town. I just sat there wondering why I had said that. There were so many other things I could have said or I could have explained what happened, but I didn't do it. *Dead* seemed to sum it all up.

After the shopping was done - in complete silence - we headed out to the parking lot. Jaxon noticed the little, dingy dive bar across the street.

"Wanna grab a beer before we head back?"

"I don't think that's a good idea. We have a ways to drive, and I don't want to ride with someone who's been drinking."

Jaxon gave me a little grin, put his hand out to me wiggling his pinky. "I'll only have one beer, pinky-swear."

I laughed at him and we headed across the street. Dave's Place was a hole-in-the-wall dive bar. It was very small with an old oak bar along the right side of the wall, a stage in the back for the band or anyone feeling brave enough to sing karaoke, and about ten small tables. The walls were plastered with neon signs from just about every alcohol brand, and an old jukebox sat back in the corner. I had been there before with Emma and Eric, but I never really noticed how small it was.

When we walked inside there was an older "cowboy" sitting at the bar, sipping on a beer, and a couple dancing on the makeshift dance floor in the back of the room by the stage. The jukebox was blasting an old Hank Williams song and I had never felt so out of place. I was standing here with a pierced, tattooed man. All eyes - granted there weren't many - but still, shifted to us when we walked in.

Jaxon led us to a table along the wall. The waitress was an older woman who looked like she was barely surviving a hard life. She had really frizzy hair that was dyed a really unnatural shade of red. Her face was covered in deep wrinkles and she was definitely a smoker. Her long fingernails were stained yellow from the nicotine. I actually felt bad for her in the few moments that I knew her, well I did until she started ogling Jaxon. She couldn't take her eyes off of him. I swear she looked at him like he was a lollipop she really needed to lick. I had to agree with her, he was lickable.

Jaxon ordered us both a beer, and then he asked a follow-up to his earlier question. "So, what happened to the twins' dad?"

I was really hoping he would just let it drop, but I knew he wouldn't, so I told him the whole story. I didn't mince any words. I gave it to him straight.

"Basically, Declan was the love of my life. We were born for each other. The term 'destiny' was used a lot when our parents were talking about us. When I was sixteen and Declan was seventeen, we were in an accident. Declan didn't make it. Shortly after the accident, I found out I was pregnant with the twins. They really saved me. I don't know how I would've survived losing him, if it hadn't been for them." I really hoped that I hadn't sounded too pitiful, when I was explaining what had happened. I didn't need the PPL (Poor Pitiful Loralei) from Jaxon. I had coined that term ten years ago when everybody gave me *the* look.

Jaxon reached over and placed his hand on my arm. His eyes were so caring. I was surprised that I felt so comfortable talking to him about this. I was never comfortable talking about Declan, but Jaxon made me feel like it was okay, like I needed to talk about it.

He never looked at me with sadness. I wasn't sure what kinda look he was giving me, but it didn't feel like he felt sorry for me.

"Seems like Declan was a really great guy. I'm sorry that the twins won't get to know him." *Wow,* he really surprised me. Those words and his gorgeous brown eyes were melting my heart.

The waitress brought us our beers. Her hand lingered a little longer on Jaxon's bottle than mine. Her eyes were just looking him up and down, and back again. I couldn't believe she was blatantly flirting with him right in front of me. Sometimes I just couldn't understand what the hell was wrong with people. It's not like we were a couple or anything. But she didn't know that.

We sipped our beers and talked a little. Jaxon told me he was from Richmond, California. "I needed to get away from the big city for a while. There was some shit going on, that well, it was just better for me to get away."

"Are you running from the law, mister?" I joked.

He shot me that sexy smirk, raised an eyebrow, and shrugged his shoulders.

He could've been for all I knew. I didn't know anything about this guy. Since he was Jake's nephew, and I trusted Jake with my life, I could only assume that he wouldn't let me spend time with Jaxon if he was a bad guy.

"What do you do? You know, for a living."

His eyes lit up as he explained, "I work on cars. Old cars are my specialty. I've always been kind of fascinated with them. My mom says when I was little, I took everything in the house apart, just so I could see how it worked and then put it back together. I kinda feel that way about cars. I like to take a look under the hood and see what I can do to make her purr."

I don't know if he meant to make it sound that way, but I was definitely blushing. He gave me a little grin and took a swig of his beer.

When we finished our beers, the waitress came over, and Jaxon ordered a couple more. I shot him a pissy look.

"I know, pinky- swear and all, but I'm really having a good time getting to know you. And it'll take more than a couple of beers to get me drunk," He said with that damn, sexy smirk of his.

I nodded as the waitress skulked away to get our order. When she got away from our table Jaxon leaned over, "Wanna dance?"

I tried to slink down in my chair. I don't dance, unless you count when I have the radio blaring and dance around my house, and I don't think you count that. "I don't really know how to dance."

"Just follow me, honey, and you'll be a pro in no time."

He grabbed my hand and pulled me out to the makeshift dance floor, pressing me against his strong muscular chest. I couldn't tell if the room was spinning, or if it was just my head. Just being that close to him was making me crazy. And then I did the one thing I shouldn't have done - I looked up. Big, gorgeous brown eyes were staring down at me. I gulped and my heart literally skipped a beat.

We danced through several slow country songs, never taking our eyes off of each other. I had never felt that connected to any other man besides Declan. *Declan.* He was never far from my thoughts, but I had to admit, I hadn't been thinking about him much while Jaxon and I danced.

When he started to lean down toward me, it just seemed natural. He brushed his lips along my neck right below my ear. I shuddered from my head to my toes and everywhere in between. He looked down at me through those long brown eyelashes and gently pressed his lips to mine. The kiss was soft and sweet.

But when he tried to slide his tongue into my mouth, I pulled away and found myself screaming, "What the hell?" I ran to the bathroom and as soon as I slammed the door behind me, he was knocking on it.

"I'm so sorry, Loralei. I didn't mean anything by it." He was quiet for a moment. "Oh, shit I did, I needed to kiss you. I still do. But if you don't want to, I won't push you, I promise. Please just open the door and let me in."

I leaned against the bathroom door. "I can't believe you did that. I didn't ask you to kiss me. I didn't want you to kiss me. Why would you do that?"

Utter silence. Jaxon didn't say a word. I slowly opened the door and he was gone. I couldn't believe he just left me there. I ran to the table and noticed my purse was gone.

I headed outside and found Jaxon sitting in the truck, holding his head in his hands. If I didn't know better I would've thought he was crying. But he was definitely not the kind of guy you would find crying with his head in his hands, right? I opened the door, and he never moved. I climbed into the truck and shut the door.

Finally, he looked over at me. "Loralei, I'm so sorry I did that. Something is wrong with me, I fuck up everything. I was having such a great time with you, and I just couldn't help myself. I wanted to kiss you so bad. I've been dreaming about what you would taste like since the first time I saw you on the farm. But you're scared. I get that. I won't let it happen again. You can trust me."

I kept my eyes glued to the floorboard, unable to look at him. "It's okay, let's just forget this ever happened, alright?"

When I finally looked at him, he nodded, and we drove all the way home in silence; not even any classic rock on the radio this time.

Jaxon

I was right, I was in trouble with this damn woman. When she explained what had happened to the twin's dad, my heart hurt for her. I could tell by the look in her eyes that her heart broke that night. I just wanted to hold her. I wanted to take all of her pain away. I hadn't known this woman long enough to feel this way about her. I have too much baggage. I can't add that shit to her life. It's bad enough that I have to deal with it, she shouldn't have to deal with it too.

When the waitress brought our beers, she was staring me down. Did she not fucking see that I was with someone? It wasn't like Loralei and I were together, together, but still. This skank needed to back the hell off.

I explained to Loralei, "I needed to get away from the big city for a while. There was some shit going on, that, well, it was just better for me to get away."

She asked, "Are you running from the law, mister?"

I wasn't running from the law, but I had had some run-ins with the law. So I just shrugged my shoulders and smirked at her.

I was so happy when she asked me about my work. I had always loved to talk about my passion for cars. "I work on cars. Old cars are my specialty. I've always been kind of fascinated with them. My mom said when I was little, I took everything in the house apart, just so I could see how it worked and then put it back together. I kinda feel that way about cars. I like to take a look under the hood and see what I can do to make her purr."

I would love to make Loralei purr. There was that blush again. I was really starting to love that blush. I took a swig of my beer and grinned at her.

We were having such a good time. I didn't want it to end, so when the skanky waitress came over I ordered us a couple more beers. Boy that pissed Loralei off. She shot me a look

"I know, pinky- swear and all, but I'm really having a good time getting to know you. And it'll take more than a couple of beers to get me drunk."

She finally agreed and I asked her, "Wanna dance?"

I could tell by the way she tried to slide down under the table and hide, that she didn't want to dance.

She finally answered, "I don't really know how to dance."

This was gonna be fun. "Just follow me, honey, and you'll be a pro in no time."

I grabbed her hand and led her out to the dance floor. Damn, she felt so good in my arms. Being this close to her was making me feel weird things. I couldn't understand what the hell was drawing me to this sweet, innocent woman. I couldn't take my eyes off of her. When she looked up at me – that was it. I was lost to her.

We danced through several songs and then, God, I had to kiss her, taste her. I bent my head down and lightly brushed my lips down her neck right below her ear. I could feel her shudder under my touch. I had to take this slow. I didn't want to scare her. I leaned in and very gently pressed my lips against hers. She tasted so sweet. I could have kissed her like this all night, but I was greedy, I wanted more. When I tried to slide my tongue into her mouth, she jumped back, screaming, "What the hell?"

Before I knew what was happening she was running toward the bathroom, slamming the door, and then locking it.

I knocked on the door. "I'm so sorry, Loralei. I didn't mean anything by it." Damn it, I screwed this up. I went too fast and scared the shit out of her. "Oh, shit I did, I needed to kiss you. I still do. But if you don't want to, I won't push you, I promise. Please just open the door and let me in."

I could hear her lean against the door, "I can't believe you did that. I didn't ask you to kiss me. I didn't want you to kiss me. Why would you do that?"

God damn it! Why did I do that? I fuck up everything. I was having such an amazing time, and then I had to screw it up and push her into something she didn't want or need. I had to get the hell out of there, and get away from her. I couldn't stand the thought of hurting her more. I threw some money down on the table to cover our tab, and noticed we left her purse unattended, so I grabbed it and headed to the truck.

I climbed in the truck and slammed the door behind. I laid my head in my hands. What the fuck was wrong with me? I was so damn close to bawling like a baby. Something about this woman was getting to me. I couldn't do this right now. My life was fucked up and I couldn't bring this sweet, innocent woman into my hell. I had to stay the hell away from her. That was the only way it could be.

She climbed in the truck. It took me a few minutes before I could even look up at her. "Loralei, I'm so sorry I did that. Something is wrong with me, I fuck up everything. I was having such a great time with you, and I just couldn't help myself. I wanted to kiss you so bad. I've been dreaming about what you would taste like since the first time I saw you on the farm. But you're scared. I get that. I won't let it happen again. You can trust me."

She couldn't look up at me either, she stared at the floorboard. "It's okay, let's just forget this ever happened, alright?"

Yes, that was for the best. We just needed to forget that any of this had ever happened. I nodded and we drove home in silence. I didn't even want to listen to the radio.

Loralei

When we got home, he dropped me off at my house before he took the supplies out to the barn office to be put away. I decided I really needed to talk to Emma about what happened at the bar. I could never understand how every time I really needed to talk to her, she didn't answer her stupid phone. I screamed into her voicemail, "Ems, why the hell don't you ever answer your phone when I need you?"

God, I needed to talk to someone about this. The only other person I could think of was, well, my mom, and since she's the one who started all of this, I didn't know if that was the best idea.

"Mom, I really need to talk, can you come over?"

Immediately she assumed something was horribly wrong. "Oh no, what's wrong, honey?"

Well, mom the world is coming to an end. This hot as hell guy that you forced me to spend the afternoon with had the nerve to kiss me while I was practically molesting him with my eyes...this was what I wanted to say. Instead I said, "Mom, everything is fine. I just need to talk to you about something, please come over."

Within a few minutes, mom was standing in my kitchen, begging me to tell her what had happened. I couldn't help what happened next. As much as I didn't want to cry in front of her, the tears wouldn't stop once they started. She pulled me into her arms and told me everything would be okay, but I didn't think I really believed her.

I explained to her what had happened. She didn't laugh at me, she didn't give me the PPL, she didn't look like she felt sorry for me, she just looked at me with love.

"Honey, you have to move on from Declan. It has been ten years since the accident, and you're not happy. I can't stand to see you like this. Please just give Jaxon a chance. He might not be the right guy for forever, but maybe he is the right guy for right now."

That last sentence struck a chord - I liked Jaxon, and I wanted to get to know him better. I wanted him in my life, right now. It didn't have to be forever. I believed in my heart that since Declan had died I only remained on the earth to raise the twins. That's why I didn't die in the accident. It didn't matter if I was happy, as long as they were. They were all I needed, and they kept me close to Declan's memory. But Jaxon was starting to change my thinking.

Once I calmed down, my mom went home with the understanding that I would take a chance on Jaxon.

Chapter 4

<u>Loralei</u>

    A few weeks passed and I saw Jaxon almost every day. We would discuss farm business over coffee in the barn office every morning. I would sometimes eat lunch with the farmhands, and Jaxon and I would always sit close to each other. Once in awhile, our legs would touch under the table. That would send a shiver up my spine. It was like we couldn't get close enough.

    We flirted innocently, well mostly, and I really thought about what my mom had said. He may not be my forever, but he could be perfect for my right now.

    The other farmhands and Jake were always teasing Jaxon about his "fancy-pants", heavy metal t-shirts, and of course his piercings and tattoos. He took it all in stride, but I could tell that some of the things they would say to him would embarrass him. They called him "Stud" because of his many piercings, and I really think they were kinda jealous of all the attention he was getting around town. Women were definitely taking notice of Jaxon. We didn't see many guys like him in this little town.

    We were all sitting around the table in the barn office eating lunch on that Wednesday afternoon. Jaxon just kept staring at his plate. He looked like he was scared to eat what was on it.

I leaned over. "What do you mean you don't know what greens are? How is that possible?" I was trying not to laugh my ass off at him.

"Woman, I have never even heard of greens. What exactly are they? Looks like spinach, and I'm definitely not Popeye." He continued to stare at his plate.

I couldn't control my laughter. He finally took a bite of the collard greens fried with bacon and onions, and he smiled. Shoveling a huge forkful in his mouth, he said, "These are awesome!"

I realized it was going to be fun introducing Jaxon to my country ways. He grew up in the city and he was definitely a "city boy". He had only been on the farm a little over a month. He hadn't really been able to experience much since he'd been here.

After lunch, Jaxon followed me back to my office and he looked really nervous. He was wringing his hands and I could tell he was sweating. He walked in behind me and shut the door behind us. I wasn't sure what was going on, and I was a little nervous now too. I tried to stifle a chuckle at him, but I didn't know what was coming next. I finally broke the silence, "Jaxon, can I help you with something?"

"Um, I have a question to ask you, Loralei. I was wondering, would you like to go out with me Friday night?" He finally made eye contact when he said, "Friday night".

Oh my God! Jaxon was asking me out. *On a date? Whoa!* I didn't know how to respond. I didn't want to say yes, because if I was being honest with myself, my feelings for him kinda scared me. But I didn't want to say no either, because my lady parts needed to be happy and Jaxon sure could make them dance just by looking at me with those gorgeous brown eyes. I had also promised my mom I would take a chance on him.

I had to answer him. I had been standing there staring into his eyes while I was having this conversation in my head. "Yes, Jaxon, I would love to go out with you on Friday. I'll just need to make sure my parents can watch the twins." Yeah, right, like that would be a problem. My mom would be jumping for joy when I told her.

Jaxon finally took a breath. I couldn't believe how nervous he was and how relieved he seemed now that I had said yes. He then placed a light kiss on my cheek as he left my office. I felt like one of those silly love sick teenagers who say, "I'll never wash this cheek again." I felt silly for feeling that way, but it was kinda true.

Thank goodness it was already Wednesday when he asked me out. I don't think I could've survived having to wait any longer; my nerves were about to overtake me. My mom had of course jumped on the opportunity to babysit.

When Friday finally rolled around, Emma came over to help me get ready for my big date.

"What are you planning on wearing tonight, Lor?" Emma asked as she held up my old Hank Jr. t-shirt between her fingers like it was the most disgusting thing she had ever seen.

"I'm not sure. That's why I asked you to come over. Now, help me pick something out," I said, sounding a little annoyed with her hatred of most of my clothes.

She gave me that devilish smirk. I'm not gonna lie, that smirk had always scared me. I saw that smirk right before she almost got us kicked out of school in the seventh grade for filling Mrs. Edgeller's desk drawer with shaving cream. "Well, luckily, I anticipated this problem and brought you some options from my closet."

That meant she had brought something that I probably wouldn't be caught dead in. She pulled out a bright red dress that was so short it would have left nothing to the imagination. "Uh, that's a no. Next." I looked at her annoyed. Then she pulled out a little black dress that I swear to God was cut all the way down to the navel. I didn't even have to say anything on that one. She could tell by my stance and expression that she better just put that right back in her magic skank bag!

Finally, she pulled out a light pink ruffle skirt. It was so cute, a little short, but definitely something I would wear. "Okay, this I might be able to work with. What should I wear with it?"

"I would wear it with a white tank and this." She pulled out a gorgeous short hot pink denim jacket with some rhinestones on the breast pockets. So country, and so definitely me. Ems had always known me so well. She knew I would never wear her first two picks.

After she helped me get ready, she headed home, and I almost wore a dent in the floor pacing in front of the door as I waited for Jaxon to arrive. I couldn't remember the last time I was this nervous. Jaxon and I had been flirting and spending time together on the farm, so this was the logical next step. But what if he expected more? What if he thought we would have sex tonight? I definitely wasn't ready for that.

When he finally got to my house I didn't even wait for the doorbell to ring. I heard his truck pull up and I opened the door. He hopped out of the truck and my heart skipped a beat. He looked absolutely gorgeous. He had on dark stonewashed jeans, and a dark grey button up shirt, with the sleeves rolled up - just enough for me to see some of his tattoos - and black motorcycle boots. His hair looked like he had run his hands through it a few times. About the time I had that thought he reached up and did it.

I giggled to myself.

"What's so funny, babe?" He asked.

Oh my goodness, he just called me babe. The butterflies were going crazy in my stomach.

"Nothing. You're just really hot - uh, I mean here - really here." I had totally just stuck my foot in my mouth.

He just chuckled and reached his hand out for me, "Ready to go?"

"Sure. Where are we heading to?"

"It's a surprise. By the way, uh, you look really, really hot tonight," he said as he looked me up and down and then smiled when he reached my eyes.

A blush crept up my cheeks. And my lady parts were definitely dancing. I didn't know how I was going to survive the night. We headed out of town toward the city. It was about a forty-five minute drive into Springfield.

For the first thirty minutes of the trip, we didn't speak. Jaxon held onto the wheel and didn't take his eyes off of the road. I was really enjoying his taste in music though. He was playing lots of classic rock.

I was staring out the window, taking in the scenery when I heard it. The sexiest voice was singing - in the car - it wasn't coming from the radio - it was Jaxon. The song playing was *Wonderful Tonight* by Eric Clapton, and he was hitting all the right notes. His voice was so sultry and low. I couldn't take my eyes off of his lips.

All I wanted to do was kiss those beautiful lips. When the song was over he glanced over at me. Our eyes met, he licked his lips, and I knew he was thinking the same thing I was.

I took a deep breath and said, "Wow, you can really sing."

"Well, don't sound so surprised. You know there is more to me than tattoos and piercings. I'm not a complete badass, just about half." He smirked, and damn it was sexy.

"Just half, huh? You're voice did surprise me, it's kinda beautiful...oh, and super sexy." I added my own sexy little smirk. I didn't know what had come over me. I didn't say things like that. And a smirk? I was seriously losing my mind.

The rest of the ride was pretty quiet. When we got into town he drove toward downtown and pulled up to a valet at RELICS a new dance club. I had seen an article in the local paper about it, but I didn't think it would be on my list of places to go anytime in the near future. Jaxon took my hand in his, and we started walking toward the club.

Downtown Springfield was such a pretty place. There were all these little bars, restaurants, and quaint shops. I didn't come here often, but I when I did I always ate at Luisa's Italian Bistro. The fettuccini there was literally to die for. Like, I seriously could die happy after eating a bowl of it. I was surprised when we walked right past the entrance to RELICS.

"Weren't we supposed to get in that line?" I asked while pointing to the line in front of RELICS.

"I thought we could grab something to eat before we go dancing. Your mom recommended a place for us. I have reservations at seven o'clock, so we better hurry." I was so excited when I saw where we were going - Luisa's Italian Bistro. My mom really was an awesome lady.

We walked in and Jaxon strutted up to the hostess desk to let them know we were there. The hostess seated us near the back of the restaurant in a secluded little corner booth. I slid in on one side and Jaxon slid in on the other. We immediately met in the middle. It was like we were drawn to each other with some sort of magnet.

I couldn't sit there and not be close enough to smell him, to feel him, to touch him.

The waitress came over to our table and took our drink orders. Then Jaxon ordered for us. He ordered me my favorite meal of fettuccini alfredo with extra sauce. Apparently, my mom had given him some pretty strong "date" suggestions.

We chatted while we waited for our food. It was so nice to have a totally adult conversation. I love my kids with all my heart, but sometimes it's nice to talk about grown-up things with another grown-up. It also didn't hurt that this grown-up was amazingly sexy and really trying to get on my good side. He didn't need to try quite so hard. He was pretty much there.

"You know I'm not a good dancer. Why would you want to take me to a dance club?"

"Well, first of all, I know you can dance. Everybody can dance. Secondly, I can't wait to get you on the dance floor and hold you tight. And last but not least, did I mention I can't wait to hold you tight and sway your body with the music?" There was that "melt your panties" look of his. *Holy hell* - I was blushing, again.

"Will you sing to me?"

"You wanna do some karaoke? I'd never turn that down." He said with a grin.

"You know that's not what I meant. Your voice is amazing. Are you in a band? Or do you sing professionally?"

He let out a big belly laugh. "Uh, no honey, I am nowhere near good enough for that. I just like to sing. Always have. My mom used to sing Elvis songs to me all the time. She was literally obsessed with that man. I swear my first words were 'thank you, thank you very much'," he said that last part with his best Elvis impersonation. It really wasn't half bad - he even had the lip curl down.

The waitress appeared at our table and delivered our food. Jaxon had ordered lasagna, but I think he ate more of my fettuccini than his own food.

"Um, excuse me. Are you going to eat your own food or would you just like to finish mine?" I chuckled.

His mouth was full of my fettuccini as he mumbled, "Oh, sorry. Yours is just so damn good. You never should have let me taste it. I can order you some more if you're still hungry."

I pushed my plate over to him and moved his lasagna to the side. "No, that's okay. Go ahead and finish mine. I'm full."

"Thanks for sharing. It's really delicious." He said.

I looked over and he had alfredo sauce on his chin. I wasn't sure what to do. I tried to kinda rub my chin, to show him that he needed to do the same. But he wasn't picking up on my hints. Finally, I said, "Uh, you have a little somethin' on your chin." I leaned over and used my napkin to wipe his chin off. Our eyes met and there was that weird electric thing again. His eyes were smoldering and I realized we had both leaned in to each other. We were so close and I had kinda forgot about wiping his chin, and was just holding the napkin in place. He licked his lips, and I just about lost it. I wanted him to kiss me again. It had scared me to death at Dave's Place, but this was different. I wanted him to kiss me – now. He grabbed my hand and placed it on the table.

"I probably better finish this...uh, don't wanna let it go to waste." He scooted over away from me and we didn't talk much after that. Jaxon was too busy shoveling food down his throat. That man definitely had a healthy appetite.

When we were done at the restaurant we started to head back toward the club. As we were walking out of the restaurant Jaxon reached over and laced his fingers through mine. It felt so nice to walk down the street holding his hand. His hand was so warm, and comforting. These small things he was doing were melting my heart. I felt sad when he had to use his hand to take his wallet out and pay our cover for RELICS.

This place was huge and so bright. A strobe light was spinning around the dance floor, making everything shine. There was a huge bar all along the right side of the club. The bar was made out of ice. It was literally and figuratively cool.

The place was packed, wall-to-wall people. I always kinda felt like I was still young and I tried to be hip, but being here made me feel old and outdated. The dance floor was huge, and the tiles were all different colors. It looked like a spazzed out version of a checkers board. I honestly wondered if any of these kids had been carded. They all looked like they had several years to go before they turned twenty-one. And the way they were dancing – they were practically having sex on the dance floor. It was like a traffic accident I didn't want to watch, but I couldn't look away. It reminded me of an orgy, not that I had ever been to an orgy, but it's what I assumed one would look like.

Since there were no seats available at the bar, Jaxon ordered us a couple of drinks and we headed for a group of small tables nestled along the back wall. Jaxon placed his hand on the small of my back and led me to an empty table. His touch sent shivers up my spine.

We sat across from each other and tried to talk, but it was so loud that we couldn't hear ourselves think. We sat there for quite a while just watching everything going on out on the dance floor. There was this blonde skank rubbing all over some guy right in front of us. She had on a super short, strapless black leather dress that zipped up the side. The guy's eyes were literally bugging out of his head. She was falling out of that dress and he was enjoying it. I couldn't quit staring. I finally tore my gaze away and looked over to Jaxon. He was staring at me. He licked his lower lip, and I had to wonder what he was thinking. Had he seen the show I had been watching? Did he expect me to dance with him like that? Uh, that wasn't going to happen.

I had a couple glasses of wine with dinner, and I wasn't sure what these drinks were that Jaxon got us, but wow! They were yummy. I was on my third yummy drink, when Jaxon stood up, leaned down and tucked my hair behind my ear. "Wanna dance?"

I shook my head, furrowing my eyebrows. I really didn't want to get out there with all those...those...*kids*. Of course they probably weren't really that much younger than me, but they were really making me feel ancient. And I was a little buzzed. I couldn't dance when I was sober, let alone when I'd been drinking.

"Sorry, but I won't take no for an answer." He grabbed my hand and pulled me toward the dance floor. It was a good thing he had a good grip on me, because my knees were wobbly.

We were packed in like sardines. The song that was playing was so sexy. The beat was slow, but the rhythm was intoxicating. I had never heard it before, but all of the people dancing were just rubbing against each other.

Jaxon put his hands on my hips and spun me until my back was against his chest. He started to move and I decided to just let the music take over. I enjoyed pressing up against him. I reached up and put my arms around his neck. This felt so good. I found myself hoping that the song would never end. But eventually it did. When it ended we didn't stop dancing, but Jaxon did turn me around so that I was facing him. His eyes, *wow*, he had the most amazing eyes. I could look into them all day. They were brown with the most beautiful flecks of gold through them. The gold made them sparkle. I could see in his eyes that he was a little buzzed too.

When he pressed me against him, I could feel *him* against my thigh. He was excited - and to be honest, I was too. I was silently begging him to kiss me. He leaned down and was so close to my lips that I could feel his breath, and then he stopped. He kinda shook his head, placed his hand in mine, and led me back to our table.

The rest of the night was pretty uneventful. We made small talk. He even talked about the weather....*the weather.* I didn't understand what had happened. I knew he was *excited* so I couldn't understand why he wouldn't kiss me. Twice...he had two openings to kiss me and he didn't do it either time.

When he took me home, he walked me to the door and didn't say anything but "goodnight" and "I'll see ya tomorrow." Talk about mixed signals - even with my very limited experience with men I could see them.

I didn't hear a word from Jaxon all day Saturday. It's not like I sat at home waiting for him to call, but I did stay home all day, just in case. He was at church on Sunday, and he came to my parents' house for lunch. He didn't have much to say to me. We mostly just made small talk. He even mentioned the weather again. I started to think that maybe I had imagined it. Maybe there weren't any sparks there.

The kids fell asleep after lunch, so I decided I would take a ride out through the property and check on the most recent shipment of cattle. It was a strong rule in our family that we didn't work on Sunday's, but to me this didn't count as work.

I went home and changed clothes, and then I jumped on one of the four-wheelers and headed out. I was riding along, looking out over our vast property and feeling lucky that it was all ours.

Knowing one day Sammy and Mags would inherit it. I couldn't help but be proud of the accomplishments I had made since taking over the management of the farm. I had handled the acquisition of most of the acreage and cattle. I couldn't even imagine all of the amazing things Sammy and Mags would be able to do when they took it over. I also couldn't help but be happy that the property was vast and they could live on opposite sides.

As I was enjoying my daydream about the future, I hit a huge rock, veered off and hit a tree. Just my luck. I wasn't hurt, but the front of the four-wheeler was caved in a little and there was smoke coming out of it, which I could only assume was not a good sign.

While I was saying a few choice words to the tree and the four-wheeler I heard someone say, "Need some help?"

Jaxon, of course, my pierced, tattooed, knight in shining armor. He had on an old pair of jeans that were worn at the knees and a wife-beater, his tattoos were prominently displayed. It was a pretty warm day and he had been working, which we weren't supposed to be doing on Sunday, so he was sweating just enough to sparkle. Oh my god the man was actually sparkling!

Realizing I sounded like a damsel in distress, I said, "It seems as though I do."

He walked around to the front of the four-wheeler. He tinkered with something under the hood and told me he would bring a trailer down to pick it up later. Then he climbed onto his four-wheeler and motioned to me. "Hop on."

I climbed on behind him and I had to hold on, so I wrapped my arms around his waist and held on tight. I told myself that, in order to be safe, I had to hold on tight; it made perfect sense.

We rode all around the property. Stopping a few times to fix some fence and help a few cattle get back with the rest of the herd. Before I knew it, it was getting dark and then I felt it – one lone raindrop. We raced back to the barn, but we were too late. The skies opened up and that one raindrop turned into sheets of rain falling down on us.

We were soaking wet. Jaxon tried to get us back as fast as possible, but in his haste he ran into a huge puddle and the four-wheeler sank in. He climbed off and asked me to try to gun it while he pushed so we could get it unstuck.

He stepped behind the four-wheeler and started to push while I accelerated. About that time mud flew all over him! He was covered in it, the four-wheeler was beyond stuck, and I couldn't quit laughing.

"You think this is funny, huh? I don't like it when you laugh at me. Come here, babe." Jaxon grabbed me, pressing his body to mine as he covered me in mud. The mud didn't bother me though, because it meant that Jaxon was pressed firmly against me. And then the sparks flew. I definitely hadn't imagined that spark.

He looked down at me as we stood in the middle of a rainstorm, and I heard him whisper to himself, "Fuck it." Then he took my mouth with such force that we fell into the mud. We both laughed until we couldn't anymore because our tongues were too busy dancing. His hands were under my t-shirt and on my breasts before I even knew what was happening. Wow, he could kiss and he felt amazing. He pulled my wet shirt over my head, and I helped him get his off. He pulled the cups of my bra down under my breasts. His lips trailed down my neck, and then he took my nipple into his mouth. I almost had an orgasm right then. I hadn't been touched like that in ten years. Ten very, very long years. I couldn't get enough of him.

He sucked and then he bit me. *Wow!* I liked it. It felt amazing. I couldn't help it though when I cried out as he leaned over and bit my other nipple.

"Shit, did I hurt you?" Jaxon panicked.

"No, it feels so good - please don't stop."

He looked up at me, gave me that sexy ass smirk and nipped one nipple, while he squeezed the other between his fingertips.

With one hand I started rubbing his chest and with the other I was pulling at his jeans. I really didn't know what came over me. I didn't know if it was the rain or the way Jaxon was kissing a trail down further and further until he found the one place that really needed his attention, but I was a freaking hot mess.

He looked up at me through those gorgeous long eyelashes, silently asking me if it was okay. I nodded and he pulled my wet jeans off and then my panties were gone. He kissed my inner thigh and then trailed kisses down to my sex. He started tracing circles on my clit with his tongue. I was so close, I was moaning as I arched my back. Jaxon inserted his finger and then two fingers, in and out, over and over again until I exploded with a loud scream, "Jaxon – Oh my god - Jaxon!"

He climbed up and kissed me, it was so soft and loving. I knew at that moment that I was falling for this guy, and not just because of the mind blowing orgasm he just gave me, there was just something about him. I really wanted to make him feel as great as he made me feel, but when I started to unzip his jeans, he stopped me. "This was for you. I just wanted to make you feel like I've felt every time I've looked at you." With those words, my heart melted.

Sometime during the last few minutes the rain had stopped and the sun was shining. I had to ask him, "Why didn't you kiss me on our date?"

He closed his eyes, took a deep breath. "You have no idea how much I wanted to. But you had been drinking, and I didn't want our first real kiss to happen when you were tipsy." I leaned toward him and kissed him softly. "Thanks for that. This first kiss was pretty amazing." Uh-oh, I was definitely falling for this guy.

Jaxon

Our date had been perfect. It was actually the best date I had ever been on. I had two opportunities to kiss her. And I wasted both of them. I told myself that it was because she had been drinking and I didn't want our first real kiss to be when she was buzzed. But the real reason why I didn't kiss her was because I knew I shouldn't kiss her. Uncle Jake had warned me away from her. He told me she had heartbreak in her past and then she confirmed it when she told me about Declan. I should've stayed away from her. I shouldn't have asked her out. But I wanted to. There was just something different about her. She was so sweet and just, I don't know, different than anyone I had ever known.

I decided after our date, that I had to keep my ass away from her. She deserved so much better than me. We didn't speak on the way home much. I didn't dream of offering her a kiss goodnight, and I didn't call her the next day. I knew I was being an ass, but I felt like that was the way it needed to be. When she found out about my history, she would run away screaming. This way we would just avoid all that.

Uncle Jake asked me to take one of the four-wheelers out and do a field check. Just to see if anything was going on with any of the cattle or anything. I was coming up over one of the hills when I saw her. Loralei. She was so damn sexy. She was cussing and screaming at her four-wheeler that had smoke barreling out of it. I drove down the hill to see if I could help her out.

"Need some help?" I asked.

She responded, "It seems as though I do."

I walked to the front of the four-wheeler and quickly assessed the damage. She had literally blown a gasket. Poor thing…it was gonna take a lot to get it back in working order.

"I'll have to bring a trailer down to pick it up later."

Then I climbed on my four-wheeler, motioned to her, and said, "Hop on."

She climbed on behind me and wrapped her arms around my waist. *Holy shit!* She felt so damn good and she was holding on so tight. *No Jaxon, this is not a good idea. You are screwed in the head and you will hurt her.* I told myself this, but I had a strong tendency to not listen to myself.

We rode around the property, stopping a couple of times to fix some fence. It started to get dark, so I was trying to get us back to the barn fast. All of a sudden it started raining. I sped up and just as I did I drove right into a huge puddle and the damn four-wheeler sank in. The rain was falling in sheets, and we were soaking wet. I was pissed. I jumped off of the four-wheeler and got behind it to push it out of the puddle. "Loralei, I need you to gun it when I say the word." I was pushing and I yelled at her, "Now."

Mud flew up all over me. I was fucking covered in it. And what was she doing? Laughing her ass off. God, she was so cute when she laughed at me. I told her I didn't like it, but secretly it was becoming one of my favorite things.

I grabbed her and pressed my body to hers. Damn, it felt good to rub all over her. There was that damn electricity again. I knew what I needed to do, but in that moment all that mattered was what I wanted to do. "Fuck it."

I slammed my mouth to hers and knocked us both to the ground. We were lying in the mud, laughing, and kissing. I slid my hands under her shirt, up to her breasts. They were so damn perfect. I had dreamed about touching them. It was amazing. I pulled her soaking wet shirt off and I had to see them, so I pulled her bra down under her breasts. They had to be kissed. I started at her neck and worked my way down. She was shuddering and I thought she was going to come right then.

I took her nipple in my mouth and sucked. I couldn't help myself, I nipped her. She cried out when I made my way to her other nipple and did the same thing.

I was freaked out, afraid I hurt her. "Shit, did I hurt you?"

She said, "No, it feels so good - please don't stop."

That was all I needed to hear. I went back to work on her nipples. They were so beautiful and they just needed to be nibbled on.

She was rubbing my chest and pulling at my jeans. I was kissing her neck, chest, stomach, I needed to taste her. She was about to come unraveled under me. She was so responsive. She wanted me, just as much as I wanted her.

I looked up at her, wanting to make sure it was okay for me to go further. Her nod was all I needed. I pulled off her jeans and panties. I kissed her thigh and then started heading for the one place I really wanted to be. I needed to taste her, so I did. I was using my tongue to draw circles on her clit. She was loving it. She arched her back and that's when I slid a finger in and then another. Watching her come undone was beautiful. It was the most beautiful thing I'd ever seen. When she screamed, "Jaxon – Oh my god - Jaxon!" I about lost it.

I wanted to kiss her - a sweet kiss to let her know how much I cared. I was falling for this woman. I couldn't stay away another minute. There were things about me that I was going to have to tell her, but not today. Right now I just wanted to be with her.

She reached down and started to unbutton my jeans. I wanted that more than anything, what man wouldn't? But this was for her. This was about me showing her how much I cared. I said, "This was for you. I just wanted to make you feel like I've felt every time I've looked at you."

While we were having this mind blowing experience the rain had stopped and the sun was now shining. She asked, "Why didn't you kiss me on our date?"

I didn't want to tell her the truth. I didn't want to tell her that I didn't think I was good enough for her. So, I told her a partial truth, "You have no idea how much I wanted to. But you had been drinking, and I didn't want our first real kiss to happen when you were tipsy."

She gave me a sweet kiss, and said, "Thanks for that. This first kiss was pretty amazing." I was in trouble. I was falling hard for this woman.

<u>Loralei</u>

I asked Jaxon if he would like to have dinner with me and the kids tonight. After he agreed we walked back to my house and

Jaxon told me he wanted to go home and shower and change. We were pretty dirty after our tryst in the mud.

He said he would be back soon. When I got inside the house I found a note from my mom:

Honey,

Jake saw you and Jaxon riding around the property and I thought you might want some "alone" time so I will keep the twins overnight. Have fun and don't think too much!

Love, Mom

My mom was a piece of work, but she was right - an entire evening with Jaxon sounded perfect. I was a little worried about what Jake might have seen, but I decided not to think about that right now. I could be embarrassed about that later.

For dinner, I made a pan of my famous goulash. And after I got the rolls ready to put in the oven, I still had time to shower. I decided to just wear jeans and a t-shirt. About the time I got my shirt on and my hair pulled up in a ponytail, I heard someone knocking on the door. When I opened the door, he took my breath away. Jaxon was standing there with faded jeans and a black AC/DC t-shirt on, holding out a yellow daisy. And those eyes, those amazing, big deep brown sparkling eyes.

"Hi, can I come in?"

I didn't realize it, but apparently I had been staring at him for a while and hadn't let him in the house or taken the flower from him.

I took the flower. "Sorry, yes, please, uh, come in."

He looked all around the house. My house was not nearly as large as my parents', but it was plenty big enough for me and the kids. He was standing in front of the fireplace, looking at my family pictures on the mantle. He turned to me, "Where are the kids?" I told him they were eating dinner at my parents' house.

We went into the kitchen and sat down on opposite sides of the table. I placed the pan of goulash I had made for dinner in front of him.

"Uh, what's that?" Jaxon said while wrinkling his nose at me. "I mean it smells pretty good, but what exactly is it?"

I really am a horrible cook. This was actually the only thing I made that the kids would willingly eat. I usually had to bribe them to force down my horrible concoctions. And we had to keep a fire extinguisher under the sink, just in case.

"It's like spaghetti, but it's made with macaroni and I added some zucchini and mushrooms. I promise it won't kill you."

He placed a large ladle full on his plate and when he took the first bite he smiled. "It's delicious, Loralei."

In my snarkiest voice I smiled and said, "I told you so."

After we finished dinner, I got up and walked over to the freezer to get out some ice cream for dessert, when I felt Jaxon come up behind me. He was so close that I could feel his breath on the back of my neck. He reached across me and grabbed some ice to put in his tea. He dropped a cube on the floor and when I bent down to pick it up, he did too, and we bumped foreheads.

"Ow," he whined.

"Really? My little head, hurt your big hard head?" I said with a giggle.

"Are you laughing at me?" he asked.

"Um, maybe?"

He leaned down over me. We were almost nose-to-nose, when he said, "I really don't like it when you laugh at me."

Well, that was that. That man was making my panties melt. He backed me up against the counter and placed his arms behind me on the cabinet. Then I felt it. He put the ice cube down the back of my shirt. I screamed. He jumped back and was cracking up.

"What's the matter, babe? You cold?"

I shimmied the ice cube out of my shirt and chased after him. "You know what they say about payback?"

"Nope. Don't believe I do. What is it they say?"

"You know…"

"Maybe? But I would really like to hear you say it." He smirked at me.

I had him backed up against the dining room table. I had one hand on his chest and the other, with the ice cube, beside him on the table. I pressed forward and while looking into his eyes, said, "It's a bitch." Right as I raised my hand from the table and put the ice cube down the front of his jeans. He was so busy looking in my eyes, that he missed what I was planning. He screamed and jumped up.

While shaking and shimmying to get the ice out of his pants, he said, "Are you laughing at me, again?"

I couldn't stop laughing. It was hilarious trying to watch this big, bad guy trying to shake an ice cube out of his pants. "Yes, I am. I really am. Because you're freaking hilarious."

He helped me clear the table and we went into the living room. I asked him if he would like to watch a movie.

"Depends, it's not a chick flick, is it?" he said with a grin.

"We can watch whatever you like. Just check out the movies and I'm gonna call my mom to check on the twins and tell them goodnight." I didn't even think about what I was saying.

"So the kids are spending the whole night away?"

Wow, I must have looked like a total slut after what happened this afternoon and then it looked like I sent my kids away for the night to be with him. I was so embarrassed I could literally hide under the couch. I could feel the blush creep into my face.

"Um, yeah. Mom wanted to keep them overnight."

And that's when the entire atmosphere changed. Before I got to the phone Jaxon was behind me whispering, "Make it a quick phone call, we have grown-up things to take care of."

Grown-up things? *Holy hell!*

I was on the phone a while. I had to describe to Mags all the reasons why she shouldn't suffocate her brother in his sleep. Apparently, he had once again hidden her iPod from her. When I talked her down and told the kids goodnight, I hung up the phone. I walked toward the living room and found Jaxon sitting on the couch. His eyes met mine.

Before I could get into the room, I don't know how he did it, but he was off of the couch and standing in front of me. His lips were on mine and he had me pressed against the wall. He lifted me up, wrapping my legs around his waist. It felt so good to be in his arms and to feel how much he wanted me. I hadn't felt *wanted* like that in a long time. It was nice to know that I excited him as much as he did me.

Before I knew it he had carried me to the couch and I was straddling him. His lips never left mine and I ran my hand down his muscular chest, then his stomach, finally I stopped at the waist of his jeans.

He pulled his shirt over his head and started to do the same with mine. My mind was racing. I was feeling so many different emotions. I wanted him. He wanted me. I could feel him pressing against me. His kisses were so intense. I kept thinking about this afternoon, and how he had made me feel. I wanted to be with him like this. But that didn't lessen the wave of fear that suddenly hit me. I didn't know how to do this. I'd only been with one man. Declan. *Oh my god, Declan.* I pulled away from Jaxon. He looked up at me, he was breathing so heavy, "Did I do something wrong? Are you okay?"

I decided I should be honest. "Jaxon, I haven't done anything like this in a while."

"How long is a while, Loralei," he asked.

"I haven't been with anyone, well besides what we did this afternoon, since Declan. And we, uh, we only did it once."

I had never been so embarrassed in my life, there was no way that he would want to be with me now. I expected him to run for the door screaming, but when I looked up he looked scared or sad, I couldn't really tell.

"Did I hurt you today, Lor? I'm so sorry, I had no idea."

Could this man be any more perfect? He was worried about hurting me, when all he did was give me the most amazing sexual experience I had had since I was sixteen years old.

I placed my hand on his cheek. "No Jaxon, you didn't hurt me. I just don't want to disappoint you. I'm a little naïve when it comes to this stuff, and I don't want you to take my shyness as me not wanting to be with you, because I want that more than anything."

"Loralei, I want to do this right. Our first time should be special and not a quickie on the couch, not that I am opposed to quickies on the couch, just for future reference." God, that smirk would get me every time.

He reached out and pressed his hand into mine and asked me to lead him to my room. When we got there he laid down on my bed and motioned for me to lay down beside him. I crawled into bed and snuggled into his chest.

Bravely, I started to kiss his chest and trace the tattoo there and then when I nibbled on his nipple he moaned the deepest, sexiest moan I had ever heard. He placed his finger under my chin and tilted my head up to look at him. He pressed his lips to mine and when he slid his tongue into my mouth I returned the moan I had received from him earlier.

I ran my hand down his chest, his stomach, and my hands were shaking as I started to unzip his jeans. Jaxon grabbed my hand, whispering, "Slow down honey, there's plenty of time for that. Tonight, let's just, well - cuddle? Women love that, right?"

I giggled, "Yeah, I think I've heard that somewhere before."

"Then it's settled. I'm going to sleep with you tonight and I'm going to cuddle the shit out of you."

"Well, when you put it like that, how can I turn you down?"

"I would never push you into anything, Lor. We have all the time in the world. I'm not going anywhere."

Chapter 5

Loralei

I couldn't understand why I was so hot and sweaty. And why I couldn't move? And what the hell was poking me in the ass? Suddenly, all of the memories of last night came back to me, along with the fear of *God*.

Jaxon kissed my neck. "Mornin' sunshine, sleep well?"

Before I could respond I heard, "Mom! Mags hid my backpack and she won't tell me where it is and I can't go to school without it!" I heard the footsteps on the stairs and before I knew it the door flew open. Sammy stood there, staring at Jaxon and I snuggled up in bed together. I didn't know what to say or how to react. I had no idea what to do so, I just laid there in stunned silence.

Jaxon broke the silence, "Hey little man, could you give your mom and me a minute?"

Sammy didn't move, his eyes were glued on us.

"Mommy, why is Jaxon in bed with you? Oh my God, did you see his penis mommy? *Grandma*, mommy saw Jaxon's penis!" That was the moment when I decided I had officially entered hell and my son was apparently obsessed with Jaxon's penis.

My mom yelled from downstairs, "Sammy, honey please come downstairs and leave your mommy alone. Oh and Loralei, I'll take the kids to school and we'll talk later. Jaxon hope you have a great day." I could literally hear the shit-eating grin on my mom's face. Jaxon laughed, and I elbowed him in the ribs. I didn't find anything about this funny. I was mortified.

As much as we wanted to spend the day wrapped in each other's arms, we knew we both had work to do. We got dressed and went our separate ways. He went out to get the four-wheeler that we got stuck in the mud yesterday, and I went to the barn to meet with the farmhands about the big cattle sale coming up next month in Joplin, Missouri.

This sale was always the most important sale of the year. It was where the best cattle were sold and if you didn't get there and get first dibs, you were stuck with the second best options. Second best was not good enough for the Harper Farm. We had to be there early and schmooze at the big Cattle Baron's Ball the night before the sale.

It was about a three hour drive from Kipton to Joplin, so I usually took Jake with me and we would stay up there for the whole weekend. Every year, I would make Jake go to the Ball with me. I think he hated it a little more each year. Maybe this year Jaxon would want to go with me. We could spend the whole weekend alone. Wouldn't he surprise the hell out of all of those cowboys that tried to get in my pants every year? I was pretty sure that I had convinced all of them that I was gay. I had tried really hard every year. I still always ended up with at least one drunk cowboy following me around all night and Jake threatening to kick their ass.

It was about time for me to head home for lunch, so I jumped in my jeep and headed that way. When I got home I had a message from Sammy's school saying they needed me to come in and meet with the principal. I immediately returned the call and asked what was going on. The secretary informed me that Sammy had an incident at school today, and I would need to come in to discuss it with the principal at three o'clock.

"There is no way I can make it in today. I have a big conference call this afternoon, and I won't be able to get away." This conference call was regarding the cattle sale. I had to coordinate with a few other farms regarding which herd we wanted to try for. I couldn't miss it.

The lovely older woman informed me that someone would need to come in to the school today or Sammy would be suspended from the fourth grade for three days. She said I could send my mom, dad, or anyone, but someone would need to come in.

I called my mom but she had driven into town and wouldn't be back in time to go. She let me know that dad was with Uncle Max fishing and wasn't expected back until tomorrow.

There was a knock at the door. Jaxon was standing on the front porch. I told him what was going on.

"Uncle Jake and I can go Loralei. I don't mind at all and I don't have anything I have to get done this afternoon. Do you think it would be okay if we went?"

The secretary just told me I had to send someone, and Jaxon and Jake would actually count as two someone's. Even though I don't know Jaxon that well, yet, I had known Jake my entire life. Jaxon is his nephew, and he wouldn't let him be around me and the kids if he was a bad guy. I could do this. They could take care of this for me.

"I would really appreciate it, Jaxon. I'm not sure what's going on, but Sammy is always getting into trouble, so it's probably nothing major. Thanks so much for doing this for me."

He grinned and pulled me towards him. "Maybe you can think of a way to pay me back later, maybe over dinner or a drink, after the kids go to sleep?"

I shook my head, "You're a bad influence on me, Jaxon!" He agreed to meet with the principal and find out what my little monster did this time and then bring Sammy and Mags home.

Jaxon

I was happy to help Lor out. She was in quite a bind and I was glad that I could be there for her. I called Uncle Jake and let him know what was going on and we headed over to the school to meet with the principal.

"Mr. Daniels and Mr. Marshall, I assume you are here today to discuss the incident with Mr. Harper." Principal Michaelson said as he looked me up and down. I didn't think he was used to seeing people who liked like me around here.

"Yes, sir. Ms. Harper was unavailable this afternoon, so we offered to take her place. So, how much trouble is he in?" I asked.

"Quite a bit actually. Samuel has had several incidents this year, well, actually every year. He is quite the prankster." Mr. Michaelson said as he raised his eyebrow. "He accosted another child on the playground today. He pushed him down to the ground and referred to him as an 'asshat'. He also told the child that he was getting a new daddy and he was big and mean and had tattoos. He also mentioned that his new daddy could kick his butt. This behavior is simply unacceptable. I'm afraid we will have to suspend him for three days." I didn't know what to say to that. Mr. Michaelson was looking at me as if to say, "Apparently he's talking about you."

"Now, sir. Isn't there something he can do to avoid the suspension? Help around the school or extra homework or something?" I really hated to let Loralei down. I couldn't let Sammy get kicked out of school.

"I just don't know, Mr. Daniels. If this was the first offense, I would say yes. But he has caused problems here since kindergarten. His kindergarten teacher retired after Samuel graduated to the first grade. Yes, it was that bad."

Uncle Jake and I couldn't help but laugh at that. Mr. Michaelson didn't think it was very funny.

"Let me talk to his teacher and see if she would be willing to work something out. I'll be right back." He said as he left the office and started down the hall.

Uncle Jake looked at me and we both broke out in laughter. "That kid is a right mess." Uncle Jake said.

"He seems to be. He really cracks me up though. I hate to see him get suspended. I hope we can work something out," I said as Mr. Michaelson walked back into the room.

"I spoke with Samuel's teacher and she feels that his punishment should fit his offense. She doesn't believe that suspension is the right answer either. She would like for Samuel to write a letter of apology to the boy he accosted and also help her in the classroom during recess for the next two weeks."

"That seems more than fair, Mr. Michaelson. I'll let his mom know what happened. Where is Sammy?"

"He's in his classroom. I'll take you down there." Mr. Michaelson stood up and led us down the hall to Sammy's classroom. When we walked inside Uncle Jake went to talk to Mr. Michaelson, while Sammy's teacher was at her desk grading papers. I sat down at a desk next to Sammy. He looked scared. I hated to see him like that.

"Hey Sammy...you got yourself in a little trouble today, huh?" I asked.

He was fiddling with his pencil. He finally looked up at me and said, "Yeah, I guess. Where's my mom?"

"She had an important call to make so she asked Uncle Jake and me to come get you. Do you want to talk about what happened today?"

He nodded and shrugged his shoulders. "Well I want to talk about it, okay?" I asked. He agreed and I continued. "You know that it's never okay to hurt somebody, right?" He nodded. "When you get really mad like that and use your fists it hurts everybody, not just the person you're hitting. You can't fix anything by using your strength. You're going to be a man. Men don't hurt people. The only exception to that is if they are hurting you. Then you can fight back, but never throw the first punch. Remember that, okay?" He stood up from his desk and put his arms around my neck. I could feel his little chest heave as he started to cry.

"He was talking about my daddy. He said I didn't have a daddy, but I did have a daddy." He was sobbing. "He died. And that makes my mommy and my grandma and grandpa so sad. I just want to have a daddy like the other kids. Jaxon, will you be my new daddy?" His words hit me like a ton of bricks. Me? Be his new daddy? How was I supposed to respond to something like that?

"Sammy, nobody will ever replace your daddy. He was very special to your mommy. I don't know what's gonna happen, but I'm here for you, little man. If you need to talk or if you feel like you need to use your fists to fix something, you come see me okay? We'll talk it out."

He stopped crying and smiled at me as he released me from his bear hug and started to put his jacket on.

While Sammy was getting his stuff ready and his teacher was lecturing him again about his stunt today, Uncle Jake pulled me out into the hallway.

"Son, I warned you. That boy thinks you're gonna be his new daddy. You need to figure out what the hell is going on back in

Richmond. Get your shit together, and decide what you're gonna do. You cannot hurt those kids and their momma. You hear me, boy?"

"I hear you. That's the last thing I wanna do."

Loralei

When I got home around five thirty, Jake's truck was in my driveway and Mags was sitting on the front porch listening to her iPod and playing with Tinkerbell, her cat. When she saw me, she came running over, whispering, "Mommy, I think Sammy is in a lot of trouble." I could tell she didn't really feel bad for her brother.

I walked into my house, and Jaxon, Jake, and Sammy were in the kitchen, Jaxon and Jake were chopping veggies for a salad. Sammy was sitting at the table, staring at the pizza boxes sitting in front of him like he was starving to death. I caught Jaxon's attention and nodded for him to come upstairs with me.

When we got to my room he gave me a quick kiss and I asked "What happened at the school?" He chuckled, and explained to me that Sammy got into a fight at school and apparently called another boy an "asshat".

"Why were they fighting?" I asked.

He explained, "The principal said that the other kid was giving Sammy a hard time about not having a dad and Sammy told him his dad had died, but he was getting a new daddy and he was big and mean and had tattoos and would kick his butt. Then he called the kid an 'asshat' and pushed him down on the playground."

I didn't know which part of this statement I should tackle first. The part where Sammy was in a fight, or when he cursed at another child, or that he thought Jaxon was his new daddy. And the worst part of the whole thing was that Jaxon thought it was really funny.

"I'm glad you find this humorous." I said in a very sarcastic tone.

He smirked. "Some parts of the story are funny, babe. I straightened everything out with the principal, Sammy didn't get suspended. All he has to do is write a letter of apology to the kid and help the teacher for a couple of weeks during his recess times."

But didn't he understand which part of the story upset me the most? "Sammy thinks you're going to be his new daddy?"

Jaxon looked confused. "I know we aren't there yet, Loralei, but wouldn't you rather him think that than not like me. I talked to him about it and explained that I wasn't his new daddy and that he shouldn't ever use his fists or his strength to solve his problems, because it doesn't work that way." When he said that, he had a look in his eyes that told me he was speaking from personal experience.

We went downstairs and Mags had set the table and Sammy was looking at me with a complete and utter look of fear on his face. I informed him he would be grounded for this, and we would talk about his punishment after school tomorrow while he was helping Jake muck the stalls in the barn. He actually looked relieved, I think he thought I was going to freak out, but amazingly enough I remained perfectly calm.

Jaxon and I were getting along so well. We were always catching each other in the barn or out in the field. We made-out like teenagers. It actually reminded me a lot of the time I spent with Declan. I noticed, since I had started spending time with Jaxon, my thoughts didn't turn to Declan quite as much as they had.

Dusk had always been my favorite time of the day. I loved to sit out on my big porch and watch the sun go down. I was doing that when I heard Jaxon's motorcycle roaring up the lane.

He drove up to the porch. I couldn't look away. He was so sexy. Like, incredibly sexy. He had on faded blue jeans with the knees ripped out, black motorcycle boots, a white t-shirt, and a leather biker vest. His helmet was all black with flames on the sides. When he pulled his helmet off of his head, it looked like a bad shampoo commercial. I couldn't look away. He took the helmet off, shook his head, and ran his fingers through his, as Emma would call it, "fuck me hair." I didn't think his lips could be any sexier. Then he ran his tongue over his bottom lip, before biting it. *Oh my God they could be sexier.* He rose up off of the bike, hung his helmet on the handlebar, and walked up the stairs to me.

"Beautiful night isn't it?" he asked.

"It really is. This has always been one of my favorite things to do. Just sit out here and have a glass of wine, enjoying the sunset." I motioned for him to have a seat in the rocking chair next to mine.

"Actually, I was wondering if you would like to go for a ride?" he asked, raising an eyebrow at me.

"I've never been on a motorcycle before."

He gasped, "We need to start by teaching you the difference between that amazing piece of machinery in your driveway and a motorcycle."

I laughed, "Uh, okay. That's not a motorcycle?"

He placed his hand on his chest, looking at me as if he was in pain. "No. No, Lor. It isn't. It's a Harley Davidson Fatboy Lo in Midnight Pearl. That my dear is so much more than a *motorcycle*."

"I'm so sorry. I had no idea."

"Well now that you do, I think we should go for a ride, don't you?"

I could do this. The kids were spending the weekend with Declan's parents. "Sure. Why not? Let's go."

"Okay, then. You might want to grab a jacket. It can get a little chilly on the back of a bike."

I went in the house and grabbed my old denim jacket. I walked outside and he was already on the bike. He was holding a helmet out for me. It was pink - bright pink. "Do you always carry a bright pink helmet around with you? You know, just in case you find some girl to take for a ride." I realized that last part sounded suggestive.

He smirked at me. "No, ma'am, I don't. I went into town and bought that today for the only woman that I want to take for a *ride*." He winked at me as I took the helmet from him.

I climbed on behind him. He grabbed my hands and placed them snugly around his waist. "Hold on tight, babe. This will be a ride you'll never forget."

I had no doubt. When he took off down the lane he scared the shit out of me. I almost jumped off the bike. "What the hell was that?"

"My baby doesn't like to go slow. She takes off pretty fast."

He took off down the road leading to town. It was such a beautiful night tonight. The wind was warm, not at all uncomfortable. The irrigation systems were going off in the field. The moon was shining down on the water, making it look like rainbows sparkling in the field. That mixed with fireflies flashing their lights all around us, was beautiful. I would never get tired of the beauty of this place I was lucky enough to live in.

Jaxon had slowed down after the initial take-off. When we got to town, he pulled into the local diner, Leona's Place. This place was famous for its pie. People drove from other states just to try a piece of Leona's pie.

Jaxon shut the bike down and stood up off the bike. He took his helmet off and damn, he looked even sexier than he had before. This was insane. He could not get sexier by the minute, could he?

"I thought we could try some of this famous pie all the guys have been telling me about."

I took off my helmet and he looked at me funny.

"What?" I asked.

He said, "Uh, you have a bad case of helmet hair. Let me help you with that." He took the helmet from me. Then he scooted in closer to me and ran his fingers through my hair. His eyes never left mine the entire time. I could look into those eyes all damn day.

His gaze drifted down to my lips and then back up to my eyes. "Whew, we better get inside. Or we might not ever make it to the pie." He said as he placed a light kiss on my cheek and lifted me off the bike.

Leona's Place didn't have many customers at this time of night. Leona was actually the only one there.

"Loralei Harper. How are ya, gorgeous? You haven't been in to visit me in ages."

"Miss Leona, sorry it's been so long. I'm just so busy. So much to do on the farm, so little time. You know how that goes."

Leona was such a sweetheart. I had known her since I was a little girl. She was a short, round older lady. She had curly brown hair and a tendency to wear a hairnet and an apron with a weird saying on it. Tonight's apron said: Big Girls Don't Cry – They're Happy Because They Eat Pie.

"Oh, baby girl, I understand that."

"What are you getting?" I asked Jaxon.

He responded with a questioning look on his face. "Uh, could I order one of everything? Would that be crazy?"

"They have eight different pies tonight, Jaxon. Can you eat eight pieces of pie?"

"I'd sure be willing to give it a good try," he said with a little grin.

Leona said, "Son, you're a man after my own heart. I'm gonna bring you out a little sample of all of the specials today."

Jaxon stood up and grabbed Leona in a big ole bear hug. "I think you're a woman after my own heart, Miss Leona."

She was blushing and smiling from ear to ear. Apparently, Jaxon's charms were effective on all members of the opposite sex. Didn't matter how old they were.

Leona disappeared into the kitchen to fetch our pie. Jaxon took my hand in his and started rubbing the pad of his thumb back and forth. He was smiling at me. The feelings I had for him were getting stronger every day. It was like we were drawn to each other. He was great with the kids and they were really starting to like him. That scared me and made me really happy at the same time. Jaxon was so different than Declan. I never thought I could fall for someone like him, but I was and I wanted more with him.

Leona came out to our table with a cookie sheet covered in pie. I mean covered in pie. I bet we had sixteen slices. So many different kinds: coconut cream, chocolate cream, lemon meringue, raisin cream, apple, blueberry, cherry, peanut butter, gooseberry, and my personal favorite chocolate-peanut butter. I ate at least one bite of each kind. Okay, maybe I also ate three bites of the chocolate-peanut butter pie. But my goodness, it was so delicious.

I couldn't let it go to waste. I was amazed at the amount of pie Jaxon ate. There was barely anything left on the cookie sheet when Leona came out to take it away.

She smiled at Jaxon. "I love to see a man with a healthy appetite. You better hang on tight to this one, Loralei."

"That sounds like excellent advice to me," Jaxon said with a grin.

He settled the check with Leona and we got ready for the ride home. On the way home he turned down the lane that leads out to the pond. I was really enjoying the ride and it didn't hurt that I got to have my arms wrapped around Jaxon, holding on tight.

When we got to the pond, Jaxon cut the engine and climbed off the bike. He took my hand and helped me get my helmet off and get off the bike. Then he climbed back on the bike. "Come here and sit down in front of me," he said.

"Um, sure." I climbed on in front of him. I leaned my back against his chest. My head was resting on his shoulder. This moment was perfect. The weather was perfectly warm. The moonlight shining down on the pond was perfect. The crickets chirping in the distance were making the perfect mood music for us.

I could feel his breath on my neck. Then I felt his tongue on my ear. He kissed my earlobe, whispering, "Thanks for going for a ride with me, Lor. Tonight, has been perfect."

How did he know what I was thinking? I thought it was perfect too.

He kissed my neck. His hands were resting on my thighs, until they started moving up to my breasts. He cupped them in his hands, and I heard a groan escape his lips as they were caressing my neck. I reached back and placed my arms around his neck and I turned my head to give him easier access to mine.

All of a sudden, he stopped. He moved his hands back to where they had been resting on my thighs and he rested his chin on my neck. He was breathing heavily.

"You don't have to stop, Jaxon."

"Oh baby, yes, yes I do. Let's just enjoy this beautiful night, okay?"

"Um, okay? You don't want to...do anything?"

"Damn, it woman. You're going to be the death of me." He said with a laugh. "Of course, I do, Lor. But I'm trying really hard to be a good boy."

We stayed at the pond for a couple of hours just talking and enjoying each other's company. I was really getting used to being wrapped up in his arms. He made me feel so safe and special. Like that was where I needed to be. This night had been perfect.

We rode home and I decided I really liked his motorcycle. He drove right up to the steps at my house. We climbed off the bike, he pulled our helmets off and hung them on the handlebars then he walked me to the door.

"Would you like to come in?" I asked.

"I would absolutely love to, but I think maybe it would be better if I didn't. I want us to take it slow, and I'm afraid if I come in I won't be able to do that." He was looking at me with a pained expression.

"Okay, I understand. But someday, hopefully soon, I want to be with you. You know that, right?"

He closed his eyes and shook his head. "Woman, you are gonna be the damn death of me. I am trying so hard to be good."

He leaned in and very softly pressed his lips to mine. He kissed me so gently, it was beautiful. He pulled away and then kissed the corners of my lips and then he ran his nose along my jaw. I could feel his warm breath on my face. "Someday soon, Loralei. Someday very, very soon."

It had been a month since Jaxon and I spent that night together in my house. I couldn't believe how right this all felt. He might be more than just the right guy for right now, he might be my forever. The kids adored him, my parents loved him, and I kinda thought maybe I did too.

I asked Jaxon last week if he would like to go to the cattle sale with me. He jumped at the chance of us spending an entire weekend together away from the kids in a hotel in another town. I was pretty excited about it too. I was nervous too, but mostly excited.

After the kids went to sleep that night, I called Emma to chit-chat. She told me she and Eric were celebrating their six year wedding anniversary with a huge party at the lake this weekend.

"Lor, you have to bring Jaxon with you to the party. I can't freaking believe you won't introduce him to me," Emma whined.

"Ems, you know I love you, but I just don't know if Jaxon is ready for a party with a bunch of country folks. You know he's not exactly a cowboy. I don't want him to feel out of place. And I explained to you that it's not that I won't introduce him to you; you're just so busy all the time with your new catering business. I never get to see you anymore."

I couldn't explain it, but I did feel kinda weird introducing Jaxon to Emma and Eric, especially Eric. He and Declan were best friends, and he and I had shared a special bond since the night of the accident. He had always treated the kids like his own. They adored their Uncle Eric, and he adored them. I was really afraid of what his reaction to Jaxon would be.

"Yeah, yeah, that's what you keep saying, but I think you're embarrassed of me. I'm not a total hick, you know. I do have all my teeth, and I don't wear overalls everyday!" I really hated to make Emma feel that way, but I felt that it was best to keep them away from Jaxon until I figured out my feelings for him.

I relented, "Okay, I'll bring him to your party, geesh, woman, calm down!" As I was saying this to Emma, I was worrying about Jaxon. I would never want to put him in a situation where he would feel out of place, and I was really afraid this party might do just that. But I decided to hope for the best and invite him anyway.

Once I got off the phone with Emma, I called Jaxon to share the invite with him.

"Hey babe, what's up?" he asked in a way that made my toes curl. I couldn't believe he hadn't pushed for us to have sex so far. I would've been concerned that he didn't want me, but we made out like a couple of teenagers every day.

"Did I wake you up?"

"Oh, no baby. I just got out of the shower."

"Well, I wanted to ask you something. I was wondering if you would like to go to a party with me on Saturday night?"

"What kinda party?" he asked.

"Emma and Eric are having a party at the lake to celebrate their anniversary. It should be fun and I would love for you to meet them." I really did want him to meet Eric and Emma. As worried as I was about him fitting in, selfishly, I wanted my friends to get to know him. And I really wanted to hear Ems thoughts on him.

"You really want me to meet your friends? I was starting to think you were ashamed of me. You talk about Emma and Eric all the time, but you haven't ever said anything about introducing us." He sounded really sad when he said that last part. Had I made him feel that way? I hadn't meant to.

"Jaxon, I'm so sorry if I made you feel that way. Of course I want you to meet my friends, please say yes."

And in the sexiest voice I have ever heard he said, "For you baby, my answer is always yes." Yes, that man could definitely make my lady parts dance. As I was standing by the bed thinking about my lady parts dancing, Jaxon asked, "So, what are you wearing right now?"

I couldn't help it. I started giggling. The way he said it was just too funny.

When he didn't say anything and I noticed he wasn't giggling, I asked, "Um, are you serious? You really want to know?"

"Baby, I just got out of the shower. I am standing in front of my bed with only a towel wrapped around my waist. And just hearing your voice has made me hard. I miss how it felt when I slept beside you. The way it felt when I held you in my arms all night. I wanted to do so much more. You know that, right Lor?"

I couldn't believe this was happening. Jaxon wanted to have phone sex with me. Surely, I was misunderstanding this.

I knew I sounded scared. "Yes, yes I know you wanted more. I did too. I was just scared, because it's been so long."

"Lor, do you want to have a new experience with me? I mean I just figured - you've never, uh, done this before, like on the phone?"

"Of course not Jaxon! You know I haven't. Have you?"

"I've never wanted to before."

"I would love to share my first time with you. I want you so much Jaxon. I'm about to explode."

I heard something crash and then I heard Jaxon say, "Holy fuck."

"Jaxon, are you still there? Are you okay?"

"Yeah, baby I'm here, um, wow, you just surprised me is all. I kind of dropped the phone." I giggled and he said "Are you laughing at me?"

"Why yes I am Jaxon, now what are you gonna do about it?" I couldn't believe I said that. But of course it's a lot easier to say things like that over the phone. I never would have said that had he been standing in front of me.

"You didn't answer my question, Lor."

"What did you ask again?" Of course I knew what he asked. I just wanted to hear him say it again.

"What – are – you - wearing?" He really drew that question out, stressing each word.

"Actually, I just got out of the shower also. But I'm not wrapped in a towel. I let it drop to the floor when you dropped the phone."

"Baby that was the hottest fucking thing I've ever heard. Are you in bed?"

"No."

"Get in bed. Naked. Get under the covers and follow my instructions."

"Yes, sir."

"Oh my God - you're killing me here."

"You could just come over. We could do this in person. Please." I was almost begging.

"It pains me to say this, but I am not coming over tonight. We are going to experience this together for the first time. Now do exactly as I say and nobody will get hurt." I laughed out loud at that.

"You know I don't like it when you laugh at me, baby. Are you in bed yet?"

"Yes."

"I want you to pretend that I am lying beside you. Can you do that, Lor?"

"Yes."

"Okay, I want you to play with your breasts for me. Take your hands and start at your stomach and make your way up to your breasts. Cup them in your hands. Now pinch your nipples, squeeze them, close your eyes, Lor, pretend it's me touching you. Can you feel my mouth on your nipple? Can you feel me squeezing them? Can you feel my teeth as I nip at them?"

"Oh wow, yes Jaxon, I can feel you. Oh, yes!" I could hear Jaxon moving around. It sounded like he was – maybe - I don't know. Sheepishly I asked, "Jaxon, are you, um, touching yourself too?"

"Uh huh...Lor, this is amazing. You're amazing."

I decided to give him a taste of his own medicine. "Can you feel me touching you, Jaxon? Can you feel me kissing you? Can you feel how much I want you inside me?" I couldn't believe those words had come out of my mouth. I didn't know what had come over me. And then I could definitely hear him rubbing himself. He was moaning, "Touch yourself, Lor. Put your fingers inside. Imagine me there. Touching you, inside you. Do it for me. I'm so close Lor, are you close?"

"Uh huh – Jaxon - I'm coming. Oh Jaxon!" My orgasm seemed to last forever. Then I heard Jaxon moan loudly and he screamed my name.

We were both panting and coming down from our amazing first phone sex experience when Jaxon broke the silence, "That was amazing for me. Are you okay? Did you enjoy that?"

How could he ask me that? Of course I enjoyed it. I really, really enjoyed it. "Yes, sir."

"Woman, you are going to be the death of me."

When Saturday arrived I decided to really play up the country part of my life. I wore skin tight black wranglers, my hottest pink cowboy boots, my belt with my prettiest silver buckle, a white button up shirt with pearlized buttons, tucked in with just enough buttons open to where you could just almost see my hot pink bra hiding below. I wore my hair down and put a few curls in it. I looked in the mirror and almost didn't recognize myself, I looked HOT!

When I heard the knock at the door, my heart started beating out of my chest. I couldn't believe how excited I was to see Jaxon. And he definitely didn't disappoint me. When I opened the door his mouth dropped open and his eyes didn't leave my chest. I couldn't look away from him either.

He was everything I wasn't tonight. He had on his "fancy pants" which were dark blue. He had on a skin tight black v-neck t-shirt tucked into his jeans, black motorcycle boots, and a black leather jacket. He was smoking HOT!

When we finally stopped ogling each other, we headed out to my old jeep and started the short drive to the lake. We rode in silence. The tension in the vehicle could've been cut with a knife. It was like there was some sort of electric current running between us and we had to have some sort of release.

Being around Jaxon did crazy things to me. I had never even thought about doing what I did next. I decided to take matters into my own hands, so to speak.

I leaned over to Jaxon, who was driving, and I licked the spot right behind his ear. I could feel his breath halt and his whole body shudder like the current had been zapped, the tension, starting to clear. I continued to lick a trail from his ear, across his jaw, to the corner of his mouth where I placed a light kiss.

He was driving, and I didn't want to have a wreck, but I just couldn't keep my hands off of him. I was rubbing his chest and then I was untucking his shirt, and trying to unzip his pants, and that's when he pulled over onto the first dirt road he came to and before I knew what was happening he had me pulled onto his lap and I was straddling him.

The kiss, this kiss was fast and furious. It was like we had never kissed before. His tongue invaded my mouth and I accepted it wholeheartedly. He unbuttoned my shirt and when he saw my hot pink bra I heard a sexy growl escape his lips. Jaxon was an expert with his tongue. He could do magical things with it. One moment he was licking the spot between my breasts, and then he was tracing a path up my chest, neck, jaw, and then my mouth.

The next thing I knew I was trying to unzip his jeans again. He grabbed my hand, "No, not here. Not like this. Not our first time, Lor. Our first time together needs to be special, not in a jeep. I think I love you, Lor."

His words hit me like a ton of bricks, mostly because I felt the same way about him. But I never thought he could love me. I'm just a little country girl and he definitely didn't fit into my world.

"You don't have to say anything; I just want you to know what I'm feeling." He said as he looked down and clasped his hand in mine.

I used my other hand to tilt his face up to look at me. "Jaxon, I never thought I would say this to another man, but I think I'm falling in love with you too."

After our "we almost love each other" declarations, we straightened our clothes out and started toward the lake again. When we pulled up, the party was in full swing. I spotted Emma and Eric out by the bonfire. It reminded of that night so many years ago when Declan and I had come back to the bonfire at the pond to pick up a very drunk Eric. And to see him standing there already drunk again really pissed me off. I wanted to go up to him and remind him of what happened that night and how if he hadn't gotten so drunk I would be married to Declan now and my kids would have their father. But I didn't. I just smiled and led Jaxon out to them.

Jaxon looked so out of place amongst all these cowboys. He was nervous, but I was the only one who knew that. He kinda looked scary. Scary probably isn't the right word. He looked intimidating.

I squeezed his hand and looked up at him, trying to let him know that it was okay. I wanted him to feel comfortable around these people. I don't know who I thought I was kidding. I hadn't felt comfortable around these people for years.

The last bonfire party I went to didn't end so well. It had been over ten years since I came to a party with my friends. It just didn't feel right without Declan. I really wished that my mind hadn't gone there. Now everywhere I looked I could see him. Jaxon must have noticed that my mind was wandering. He squeezed my hand and looked at me like he really wanted to help, but didn't know what to do.

"Lor, you're here! I can't believe you actually came!" Emma hollered as she came running up from the other side of the beach. She looked like one of those bad tampon commercials where the girl is running across the beach towards her lover. This really helped my mood. I was laughing inside and started running toward Emma, pulling Jaxon with me.

Emma couldn't take her eyes off of Jaxon. She looked him up and down and up and down again. Then she looked at me and gave me a not so subtle wink and nod of approval. "And this must be the amazing Jaxon I have heard so much about?" Emma said to Jaxon.

"Well I don't know about amazing, but I am Jaxon. It's really nice to finally meet you Emma." Jaxon wouldn't let go of my hand and I was really glad he didn't. We both needed each other to make it through this night.

"Eric is dying to meet you," Emma said and then yelled, "Hey Eric, get your ass over here and meet the amazing Jaxon."

Eric came walking over, assessing Jaxon from his motorcycle boots, to his "fancy" pants, to his pierced eyebrow and shaggy hair. I could tell by the glaring look of disapproval on his face that he didn't like what he was seeing. "Hey, man, nice to meet you. I've heard so much about you from Lor and the kids." Jaxon said to Eric as he stuck his hand out to shake hands.

Eric didn't move. He didn't say anything. He just stood there staring at Jaxon and then he looked over at me. "Can I talk to you for a second, alone?"

Jaxon dropped his hands to his sides. I winced at the loss of that connection to him. Eric grabbed my arm and pulled me toward the bonfire. Emma just looked at me with raised eyebrows. Silently saying, "I don't know what he's doing." She asked Jaxon if he wanted to go get a beer. They headed off to the coolers as Eric, and I walked away.

"What the hell are you doing with a guy like that? Do you really think that's the kind of person Declan would want around his kids? You do remember whose kids they are, right?" Eric was being so hateful. This man had helped me so much since Declan died and now that I was finally finding happiness he was pissed at me. I couldn't help myself.

The words flew out of my mouth. "Yeah Eric, I remember who's kids they are, do you? They aren't yours, they're Declan's, and he's dead because we had to come get your drunk ass and drive you home! And that's the reason why I've been so miserable for so long. Now I'm finally finding a little bit of happiness and you're mad at me? Are you fucking kidding me?"

I didn't need this shit and I wasn't going to deal with it tonight. I made my way over to Jaxon and I couldn't contain the tears that started falling. I grabbed Jaxon's arm and asked him to get me out of there. He put his beer down and we rushed over to the jeep.

Emma asked as she followed Jaxon and me to the jeep. "Where are you going, Lor? Please don't leave, the party is just starting. What the hell did he say to you?"

"I can't do this Emma. I thought I was ready but I'm not. And Eric doesn't think Jaxon is the right guy for me? What the fuck? Why should I give a shit about what he thinks? How dare he say anything about my life choices!"

I pulled the door open on the jeep and climbed in. Jaxon shut the door behind me and ran around to get in. He started it up, and I watched Emma run over to Eric. She was beating at his chest and screaming at him. Eric couldn't take his eyes off me. He wasn't angry, he looked sad. I started to tear up again and when I looked over at Jaxon he was just staring straight ahead as we drove down the road. He was acting like I wasn't there. I reached over to grab his hand and he pulled away.

"I'm sorry you had to hear that. I shouldn't have said that in front of you. I am so sorry."

Jaxon finally looked over at me and said, "Eric's right, Lor. I don't know who the hell I was trying to kid. I'm not the right guy for you. I was just fooling myself thinking I was good enough to be with a lady like you. I'm not. You deserve so much better than me."

Then he stared off into the distance in front of us again. "I'll talk to Uncle Jake and leave tomorrow. I don't want to hurt you anymore than I already have. You'll always be special to me, and I hope that you'll always remember me."

I was crushed. I had opened my heart, my life, and my body to this man and we hit one little bump in the road and he was ready to leave?

"Well apparently our time together meant nothing to you if you're willing to just leave when the going gets tough. I thought we were falling in love, but I guess I was really, really wrong." I tried to hold back the tears.

Jaxon pulled the jeep over and grabbed my face in his hands. His eyes were so intense. We sat there for a long time just staring at each other until he said, "God damn it, Lor. I don't think I love you."

My heart sank in my chest. He doesn't love me. That's why it was so easy for him to just walk away.

"I fucking know I love you. I have never felt this way about anyone before. Saying all that shit just now about killed me. I can't stand the thought of not being with you. Not seeing you every day. I love you and I love the kids and I want to see where this goes. I want us to try for our happily ever after. Don't you want that too, Lor?"

I wanted to scream "yes" and "I love you too", but I couldn't say anything. I reached up and swiped my knuckles across his jaw. "Eric is an asshole. He doesn't know what's best for me and the kids. But I do, and I think that's you."

He kissed me, a sweet, soft, meaningful kiss. A kiss that told me that we were going to be together and that it didn't matter what anyone else thought.

Chapter 6

Loralei

The next few days were great. Jaxon and I spent every minute we could together. The fact that we worked together was really convenient. That's one of the perks of being the boss, you can make-out with your farmhand boyfriend in every possible place you can think of on the farm. The barn, the field, the garage, the garden, my office - so many places, so little time.

I walked into one of the horse stalls and suddenly felt warm breath on the back of my neck.

"Morning, babe," Jaxon said, placing a kiss on my neck. I felt his tongue as he licked a trail from my ear to my jaw. I shivered from my head to my toes.

"Jaxon, stop. Someone will see us."

"No, they won't. Everyone went into town for the sale this morning. We have the barn all to ourselves. Of course, we have to share it with the horses, but I don't think they'll mind if we roll around in their hay for a bit."

I turned to face him. "Did you just insinuate that I would roll around in the hay with you?"

He nuzzled my neck and nipped at my ear. "Why yes, ma'am. I believe I did." He laughed against my neck and pushed me onto the bales of hay in the corner of the stall.

I giggled as he was fumbling with the buttons on my shirt. "You need help with that, stud?"

Jaxon pulled away. "You know I hate it when the guys call me that, but when you do it, it really turns me on." The sexy smirk was back. "I'll make you think stud." He kissed me hard.

As his tongue thrust into my mouth, I pulled my knees up so I could get him closer to me. He pressed into me and let out the sexiest moan. "God, you feel so good. I want to bury myself inside you, and never come out."

"Then do it already. Please, Jaxon, I'm ready. I need to be with you." I was breathing heavy and probably sounded like a crazy person.

"Not like this, Lor. Not out in the barn, literally rolling in the hay. It needs to be special."

"How about tonight? My parents are keeping the kids. We'd have the whole house to ourselves."

Before I got the words out of my mouth, he picked me up off of the hay and started swinging me around in circles. "Whoa, calm down stud. I'll take that as a yes?"

He stopped spinning and sat me down. "Yes, for you the answer is always yes."

The rest of the afternoon dragged. It seemed like the day would never end. I got home and called my mom to make sure the kids were okay. I told them to get their homework done, be good for their grandparents, have sweet dreams, and mommy would see them tomorrow.

I could do this, right? It's just sex, Loralei. I tried to tell myself it was just sex, I really did. But it felt like so much more. Like when Declan and I were together, it wasn't about the sex, it was about our connection. It was about our future. I felt like this night with Jaxon was going to change things.

I was an excited, scared ball of nerves. We were going to be together. He could be my future. And that was huge. If he was going to be in my life, that meant he was also going to be a part of my kid's lives. I had thought of nothing else since that first night we spent together. I had finally come to the conclusion that I loved him, and he wasn't going anywhere. So, yeah, I decided I could do this.

I took a long, hot shower. Towel dried my hair and put on my sexiest nightgown. While I was searching for something to wear, I realized I probably should have gone with Ems one of the many times she invited me, to pick out something sexier. My sexiest nightgown was just a short, white baby-doll gown. It was trimmed in lace and very feminine. Not super sexy, but I had to work with what I had.

I left my hair down and went downstairs to the kitchen. I decided maybe a glass of wine would help calm my nerves. I poured a large glass and headed to the living room to wait for Jaxon. When I walked into the room, my eyes immediately flew to the mantle, to the picture of Declan and I. I walked over to it, picked it up, and almost cried. Almost.

My feelings were changing. Declan would always be my first love. But I was starting to realize that he wasn't the only love of my life. Jaxon had done this. He had made me forget, no not forget, I could never forget my past. But he had made me reevaluate my future, or my destiny.

Tonight would change everything, but I wasn't nervous anymore. It was like Declan had released me. Something had happened in my head and my heart. Something that made me know how right tonight was going to be. How right Jaxon was for me and my future. Tonight was going to be life-changing.

When I heard the motorcycle barreling down my driveway, I went into the kitchen and rinsed my wine glass and put it in the dishwasher. I didn't want Jaxon to think I had to drink to do this.

He knocked on the door and I ran to answer it in just my nightgown. He was dressed in his signature "fancy pants" and a blue Eagles t-shirt. His shaggy hair was perfectly tousled and those big brown eyes were taking in every inch of my body.

I cleared my throat, and he finally made eye contact. "Babe, you do realize that sexy-ass nightgown is completely see-through in the light? You may have just given me a heart attack." His eyes were lingering on my breasts. Men - they're all the same.

"We have plans tonight, mister. You can't die on me now." He walked in the house and immediately picked me up and pressed me against the wall.

He whispered in my ear, "I don't plan on dying until I see you with that gown off."

Thank goodness he was holding me up, because those words, and the way he said them, almost caused my knees to give out. He kissed my neck right below my ear, and made his way up to my ear. He nibbled on my earlobe, and I giggled.

In a low, sultry voice he said, "You know how I feel about you laughing at me." He kissed me, picked me up, and started carrying me upstairs toward my bedroom.

We were still kissing when he sat me down at the foot of the bed. He looked down at me through those long lashes and grabbed the hem of my nightgown, pulling it over my head. I stood in front of him in just my white panties. I instinctively crossed my arms over my naked chest. Even though he had seen my breasts before, it was just an instinct to cover them.

"Please don't do that, babe. I want to see and experience all of you. Please don't be nervous or shy. It's me, and I love you. I don't plan on having sex with you tonight, Loralei. What we are going to do means so much more to me than just sex. I'm going to make love to you. I'm going to show you how much I love you. And I want you to feel comfortable enough to tell me what you want or don't want. I want you to know that you can't do anything wrong here. We love each other and anything we do in bed together will be perfect. Now, I want to ask you one more time, are you sure you're ready for this?"

I was in awe of this man. His words just melted my heart, not to mention what they did to my panties. I didn't answer him. Instead I reached for the hem of his t-shirt and pulled it over his head. Then I unzipped his jeans and slid them down to the floor. He kicked them off and we both stood in silence, staring at each other. Jaxon placed his hand on my cheek and started to gently rub his thumb back and forth over it. He leaned in and placed a very soft kiss on my lips. I needed more. I threw my arms around his neck and pulled him toward me. I kissed him with everything in me. I wanted him, and I wasn't going to wait another minute.

He pressed me back onto the bed. His lips never left mine while he laid down beside me on the bed. He slowed the kiss down. I couldn't control the whimper I released when he pulled his lips from mine. There was that sexy smirk again.

"You miss me already? I'm not going anywhere, Lor. You are mine." He kissed my neck and moved down to my breasts. He was caressing one with his hand and kissing the other. I couldn't decide which felt better. They both felt pretty amazing. He kept looking up at me. I couldn't take my eyes of him. He was so beautiful.

He removed his hand from my breast and slid it down to my panties. Never breaking eye contact, he removed my panties. Then he leaned up and started looking at me, like really looking at me. When his gaze got to my c-section scar, he leaned down and placed soft kisses along it. It felt amazing, but I was shaking. He was getting really close to the place I wanted him to be.

"Babe, are you okay?"

I guess he felt me shaking and it worried him. "I'm just a little nervous."

He stopped what he was doing, gave me a long, sweet kiss and said, "What did I tell you, Lor? There is no reason to be nervous. It's just me. I love you."

I shook my head. "Maybe I wouldn't be so nervous if I wasn't the only one lying here naked."

"Your wish is my command." He took off his boxers and I was shocked. Okay, yes I was shocked to see his penis, but I was even more shocked to see *that*.

I guess I was staring, because he said, "Remember when Sammy asked me about my piercings? I didn't tell him I didn't have one, I just told him we shouldn't talk about it. If it scares you, I can take it out."

I reached down and touched it. Jaxon let out a small gasp. I asked, "Um, will it *hurt* me?"

"No, babe, it will feel really, really good. I promise."

Jaxon started kissing me again. He pulled away from my lips and his mouth trailed down my stomach toward my inner thighs. He said, "I want to kiss you there, Lor. Do you want me to do that?" I couldn't speak, I nodded. He pressed his face into me. "You smell amazing. I cannot wait to taste you."

Before I could think about what was happening, his tongue was inside me. He was licking me and then he was sucking my clit. He grazed it with his teeth and everything went blurry. I arched my back, which only made his tongue go deeper and I screamed out, "Oh my God."

Once I came down from my glorious high, he climbed up to my mouth and whispered, "You can just call me Jaxon."

I had to smile at that.

He placed his knee between my legs and spread them further. "Are you ready?" he asked.

"Yes, Jaxon, I am."

He was leaning over me and then he started to press himself into me. When I felt the piercing hit my clit, I flinched. He stopped, "Okay?"

"It just felt *weird*, it's okay. Please keep going."

He pressed deeper and deeper until he was all the way in. I could feel the piercing the entire time. It had been so long since I had done this; it felt like I never had.

"I'm going to move now, okay? Tell me if you want me to stop." He started moving. Very slowly at first and then when our bodies became accustomed to each other, he sped up. His piercing was rubbing me and I was getting so close. He was thrusting so hard now. The headboard was hitting the wall. I was moaning, he was moaning. "I'm so close Lor, are you close?' I nodded and he said, "Let's come together, okay? Ready?"

I was having a really hard time speaking, but I finally got out, "Yes."

He started thrusting into me. Once, twice, and then we came together. He was breathing heavy, nuzzling my neck. "I love you, Loralei Harper. Oh my God, I love you."

We spent the rest of the night holding each other. It was the most amazing night I had had in my twenty-six years. Jaxon and I were in love and nothing could change that.

The next morning when I woke up, I was suddenly panicked. Last night I was so happy to be with Jaxon that I never even thought about it. How did I not think about it? After what happened with Declan, how could I have not thought about a condom? I had never needed birth control before. I honestly didn't think about it last night. But why didn't Jaxon? He knew why he was coming over. He knew I hadn't been with anyone in ten years. He had to know that I wasn't on birth control.

I had to ask, "Baby, are you awake?"

He peeked at me with one eye, "Yeah, everything okay, babe?"

I just needed to spit it out. We had just spent the night together, so why was asking him this question so embarrassing?

I finally just blurted it out, "Um, why didn't you use *protection* last night?"

He closed his eyes and took a deep breath, "I'm clean, Lor. I knew your history and knew you were too."

That didn't really answer the big question though, did it? I didn't want to get pregnant again, especially not this early in our relationship. With the twins I could write it off as being a careless teenager, but this would be different. "What about getting me pregnant? I'm really not ready for that, Jaxon."

"I'm sorry, Lor. I don't know what else to say. I just wasn't thinking." That didn't really calm my nerves any, but I guess it was the best answer I was going to get.

We really needed to get to work. We didn't want to leave each other, but we knew we would be able to see each other all day.

The next week was great. Jaxon and I spent as much time together as we could. I thought it might be awkward between us, but it was the opposite. It was so easy to talk to him, to be with him. Actually, we wanted to be together all the time. But that was kinda hard to do with the kids and the farm. But we tried to eat lunch together every day.

I was sitting at my desk that morning, when he walked in. He sauntered over to me, picked me up out of my chair, and sat me down on the desk, he slid in between my legs and kissed me so passionately, "I've missed you, baby."

He was doing all of the right things, in all the right places. Before I knew it we were panting and had moved past heavy petting when all of a sudden the door flew open. Jaxon's eyes shot up and he got this look on his face. This look that said he had been caught doing something he wasn't supposed to do.

He backed away from me and went running toward the door. I looked over and saw a beautiful blonde woman standing in the doorway with tears in her eyes. She was a very small woman with a perfect body, long blonde hair, and she was wearing a shorter than short mini-skirt with a barely there halter top with 4 inch stilettos. She looked even more out of a place on a farm than Jaxon did.

She screamed at me, "Who the hell are you?" I couldn't understand why she was so mad at me, why she was crying, or why Jaxon was just standing there staring at her.

"I'm Loralei, and you're in my office. So, I think I should ask the questions. Who the hell are you?"

The words that came from her mouth literally made my heart break. "I'm his wife." She pointed at Jaxon. He looked over at me and didn't say a word. I couldn't help the tears that came into my eyes.

He finally spoke, "Stacy, please wait outside. I need to speak to Loralei."

Stacy replied "Like hell I will, you fucking bastard! What the hell are you doing with your tongue down her throat, you're my husband, you asshole!"

"Don't worry about it, I'll leave you two alone," I said on my way out the door. Jaxon didn't try to stop me, and I was actually glad he didn't. I was too upset to talk to him. I really didn't want him to see how much this was affecting me. How much he was able to hurt me.

When I got home, I called mom.

"Would you be able to keep the kids an extra day? I think I'm gonna go to Joplin today, instead of tomorrow."

"Everything okay, honey? You don't sound so good." Mom asked.

"I'm okay. I'm not, but I just don't want to talk about it right now, okay?"

"Is Jaxon still going with you?" She asked, knowing he wasn't.

"Something happened. Long story – I'll explain it later. I promise."

I got the kids stuff packed for their long weekend with their grandparents and started my three hour drive to Joplin.

I finally turned my phone off about half way to Joplin. Jaxon wouldn't stop calling. I had nothing to say to him. I couldn't believe he lied to me. How could he be with me if he was married and why didn't Jake tell me he was married. I really didn't understand what was going on, but I couldn't think about it right now.

I turned my phone back on long enough to call Emma. I needed to talk to someone about what had happened.

"Hey, Lor, what's going on?" She answered with her normal, perky voice.

I was sobbing. I could hardly respond. "He's, he's married, Ems."

"Who's married, Lor?" She asked.

"Jaxon. Jaxon's married. His wife showed up today. He has a wife." I was still crying and trying to focus on the road.

"That fucking bastard. I'll castrate him for you." Ems was always supportive. "Why the hell didn't he tell you he was married?"

"I don't know. When she showed up, he acted like I wasn't even there. When she saw us together, kissing, he looked like a kid who got caught with his hand in a candy jar. He looked like he was doing something wrong."

"I'm flabbergasted, Lor. I don't, I just don't even know what to say. I'm here for you always. Whatever you need, you just let me know. Don't you dare cry over that bastard. He doesn't deserve you."

"Oh, Ems. What about the kids? They love him. This is going to break their hearts. This is why I didn't want to be in a relationship. Don't you see? This is what I have always been afraid of. I can't stand the thought of my babies hurting over this, over my bad decisions."

"You listen to me, Loralei Harper. This was not your bad decision. He seemed like the real deal. You didn't do anything wrong. He's a liar, not you. Now, you're scaring me. I don't think you're safe to be driving. Just pull over and let me come get you," she pleaded.

"I'm okay, Ems. The tears are drying up. I'm fine to drive. I'm going to be there in a couple of hours. I'll call you when I get checked in."

"You better. Don't make me drive my ass to Joplin to check on you."

"I promise. I love you, Ems. Thanks for listening."

"I love you too, Lor. You drive safe and take care of you, for me."

"Will do."

I hung up the phone and turned it off again. I didn't want to talk to Jaxon anymore today. Nothing he could say would make this better. The look on his face when Stacy walked in was engraved in my brain. I would never forget how guilty he looked.

When I arrived at the hotel, I was drained physically and emotionally. I checked in and gave my bags to the bellboy as I headed upstairs to my room. I loved this trip every year mostly because of this beautiful hotel and the amazing suite that I splurged on. The suite was huge and very traditional. There was a huge four-poster bed in the middle of the room. The bathroom was gigantic and so relaxing. There was a large claw-foot tub in the corner that was the perfect size for two. I had fantasized about Jaxon and me taking a bath together in that tub.

Jaxon. Why did he lie to me? Why didn't he tell me what was going on? Why would he hurt me like this? I just couldn't understand.

When I turned my phone back on, I saw that I had more missed calls and several voicemails, all from him. The more I looked at the phone the madder I got. *Screw him* - this was not my fault. I opened my heart, body, and soul to him, and he neglected to mention he was married. How could he do that? What kind of a person was he?

I decided to go down to the hotel bar and get a drink. I was here to relax and have fun and that's exactly what I planned to do.

Before I left the room, I called mom and checked on the kids and told them goodnight. I reassured mom that I was fine and headed downstairs to the bar. I decided I should try to eat something before I started drinking so I asked to be seated in the restaurant. There was a gentleman standing by the hostess station. I assumed he was waiting for a table also.

He was tall, like abnormally tall, I would guess him to be 6' 7". He looked to be about my age, he had light blonde hair and really intense green eyes. He was also a cowboy from his hat to his boots and the wranglers in between. His body was very muscular and you could tell by looking at his calloused hands that he worked hard, definitely not afraid to get his hands dirty.

He shocked me when he walked over and said, "Evenin' ma'am, dinin' alone tonight?" I didn't think he could get any sexier, but I was wrong. His slow, southern drawl was hot.

I answered with, "I've kinda had a shitty day actually, and I wouldn't be good company for anyone tonight. I just came down to grab a drink, well actually probably a few drinks, and I thought I better eat something first."

"Well we can't have that now, can we?" He motioned for the hostess. "Excuse me ma'am, we'll need a table for two."

"My name is Cade Walker, nice to meet you Miss....?"

"Oh, my name is Loralei Harper. Nice to meet you too, Mr. Walker."

He looked at me funny. "Please call me Cade and I'll call you Loralei, okay?"

I nodded in agreement and the hostess came over to escort us to our table.

We sat down. Cade asked what I would like to drink. I told him to surprise me. He headed off for the bar, and the waitress brought me our menus. She explained that she could have taken our drink orders. I wasn't really paying attention to anything that was going on, so I just nodded and waited for Cade to get back with my drink.

Cade brought me a bottle of Corona with a lime in it. I was not a big fan of beer, but I started chugging it anyway.

"I think you might ought to slow down, hon'"

I sneered at him, "I warned you I had a really crappy day, but I forgot to mention that I plan on getting really drunk tonight, so if you don't want to be a part of that you better get your ass out of that chair and go find some other woman to hit on."

He looked completely stunned, but he just gave me his best shit-eating grin. "So what makes ya think I'm gonna hit on you?"

In my snarkiest voice I said, "You aren't planning on it, really?"

He couldn't even argue. He just laughed this deep belly laugh as the waitress came over to take our order. "Just bring us a couple of steaks, medium rare, baked potatoes, and do you have dinner rolls?" The waitress nodded, took our order, and headed off to the kitchen.

"You realize this is 2013 and not 1950, don't you? I am perfectly capable of placing my own dinner order!" This man was so arrogant.

He just shrugged his shoulders. "Well yeah hon' I do, but you didn't seem to mind it, you know, I bet there are lots of things I could do for you that you wouldn't mind."

When he said that, I choked on my beer. He was looking at me like he could eat me alive, and I didn't know if it was the fact that I was pissed at Jaxon or that Cade was just so damned gorgeous, but my lady parts were doing a little happy dance.

We ate our dinner and I had a few, well more like seven, beers. I was feeling no pain. Screw Jaxon, actually no, been there done that, won't do it again. Before I knew what was happening, I was trying to get my keycard to unlock my hotel room door, and Cade had his tongue in my ear.

What was that noise…seriously, why did I feel like my head was going to pop off and that that wouldn't be the worst thing to happen? I very carefully turned over and then I really wished my head would just pop off. Cade was in my bed and he was buck naked, except for his socks. And what I couldn't decide was if I was more upset that he was in my bed, or that he hadn't taken his socks off before we had sex. I felt like a total slut at that moment. I very carefully crawled out of bed and headed toward the bathroom.

When I looked in the mirror I scared myself. I looked like a hooker. Well, what I assumed a hooker would look like after a really rough night. I had raccoon eyes from my mascara, my hair looked like rats could be living in it, and I was wearing - what was I wearing - apparently I got cold in the night because I had on Cades undershirt.

I decided that I really needed to take a shower and try to remember more about what happened last night. Everything started flooding my mind...the intense flirting during dinner, his foot sliding up my inner thigh under the table, and then me asking him to come to my room for sex. Oh my god, I asked him to come to my room and I told him I just wanted to forget about everything and have meaningless sex and he agreed and came to my room with me. I can't even blame him for what happened. I did this. It was all my fault.

Why was I so sore? I literally hurt all over and the warm water in the shower was only helping a little, I needed to remember more about what happened after we got back to the room last night.

I remembered trying to get into the room and Cade sucking on my earlobe and then sticking his tongue in my ear. Then he used that tantalizing tongue to lick a line from my ear to my nipple, where he sucked and pinched until I screamed out in pain or ecstasy, or both. That thought sent a shiver down my spine.

Then somehow I was naked and he was naked. I remembered seeing a tattoo on his chest and thinking I had to trace it with my tongue, and then I did just that.

All of these memories were coming back to me - me insisting he wear a condom and then Cade entering me as he bent me over the couch. I remembered how big he was and how it felt to be so amazingly full, he was bucking and riding me like an animal. That must be why I was so sore today.

More memories appeared of me in bed with Cade lying on top of me, him screaming how tight I was and how amazing it felt to be inside me. Oh my god, I am so glad I was drunk at the time, or I probably would have died of embarrassment. This memory couldn't be right, surely not. There was no way a man would howl when he came, but, oh my god, I remember him doing just that.

I decided that I better learn to enjoy the heat because I was definitely going to go to hell for being a slut. I hadn't had sex in ten years and now I was just screwing random cowboys that I met in hotel bars. I asked myself, "How did it come to this?" But I already knew the answer. I fell in love with a pierced, tattooed, knight in shining armor who just happened to forget to mention he was married.

Cade

Damn, I hated coming to this thing. Since I was in charge of my family's ranch, I had to attend this event every year. Normally, I would find a warm body to keep me company for the weekend. Then I would make some deals as I wined and dined a few prospective sellers.

I really needed a beer and to find that warm body for the weekend. The best place to do that was at the restaurant downstairs. There would be some little cattle heiress just waiting for a big strong cowboy like me to sweep her off her feet, or in my case fuck her senseless.

While I was standin' at the hostess station I saw her. She looked like an angel. All she was missin' was a damn halo. She had long blonde hair laying in curls down her back. She was wearing blue jeans, cowboy boots, and a red plaid button-up shirt. That shirt had just enough buttons unbuttoned to make me want to take a closer look.

I walked over to her. "Evenin' ma'am, dining alone tonight?"

She looked like her cat had just died. She said, "I've kinda had a shitty day, I wouldn't be good company for anyone tonight. I just came down to grab a drink, well actually probably a few drinks, and I thought I better eat something first."

"Well we can't have that now, can we?" I motioned for the hostess. I let her know I would be needin' a table for two.

I decided I should probably introduce myself. "My name is Cade Walker, nice to meet you Miss….?"

"Oh, my name is Loralei Harper. Nice to meet you too Mr. Walker."

What the hell? Nobody calls me Mr. Walker. "Please call me Cade and I'll call you Loralei, okay?"

The hostess took us over to our table.

I asked Loralei what she would like to drink. She told me to surprise her. Corona with lime it is. I could tell she wasn't really excited about my drink choice, but she started to chug it down anyway.

"I think you might ought to slow down, hon'"

She shot me a look, that I'm pretty sure would've killed a weaker man, "I warned you I had a really shitty day, but I forgot to mention that I plan on getting really drunk tonight, so if you don't want to be a part of that you better get your ass out of that chair and go find some other woman to hit on."

Oh, I was gonna enjoy this. I couldn't help but grin. "So what makes ya think I'm gonna hit on you?"

She said, "You aren't planning on it, really?"

I couldn't disagree with that. Of course I was plannin' on it. Why the hell else would I have bought her a drink and offered her my company for the evening? I just laughed at her.

The waitress came over and I ordered our dinner. This did not make Loralei very happy. And by the look on her face, I knew I was fixin' to hear about it.

"You realize this is 2013 and not 1950, don't you? I am perfectly capable of placing my own dinner order!"

Yep, I was gettin' a hell of a kick out of this woman. "Well yeah hon' I do, but you didn't seem to mind it, you know, I bet there are lots of things I could do for you that you wouldn't mind." *Damn,* the things I could do to this woman.

I guess I was kinda looking at her like she was my next meal. She was blushing, and in my vast experience, that was always the sign of a good girl wantin' to be bad.

Wow, Loralei Harper could drink. While we ate our dinner she chugged seven or eight beers. She was pretty buzzed. Actually, I was too. I was matching her drink for drink.

"So, you run Harper Farms, huh?" I asked in between bites of steak.

"Yep, sure do. I've been managing it for several years. It's so much more than just a business, you know? It's my future. It's my family's future. It's what I have to show the world I was here. And I accomplished something while I was in this world."

It was like she was inside my head. That was exactly how I felt about my ranch. It was my life. And I would do anything to make it a success. Damn, she had the most beautiful honey colored eyes. I couldn't wait to see the look in those eyes when I made her come. If I had anything to do with it, that would be happenin' real soon. I ran my boot up her leg starting at her ankle and ending at her inner thigh. She was looking right into my eyes the entire time.

"So, Cade Walker, you wanna have sex with me?" She asked. I almost choked on my beer.

"Excuse me?"

"Cut the shit. We both know that's what you've been planning all night. I'm just making it easier for you. But let me make this clear - this means nothing. It's just two people having sex. And I have a rule. If you follow the rule, I will do anything to you that you want."

"Anything?" I asked.

"Yep, anything your little heart desires."

It definitely wouldn't be my heart that she would be servicing soon. I wouldn't have any problem coming up with something for her to do to me.

"What's this rule I have to abide by?" I asked.

"You have to wear a condom. You can't be like asshat and try to get me pregnant, kay? That's not too much to ask, right?"

"Not at all, hon. I promise I'll wear a condom."

"Then we're on cowboy. Let's get upstairs."

"Your room or mine?" I asked.

"Mine."

I took care of the check and we started walking to the elevator. When the doors closed after we stepped on, she jumped me. No joke. This woman was fuckin' amazing. She had me pushed up against the wall, her tongue was in my ear, and her legs were wrapped around my waist.

I peeled her off of me as the elevator doors opened. We walked to her room. She had a hard time getting the door open, but finally she did.

I couldn't wait another second. I needed to be inside her. I grabbed her shirt and ripped it off of her. I threw it to the ground and she smiled the sexiest little smile at me. She started to take her jeans off, so I decided to help her. I pulled them down and had her step out of them. I threw them somewhere in the room too. I was in a hurry. I wasn't too worried about her clothes.

She was standing in front of me in a lacey black bra and panties. I stripped down to nothing but my socks. I didn't have time to take them off. Priorities.

I couldn't wait another second. I grabbed her and kissed her hard. I thrust my tongue into her mouth. I didn't want this to end. There was something about this woman. I couldn't say for sure what it was. But it just felt right.

I started licking a line from her throat to her nipple. When I bit down she hollered. I straightened up and looked into her eyes. Those beautiful, fucking eyes. She saw my tattoo on my chest and leaned in and licked a trail all the way around it. I couldn't take another second of this. I had to be inside her, now.

I motioned for her to follow me over to the couch. I turned her until her stomach was pressing against the arm of the couch. I covered her body with mine. Grabbing her panties, I ripped them off of her and threw them across the room. I unhooked her bra and started to massage her breasts, paying special attention to her nipples. They were so hard.

She wanted me just as much as I wanted her. I could feel it. My hand found its way to her pussy. She was so wet and ready for me.

I started to press into her from behind, when she said, "Condom. You promised." She was breathing heavy and rubbing her backside up against me. I was about to explode and I wasn't even inside her yet. I left her just long enough to grab my wallet and get a condom. I got back over to her and entered her in one hard thrust. She screamed out, "Oh my God, Cade."

After the couch, I took that woman in every position I had ever tried or imagined. She was fuckin' amazin'. She made me howl more than any other woman ever had. When she finally had enough and fell asleep, I laid awake just watching her breathe. She was the most beautiful woman I had ever seen. There was somethin' about her. I ran my hand along her jaw and she twisted to press her cheek into my palm.

This woman was gonna be trouble. I could already feel it in my...heart. Seriously? What the fuck was happenin' to me? I don't have feelings for women. I fuck women. That's it. No sappy love stories here. What the hell was makin' me want to know more about her?

Jaxon

"What the hell are you doing here?" I asked Stacy.

"I should ask you the same thing. I've missed you so much, baby. Why are you here? Why did you leave Richmond?" Stacy sashayed over to me and wrapped her arms around my neck. I pushed her away.

"Are you still using?" I asked.

"No, baby, I quit that shit a long time ago. I've been looking everywhere for you and finally your mom told me where you were."

She looked sincere, but with Stacy you could never tell. Her pupils looked normal and she didn't look like she was using. She had actually put on a little weight. She was still really small, but she had some meat on her bones.

"Where have you been, Stacy? I looked everywhere for you. It was like you fucking vanished."

"I was in rehab, baby. Trying to fix me, so I could come fix us. I love you, Jaxon. I have loved you since I was a kid and I always will."

Before I knew what was happening, she was kissing me and touching me and trying to push her tongue into my mouth.

I pushed her away, using a little more force than I meant to, and she fell to the couch. "I can't do this with you Stacy. When you left I filed for divorce. All I need you to do is sign the papers. As far as I'm concerned, we have been divorced for almost two years."

She burst into tears. "Is this because of that country bumpkin you were banging on the desk when I walked in here?"

I couldn't even look at the woman sitting in front of me. This was not the same woman that I had loved. I had to keep telling myself that. She was not the love of my life. She was just my ex-wife.

"I love her, Stacy. I really love her. She's my future, and I need you to remain in my past. I need you to sign the papers and move on with your life. Can you do that for me?"

Stacy was still crying. "I have something to show you that might change your mind. You need to come out to the car with me?"

I agreed and followed her out to her car. I noticed as we got closer that there was a woman sitting in the front seat holding something in her lap. When we reached her car I realized the woman was Stacy's sister Megan and the "something" she was holding was a little girl.

She looked to be about a year old – maybe, I don't know, I couldn't really tell. When I looked over at Stacy she was smiling from ear to ear, "I would like to introduce you to your daughter. Her name is Jazmine, but I call her Jaz."

I couldn't move, I couldn't speak, all I could do was stare at the beautiful little girl sitting in front of me. She looked just like Stacy. But how could she be mine? Could she be mine?

"Stacy, she's mine? Are you sure?" I asked.

"Of course I'm sure, Jaxon. I always used a condom with everyone but you. She has to be yours."

"That's bullshit, Stacy. You were so high most of the time, you have no fucking idea if you used a condom or not."

She looks just like you Jaxon. I know she's yours. I have no doubt that she is ours. We made her with our love. How can you deny that?" Stacy pleaded with me.

"I'm sorry Stacy, but I can't take your word on this. I need a DNA test. If she's mine, I want to be a part of her life, but we are through. I don't love you, and I don't want to be married to you." I didn't mean to sound so harsh, but I needed to make her understand. I couldn't stay married to her even if Jaz was mine.

Jaz was so beautiful, little, and sweet. I would love for her to be mine. I know that would complicate my relationship with Lor, but had always wanted to be a daddy, and Stacy and I tried for so long and it didn't happen. I was so afraid I couldn't have kids of my own. I needed this test, I needed to know, and I needed to know as soon as possible.

I couldn't hold Jaz yet. I didn't want to have any attachment to her until I knew for sure. "I can call the clinic in town and see when we can schedule a DNA test," I said.

"It's not fucking necessary, Jaxon. She's yours. I know that with all my heart." Stacy said as she stepped closer to me and tried to put her arms around my neck.

I pushed her back and said, "I want the damn test, Stacy. I'll call and get it scheduled."

Stacy nodded and I went back inside and made the call. The clinic said they could see us first thing in the morning and we would have the results in a couple of weeks.

Stacy informed me they were staying in town and she would meet me at the clinic in the morning.

I had to try to fix what I fucked up with Loralei. I didn't handle any of this well. I should've ran after her, but I didn't. I didn't do a damn thing to stop her from leaving.

I drove to her house and she wasn't home. Since she wasn't there I went to her parents' house.

"Mrs. Harper, is Loralei here," I said sheepishly when she answered the door.

"No, Jaxon. She isn't here," She answered with a "go to hell" look on her face.

"Do you know where she is?" I asked. I was having a hard time making eye contact with her. I knew that she knew what had happened earlier.

"She doesn't want to see you right now, son. You need to give her some time. To be perfectly honest with ya, I'm not real happy with ya either."

How could she be? I had just hurt her daughter. I hadn't meant to, but I was shocked when I saw Stacy. I didn't know what the hell to do.

"Mrs. Harper, it was never my intention to hurt Loralei. I love that woman, so damn much. I need to fix this. Please tell me where she is." I was almost begging.

"I think you need to go home and sleep on it. Think about what's happened and how you intend to fix it. Give Lor some time to think about things too," She said.

I couldn't argue with her. I was sure Lor needed some time to think. I couldn't stand the thought of not seeing her until tomorrow, but it was better this way.

"Did she go on to Joplin?" I asked sheepishly.

"She did, Jaxon. But I'm asking you to give her until tomorrow. I think you both need to calm down before you do something you wish you hadn't."

I agreed to not go to her until tomorrow, but that didn't keep me from calling her. I knew she wouldn't answer, but I called anyway. I didn't sleep a wink and didn't even change my clothes. Nothing mattered until I could speak with Loralei tomorrow…just a few hours and I could try to fix this.

Chapter 7

Loralei

I had to get away from Cade, but how? We were in my room and once again I was struck with disbelief at what I had done. I called home to check on the kids and wish them good luck at school while I thought up a polite way to get Cade to go the hell away.

When I finally walked back into the bedroom, Cade was awake and on the phone.

"Yeah, a couple of western omelets, fried potatoes, and some biscuits. Thank ya kindly ma'am."

He looked up at me. "I thought you might be hungry after last night, so I ordered us some breakfast."

All I could say was, "Thanks." I was having a hard time even looking at him, every time I did I could hear him howling or see a flash of him on top of me or hear some of the dirty things he said during sex.

He got out of bed and walked to the bathroom, still naked, not a care in the world. When I saw him walk away, I realized why my lady parts were so damn sore - that man was huge and I mean *huge* in every way. I was surprised he didn't split me in two with that damn thing.

But if I was so repulsed by it, why did I get kind of excited when I thought of him maybe wanting to do that again? I really was a slut. What had happened to sweet little naïve Lor? I didn't know, but this Lor was going to enjoy life and do whatever she needed to do to forget all about what's-his-name. The man I would now refer to as "asshat."

Breakfast was delivered, and Cade came walking in with a towel wrapped around his waist while he used another towel to dry his short blonde hair. We sat and ate in silence. A couple of times when I ventured a look up, I noticed he was staring at me. With the whole "Cade's in my bed naked" debacle this morning I forgot to turn my phone off. Apparently Jaxon was awake because it was now ringing non-stop.

"Aren't ya gonna answer that, hon'?" Cade said, scrunching his eyebrows at me.

I just shook my head and shoveled a huge bite of omelet into my mouth.

All of a sudden Cade's face got really serious. "I need to ask you a question hon. Is that your husband you're ignorin'?"

I couldn't believe he thought that. How could he think I would do something so horrible? I mean I knew he didn't know me at all, but what kind of woman would do something like that?

"I would never do that. I'm not married now. Actually, I've never been married."

He looked really relieved. "That's good to hear hon, real good."

As we finished breakfast Cade asked, "Any big plans for today?"

I didn't expect him to hang around; I kinda thought this would be more of a "wham-bam-thank-you-ma'am" type of thing.

"I do have plans while I'm here, so it would probably be best if you went ahead and left and got back to your business."

He stood up, dropped his towel and stepped around the table to me. "I would rather you do what you promised me you would do last night."

Holy hell, what had I promised to do?

This couldn't be good, the man was standing in front of me, naked, and I couldn't remember what I had promised while I was drunk, and in the throes of passion. I looked up with my eyes bulging out of my head, I gulped. "Uh, what exactly did I promise to do?"

He grinned. "You told me if I would wear a condom and not try to get you pregnant like the asshat did, you would do anything I asked you to do to me."

Had I really promised something like that? I didn't think I would do anything that stupid, but that part about the asshat sounded about right.

"So what would you like for me to do for you Cade?"

He let out a little chuckle, leaned down to my ear, and whispered, "I would really like for you to suck my..." before he could finish his request someone pounded on the door, yelling my name. I knew who it was, but I sure as hell didn't want to talk to him not now, not ever. He wouldn't let up, yelling, "I am going downstairs, and I will make them give me a key to your room. You are going to talk to me whether you want to or not."

Cade gave me a puzzled look, asking, "Asshat?"

"Yep that would be him. We are not married, he apparently is, but he didn't bother to tell me that before he slept with me, so I don't really think we're anything right now."

"It sounds like you have some stuff to work through, and it would probably be a good idea if I was gone before he gets back up here. Unless, do ya think he'd hurt you? Are you scared of him? I can make sure he doesn't lay a hand on you."

"No, Cade, I'll be fine, but I do think it would be best, if you went to your room now."

"Will I see you again?"

"I don't think that's such a good idea, Cade. I have some stuff I need to figure out. This was a mistake. I never should have let it happen. I'm so sorry I used you like that."

He closed the distance between us and put his arms around me. "Hon, you can use me like that anytime. Last night was not a mistake. It was amazin'. Didn't you feel that spark, I felt?"

I pulled out of his embrace. "Sorry, no spark, but thanks for helping me make it through last night; I don't know that I could've done it without you."

He leaned down and whispered in my ear, "Hon, most of the things we did last night you definitely couldn't have done without me." He gave a low chuckle and pulled his jeans on. I watched him a little too closely as he buttoned up his shirt and slipped his boots on.

He got out of the room about a minute before Jaxon barged in. He looked awful. His eyes were all red and puffy, like he'd been crying and probably not sleeping. He had on the same clothes he had on the last time I saw him.

"What the hell do you want? I don't have anything to say to you. Your wife said it all."

"I need to explain, Loralei. Stacy and I are married, but we've been separated for over a year. She was addicted to heroin and that's a big part of the reason why I came to stay with Uncle Jake. She has been in rehab for the last three months. When she got out, my mom told her where to find me. I had no idea she was coming here. I didn't know where she was. I haven't seen her in way over a year. She disappeared. I filed for divorce, but since we couldn't find her to sign the papers, it hasn't been finalized yet. I swear to you, Loralei, I would never hurt you like that. I considered myself divorced since we haven't been together for so long."

I couldn't look at him. I had my hands balled up into fists at my sides. "That doesn't explain the way you reacted when she came into my office yesterday. Jaxon, you acted like I wasn't even there. The look on your face, well, you looked like a deer caught in the headlights. All I wanted was an explanation. You didn't even try to stop me. You just let me leave."

"I was so shocked to see her that I didn't know what to do, Lor. She looks so different from the last time I saw her, I was in shock. I've been calling you non-stop since you left. Your mom asked me to give you the night to think things over. I don't love Stacy anymore, Loralei, and I haven't in a long time. Our marriage had been over for months before she disappeared. Her addiction almost killed her, and me, in the process and it was all my fault. I introduced her to that life. I'm not a good guy, Loralei. There are a lot of skeletons in my closet. I was trying to turn my life around, and I thought meeting you and falling in love was a gift from God. Maybe a sign that I wasn't as bad as I thought. That maybe I was worthy of being loved by an amazing woman like you. And then I fucked it up. I told you that day in the truck, I fuck everything up. I'm so sorry I hurt you Loralei, but I had to explain the situation. I know you hate me, and you have every right to, and you can do so much better than me, but I'm in love with you and I think I have been since the moment I laid eyes on you on that four-wheeler my first day on the farm."

I couldn't hold it in any longer. The tears started pouring down my face.

"I'm so sorry Jaxon. I'm so sorry that I didn't pick up the phone."

And then I started pounding on his chest. "Why didn't you stop me? Why did you let me leave? Why did you let me come here alone? Why Jaxon? Why? You have no idea what I've done!"

I couldn't look at him. I couldn't stand to see his face when the realization hit him. When he noticed the bed in shambles, or my clothes strewn all over the room, or my panties ripped to shreds at the edge of the couch. I couldn't stand to see his face when he realized what a horrible person I was and what I had done to us, to our future.

Jaxon didn't say a word. I watched as his jaw clenched and a tear came to his eye. I didn't think he was sad, but I knew he was pissed. His hands were curled into fists, "Where the fuck is he?" I had never seen this side of Jaxon, he was beyond mad, he was shaking with anger.

"He's gone. It was a mistake. I'm so sorry. I was so upset and I got really drunk and I just wanted to forget about you. I wanted to forget how much you hurt me. Jaxon, please understand; please know that if I had known everything you just told me this wouldn't have happened. If you had stopped me yesterday or if I would have answered the phone. Please Jaxon, please don't hate me! I love you. I'm so sorry!"

"I poured my heart out to you. I have been honest with you the whole time about how fucked up I was. But I guess I didn't realize how fucked up you are. You waited ten years to have sex after you killed your boyfriend and had his babies and then you can't give me one day? Just one fucking day to explain to you what happened before jumping into bed with some asshole you met in a bar?"

"You're not the person I thought you were, and I can't believe that I fell in love with you. Get your fucking hands off of me so I can get the hell away from you. I never want to see you again. Just pretend I died, you shouldn't have a problem with that!"

With those words, Jaxon turned around and ran out of the room. He slammed the door so hard, that the pictures on the wall shook. I was sobbing uncontrollably. What the hell had I done? How could I have done that to Jaxon? Jaxon was right, I was totally fucked up. I was in love with him yesterday and instead of giving him the opportunity to explain what was going on, I had hooked up with some random cowboy. What kind of person did that make me? I knew the answer to that, the horrible kind.

I couldn't move. I curled up in a ball on the bed and cried. I called Emma and told her what happened. I had to talk to someone about it. She insisted on coming to see me. She knew how important it was for me to attend the Cattle Barons Ball that night. The ball was the kick-off for the actual sale. It was where everyone got together and schmoozed and it's where all of the deals were really negotiated. If you could get the seller to agree to something tonight, then tomorrow the deal was already made before the actual sale even began.

No matter how bad I felt, I had to go to this event. There was no way around it. This was for the farm and it had to be done. I was so thankful that Emma was coming to go with me.

I always splurged and bought a sexy new dress for this event. The sexier I looked the better price I could get on the new herd. It was sad, but true. I had to use my DD's to get what I needed for the farm tonight. This year's dress was candy apple red, floor length, with a deep v-cut in the back and it had a sweetheart neckline that accentuated my assets. The last thing I wanted to do tonight was to go to a party. But there was no question, I had to be there. And I would have to put a smile on my face, and pretend that everyone was hilarious and I was having a great time. I planned on drinking - a lot.

When Emma arrived she immediately went to work on my hair and make-up. I was so glad she was here to go with me. I really didn't think I could face this alone. She didn't ask me for any more details about what happened, but she knew the basics.

The event was always held in the grand ballroom of the hotel. When we stepped out of the elevator and headed that way you could already hear the band playing some old country music and you could hear everyone mingling around the room. The ballroom looked like a set from "Gone With the Wind". The color palate was rich golds, dark greens, and deep burgundies. The walls were covered in velvet fabric. It looked like we were stepping into Tara.

This year's big sale that everyone was interested in was from Cattleman Farms out of Ohio. They had the best herd this year, and I planned on taking most of them home with me to Harper Farms. George Davidson was an older, graying, overweight gentleman, who happened to be the controlling interest in Cattleman Farms, and therefore the man I needed to see about some cattle.

Emma, who was very petite, with short black hair cut in a pixie cut, was wearing her short little black dress to the ball. She walked over to the bar to get us a couple of drinks. I was looking for Mr. Davidson. Before I could catch his eye I noticed another gentleman walking up to him. No, it couldn't be. What the hell was he doing here?

"Well hello hon', how are ya feeling? I heard you had a rough night last night," Cade said in a snarky tone as I walked up to find him talking business with Mr. Davidson.

"I'm feeling just fine. That thing last night was so insignificant it didn't have any effect on my day at all, but thanks so much for your concern."

"It was definitely my pleasure ma'am. Well, George sounds like we got some more business to talk about, you wanna go grab another drink at the bar?"

I pushed right in front of Cade. "Mr. Davidson, I was really hoping we could get a chance to talk tonight. I would love to give you some information about Harper Farms. I believe our reputation precedes us."

I pushed out my chest so my cleavage would just about pop out of the front of my dress. Cade and Mr. Davidson both noticed immediately. I didn't know who looked hungrier.

"Harper Farms, huh? Yes, ma'am. I believe I would like to talk to ya a little more tonight. Why don't you let me finish my discussion with Mr. Walker, and then I'll come find ya?"

"Sounds like a great idea Mr. Davidson, or can I call you George?"

"Why of course you can, hon, I look forward to seeing ya real soon."

Cade glared at me from the bar, but the glare quickly changed. It became more intense, more sultry, just damn hot. Why was he looking at me like that? Didn't he understand that last night meant nothing, and I would never do that with him again? I thought I really loved Jaxon, I mean I did love Jaxon - but why was I drawn to this arrogant asshole?

It seemed like this event would never end. We had schmoozed with everyone in the room. We had been pawed. I had at least twenty offers to dance, buy me a drink, or take me up to their room. But the good news was I talked to George, and he had agreed to sell me half of his herd at a great price. Emma was having a good time drinking and dancing and pretending she was single. She would never do more than flirt, but she was really enjoying herself.

"I am really tired Lor. You about ready to go upstairs?"

"Why don't you go ahead Emma, I'm not quite ready to go to sleep yet. I'll be up soon. I'll be fine, go get some sleep."

"Okay, but if you need anything call me, I'll leave my phone on." She then disappeared down the hall.

Not moments after Emma disappeared I felt warm breath on my neck and then a tongue on my ear. I shuddered all the way down to my toes.

"Dance with me?" I turned to see Cade looking at me, waiting for my answer.

"I don't dance, sorry."

"You can just follow my lead."

"I don't think so. Not tonight. I think we did enough last night, don't you? And besides, I really need to get upstairs to Emma."

He grabbed my hand and pulled me out into the hall. Before I knew what was happening, his tongue was in my mouth, his hand was sliding up my thigh through the slit in my dress. He murmured, "So wet", when he ran his fingers inside my panties.

I didn't know what came over me, but I didn't stop him. I let him raise my leg up and press his erection against me. I let him kiss me and take over my mouth with his tongue, and then I let him slide his other hand down the back of my dress to cup my bare cheek. I didn't want him to stop and the only reason he finally did was to say, "I don't have a condom with me. We need to go to my room, now."

In his room, we picked up right where we left off. He had me pressed against the wall with my legs wrapped around his waist as he held me up over his very strained erection that was about to poke right through his pants. I reached between us and unzipped his pants, letting them fall to the ground.

"Condom," I said as I pushed his tightie-whities down his legs.

He carried me over to the nightstand, bent over and opened the drawer. There was a giant box of condoms in there. "Like a good Boy Scout, I'm always prepared."

He put me down just long enough to put on the condom, and then he pushed me back up against the wall and held me up to where I was hovering over his erection. Our eyes met and he teased me by inserting just the tip and then he did this amazing thing with his hips and pressed in a little further. His eyes never left mine. Then a moan escaped his lips as he told me, "Hold on, wrap your arms around my neck."

I did as I was told and he grabbed my ass and slammed me down on him. I screamed out "Cade - oh my god - Cade," as I came again and again.

He was relentless; he didn't stop pounding into me. It hurt, but in such a good way. Nothing like my time with Declan that was so sweet or my time with Jaxon that was so loving. This was just hard, rough sex. I really never thought I would enjoy that. When I had fantasized about sex, it was always gentle, but Cade was anything but gentle.

After he had given me too many orgasms to count, he let go and when he did he howled - *wow,* I guess I didn't imagine that after all.

The next morning the light was so bright coming through the windows. I felt his warm body pressed up against mine, and the realization of what had happened yesterday hit me. I had lost Jaxon forever. He hated me. I couldn't blame anyone for this. It was all my fault.

The thought of laying there with Cade was literally making me nauseous. I needed to get out of this room and get back to Emma. I needed to call the kids and I really needed to talk to Jaxon. First things first, I had to get away from Cade.

I tried to pull out from under his big, muscular arm, but the more I tried to wiggle out from under it, the closer Cade pulled me back.

"Where ya tryin' to rush off to, hon?" Cade whispered in my ear.

"I need to get back to my room. Emma will be worried sick, and I have to call and check up on my kids."

"Kids? As in 'more than one'?"

"Yes, Cade, I have nine year old twins."

Cade looked like I had surprised the hell out of him. "But you're too young to have kids that old, aren't ya?"

"Obviously, I'm not that young, because I do have kids that old. I'm twenty-six."

"Started young, huh?" he laughed as he kissed my shoulder.

There was no way I was going to go into the details of my life with this man. I didn't plan on ever seeing him again, of course I didn't plan on last night either.

I sat up and decided it was time to be honest with Cade. "This can never happen again, Cade. I am only in town one more day and then I will be heading back home to my kids and...." Cade interrupted me, "Asshat?"

Then it hit me - Jaxon, what I was going to do about Jaxon? He hated me now, we both said some horrible things yesterday and then I did the one thing that I knew would break his heart - *again*.

How could I sleep with Cade again? What had come over me? I knew that he was sexy and he made me feel like a completely different person, but how could I want to be with him? I didn't understand why I wanted him, when I was in love with Jaxon. But was I in love with Jaxon? Maybe I wasn't. Maybe I just thought it was love. Right now all I could think about was my need to get home. I needed to figure out what was going to happen with Jaxon. But most of all I just needed to get the hell away from Cade.

Chapter 8

Jaxon – 17 years old

"Son, its time for you to make some difficult life choices. You've been in front of me on more than a couple occasions. I've watched you get a little more lost each time you're brought in. I know you haven't had the best lot in life, but when a boy gets to a certain age he has to decide what kind of man he wants to be, and son, you need to be making that decision soon."

I knew Judge Powell was right. If I didn't make some changes I was going to end up in prison or in the ground. This was a fact - true history - as my mom would call it, but I just couldn't get my life straightened out. I didn't care what happened to me. I never had really.

I grew up in Richmond, California. My mom, Sue, tried to raise me right, but my dad left when I was a baby so everything was much harder for her. My mom was born and raised in a small town in Missouri. She met my dad, Jack, when she visited Camp Pendelton for a cousin's bootcamp graduation ceremony. He was a contractor who worked on the base there. They had a whirlwind week long romance.

When she got back to Missouri and found out she was pregnant, she contacted my dad. He apparently wasn't real excited about being a dad, but he told her if she would move to Richmond with him he would marry her and raise me. That marriage lasted until I was two months old. Then he took off and that was that.

Life was hard for my mom and me. After my dad left, mom had to work three jobs just to keep a roof over our heads and food on the table. I loved her with all of my heart. She was the most amazing woman ever, but after my dad took off on her, she was never really the same, or so I'd heard.

She could've moved back to Missouri and lived around family, but she was embarrassed and ashamed of what had happened with my dad. So we stayed in California and she tried her best to raise me right. I did not help her with that at all.

I started out drinking when I was about twelve. Drinking was an awesome way to get my mind off of what was going on in my life. I got my first piercing when I was thirteen. I was drunk. Some guy at the party I was at took a needle and pierced my eyebrow. It hurt like a son-of-a-bitch, but in a room full of badass kids I sure wasn't going to show any pain.

Soon drinking just wasn't enough, I needed more. My friend Ratz, - his real name was Toby Ratzen - started dealing drugs when we were fourteen. He introduced me to a whole crazy world of hell. I just wanted to get out of my head, but what Ratz got me into almost got me out of this world.

I woke up and I couldn't figure out why I was so hot. I was smothering and I couldn't quit shaking. I felt like I was literally going to shake out of my skin. And it was so fucking bright in that room. I felt like if I tried hard enough I could reach out and touch the sun.

"Baby, *oh God*, baby. Please wake up. Please be okay. I can't live without you Jax, wake up!" Stacy was screaming at me. Stacy and I had been together for two years. We planned to get married and get the hell out of this horrible town as soon as she finished high school. I quit last year, I didn't need school, I just needed her and my next fix.

Soon pot wasn't enough, and I had to start dealing with Ratz so I could feed my own addiction. Stacy was so fucking pure. Like the snow. No matter what I tried to give her, she wouldn't use drugs. She really loved me and wanted a future with me. Why couldn't she understand how fucked in the head I was? I never understood why she wanted to be with me. But she did, so I decided I was going to straighten up. I didn't give a shit about me. I had to do it for her.

That's what had started the downward spiral that got me in front of Judge Powell today.

I tried to open my eyes. Stacy was still screaming, and I could feel something seeping down my face into my eye. My pants were wet. Oh shit, I'd pissed myself. I couldn't do this to her. I had to get away. She deserved so much better than me and my fucked up life.

"Jax, please tell me you're okay baby, please. I'm so sorry I was late, I had to take Megan home after school. Mom couldn't pick her up. I should have been here with you. I'm so sorry I *wasn't here to help you."* Stacy cried. *I finally got my eyes open and the look on her face absolutely broke my fucking heart. The time was now, I knew what I had to do.*

"Get the fuck off me bitch! Get the hell out of here. I don't want you. I don't want to ever see your fucking face again. GET OUT!" I didn't want to do this, and it was breaking my heart, but I couldn't put that look on her face ever again. She would be so much better off with some nice guy that could give her what she needed. Stacy sobbed and ran out. *Mission accomplished.*

After I kicked Stacy out, I went cold turkey. I quit the drinking, I quit the drugs, and I told Ratz that I couldn't work for him anymore. I'd almost OD'd. I'd fallen and hit my head and was bleeding all over everything, I'd pissed my pants. I'd lost so much weight that I was barely even myself anymore. I was going to become a better man and maybe then I would deserve Stacy. I could beg her to take me back. After everything I said to her, it probably wouldn't happen, but I had to try.

The day before I appeared in court, had started off like any other day in my new world. I woke up, took a shower, and headed off to the garage I worked at to start my shift at eight a.m. I got the call at eleven-thirty a.m. Ratz, what the fuck could he want?

"Uh, man, I need you to do a job for me tonight."

"You know I don't do that shit anymore Ratz, leave me the hell alone!"

"I need you man, I know you gave it up, but I need you to do this. Don't make me do something you'll regret," Ratz threatened.

"What the fuck, man? You're gonna threaten me now. Fuck you!" I screamed and slammed the phone down. What the hell did he think I would do, just drop everything and go do a job for him? I didn't do that shit anymore and I wasn't getting back into that life.

I'd been clean for six months, trying to work up the courage to go back to Stacy and beg forgiveness. It had been so long since I had seen her, I just needed to make sure I was completely out of the life before I went back to her.

When I got off work, I started for home. I looked over and saw Ratz's jeep parked across from my garage. I walked over to him ready to knock his head off, when I noticed someone sitting in the front seat. It was Stacy.

She was completely wasted out of her fucking mind. She was skin and bones, her hair was falling out, she had on an outfit that a hooker wouldn't wear, and Ratz had his tongue down her throat.

Ratz had planned this whole thing. He knew how upset I would be about Stacy, and he thought that I would just give in and use. Do whatever he needed me to do. I think I changed his plans a little when I punched through the window, grabbing him by the throat. I pulled him out of the window with my bloody arm and cut the hell out of him and myself. Then I started pounding him. I heard his nose break. His jaw was cracking.

I wanted to bash his skull in for what he had done. When I got to jail, they told me I almost killed him. He fucking deserved it for what he did to Stacy. My sweet, pure, innocent Stacy.

"What do you have to say for yourself, son?" Judge Powell asked me.

"Sir, with all due respect, the bastard deserved it. I know I shouldn't have done it, but you have no idea what he's done."

I tried to control my anger, but I could feel it raging through my body. My hands were clenched into fists and I could feel the sweat beading on my forehead.

The judge said, "I know Mr. Ratzen. He has appeared in my court several times, and I believe you when you say he deserved it. I don't like what you did, but I understand that you were trying to protect Ms. Roberts. I'm going to sentence you to community service and one year probation. I want you to know that Ms. Roberts was taken in and she will be placed in a mandatory rehab program for three months."

I was so relieved not only for myself, but that Stacy would get clean. This was all my fault. I had done this to her. I knocked her down with my words and she went to the one thing that would make her forget, just like I had done so many times before.

I waited thirty days before I visited Stacy in rehab. We talked for hours every day, and I explained to her why I had said such horrible things to her. She told me she understood that I was trying to protect her from that life.

By the time she got out of rehab we had decided to get an apartment together. Stacy started cosmetology school, and I continued to work at the garage. Within a year we were married and talking about buying a house and having kids. I was so happy to be with her and together we were happy.

<u>Jaxon- 25 years old</u>

Stacy and I had been married for almost seven years. For the most part we were really happy. She worked full-time at a beauty salon by our house. I still worked at the garage, but now I was the manager. We had been trying to get pregnant ever since we got married, but it hadn't happened. I would wake up sometimes in the middle of the night to Stacy crying in the bathroom because she started her period. I knew how bad she wanted a baby, and it killed me that I couldn't give her the one thing she wanted more than anything.

The past couple of months Stacy had been acting weird. She would go out with her girlfriends a few nights a week and I would hardly even see her on the weekends. I decided I should give her some space, because I knew she was so upset about the baby situation. But her behavior was really starting to worry me.

When I opened the door to our house that night I knew something wasn't right. I took off early so I could surprise Stacy. I stopped and bought her a dozen red roses and got her a box of her favorite chocolates from the little store on the corner.

I heard voices when I started for the stairs, and then I heard something I never thought I would hear. I heard Ratz scream out "Stacy" and then a loud moan. I walked into my bedroom and found him on top of her. She was so wasted that she actually reached for me and asked me to join them. I wanted to kill him, I wanted to kill her, but all I could do was stand there and stare as my life was ruined.

I turned around and walked out of our house. I got in my car and drove to my moms house across town.

"Son, is she using drugs again?" My mom asked.

"I think so. She's been acting really strange. I wanted this to work so bad. I love her, mom," I said as I held my head in my hands sitting at the table in my mom's kitchen.

"She's your first love, Jaxon. We all think that our first love is forever, but ninety-percent of the time it isn't. I've been concerned about that girl for awhile. I was wondering how long it would take you to see it."

"Why didn't you tell me?" I asked, looking up.

"You needed to see it for yourself, son. This isn't something your mom can do for you. You needed to figure it out yourself. And now you need to plan your future. You have to decide if Stacy is going to be part of it."

"I honestly don't know. I thought she was my future, but now I'm not so sure. Can I stay here with you for awhile? Until I work some stuff out."

Mom stood up and walked over to me. Placing her arms around my neck, she said, "Of course, you can, Jaxon. You can stay here as long as you need to. Whatever you need, son. I love you. Don't ever forget that."

The next day I went back to my house and found a note from Stacy:

Jaxon,

I'm so sorry for what I've done. I hope one day you will forgive me. I'm leaving and I don't know if I will ever come back. Please don't hate me.

Love, Stacy

I waited a year for Stacy to come home. I searched for her in every hole I had ever been in and in every rehab I prayed she had checked into. I finally filed for divorce, sold the house, and moved in with my mom. Since nobody knew where Stacy was, I couldn't finalize our divorce. I didn't see anyone, I didn't go out, I didn't do anything but work. I didn't care what was happening in the world. All I knew was that mine was shattered.

Another year passed, and I was leaving work one night when I looked over and saw a familiar jeep parked across the street. I really didn't think Ratz was that fucking stupid, but he surprised me. He stepped out of his jeep and motioned me over to him. The look on my face should have told him to get the hell away, but Ratz never was the brightest bulb in the box.

I tried not to hit him. I swear to God, I tried not to slam his head into the front of the jeep. I really did, but I just couldn't control my anger. I couldn't move past the last time I saw him and the sounds he was making and what that meant to my world.

I asked him where the hell Stacy was and he swore that he hadn't seen her since that night. He swore this as I held him by the throat over the hood of his jeep with a look on my face that had to scream "I'm gonna kill your ass." So I believed him. To this day I don't know why he was there that day, and I really don't give a fuck.

That was the day that I decided I needed to get the hell out of this town, this state, this life. That was when my mom called my Uncle Jake and asked him if I could come stay with him for awhile. He told her to send me his way, and I was welcome to stay with him as long as I needed to.

Chapter 9

Loralei

I hadn't seen Cade since I left his room yesterday morning. I hadn't really been trying to avoid him, I had just been lucky. Emma left last night. She needed to get home to Eric and I needed to go back to being Loralei. I didn't know what had happened to me over the past couple of days, but I needed to get myself back. I had been acting like a totally different person. The Loralei I had always been was not the person in this hotel room today. I had changed, and not for the better.

I just had one more event that I had to attend. Then I could head home. The final event was basically a "we're so glad you came and spent all of your money on our cattle" party, but it was really an integral part of the schmoozing process. I had a bad feeling that I wouldn't be able to avoid Cade tonight, but I knew I wouldn't be ending up in his bed.

The event tonight wasn't formal, so I brought a lacey white dress and my hottest pair of pink cowboy boots to wear. I had to look the part of the country bumpkin, and I was pretty good at it. I took a long bath in the amazing tub in my suite, applied a little bit of make-up, and pulled my hair up into a ponytail, tying it with a pink ribbon.

I headed downstairs and prayed I wouldn't run into Cade. I never expected what I found when I got off the elevator.

The elevator dinged, the doors opened, and before me stood Jaxon, my pierced, tattooed knight in shining armor. He had on his "fancy" jeans, a white button up shirt, and a pair of cowboy boots, that he must have borrowed from Jake. He gave me a really sheepish grin and reached his hand out to me.

I was so surprised to see him. "What are you doing here?"

"Do you want me to leave?" he said with a really sad look on his face.

I ran over to him and threw my arms around his neck and screamed, "No!"

He pulled back. "We need to talk, but I know that you have to go to this party. So can we just put a hold on the bad feelings and enjoy this party before we go upstairs and talk?"

"Yes, I think we can do that. We do have a lot to talk about, but right now, I am just so happy to see you, you have no idea."

"Oh, babe, I think I have a pretty good idea."

We walked into the party, and I could tell that people were looking Jaxon up and down. He had the sleeves of his white button-up rolled up to his elbows so his tattoos were prominently displayed and his eyebrow ring was shining.

I was so proud to be there with him, even though I couldn't forget everything he said. I was just so happy that he made the first move to fix things.

The sultry voice of Patsy Cline singing *Crazy* filled the room. Jaxon reached his hand out to me. "Loralei, would you give me the honor of this dance?"

I jumped at the chance to be that close to him. He wrapped his arms around me, pulling me close to him as we began to dance. We were swaying to the rhythm of the music. We danced and he held me. All of the horrible things we said were disappearing from my mind as his eyes danced with my heart.

Before I knew it, we had been dancing for over an hour. We finally had a seat at one of the tables in the back of the room.

"I'm sorry, Lor." Jaxon said as he leaned over and took my hand in his.

I squeezed his hand, "Me too, Jaxon."

"You look beautiful tonight, baby," Jaxon said as he leaned over and kissed my cheek. That kiss sent shivers down my spine. "You thirsty?" he asked.

"Um, yeah. I am actually."

"I'll go grab us a couple of drinks. I'll be right back."

As I was watching him walk away, I felt a large hand on the small of my back and immediately knew it was Cade.

He leaned down and whispered in my ear, "Looks like you and asshat have kissed and made-up. So I guess that means you won't be in my bed tonight, hon." I could tell he was not happy about this.

He grabbed my waist, pulling me up to him. "Does he know you woke up with me today? Does he know the way I make you feel with just the touch of my hand or the sound of my voice?"

I flipped around, looked him square in the eye and pleaded, "Cade, you have to get out of here. I don't feel anything for you. I love him and I want you to leave, now!"

"That's sure not what you were screaming at me last night, hon." He swooped down and kissed me hard. Without even realizing what was happening he had walked me toward the bathroom and pushed us through the door locking it.

He reached around and started to unzip my dress. It was hanging halfway down my back before I broke away from him. I tried to tell him to get away from me, but I couldn't say anything. The look on his face was mesmerizing. I couldn't break away from his stare, and I couldn't speak.

We just stood there staring until I heard a knock at the door that broke the trance between us. Cade gazed at me with a look I never dreamed I would see from him - defeat. He said, "Here let me help you with that," as he zipped up my dress.

"I don't know what's happening here, but I love him Cade. I can't be with you. Please just stay away from me. If you care about me at all, you will stay away."

I had to get out of this room. It was so hard fighting my attraction to Cade while standing so close to him. I had to get back to Jaxon.

I took a few minutes to relax and gain my composure, and then I headed back to the party and found our table empty. Where did Jaxon go? Oh my god - did he see what just happened? Did he see Cade kiss me? I ran to the elevator as fast as I could. I had to get to our room. I prayed that Jaxon would be there.

On the ride up I kept thinking about Cade. About the look on his face when I told him I loved Jaxon. He looked so defeated, so sad.

Everything with Cade was intense. We were only in that bathroom for a couple of minutes, but it felt like forever. I couldn't fathom who I had turned into. I was not this person. I was not a woman who did things like this. I was a good Baptist girl. I was a mother, and a daughter. I was not whoever this was that I had been for the past few days.

I needed to get back home. I needed to get back to my life and get away from all of this craziness. The craziness called Cade.

I stepped off of the elevator and made my way down the hall to my room. When I opened the door, the room was empty. Finally, I heard water running and headed toward the bathroom. Jaxon was standing at the sink with his shirt off. He looked *different*. He didn't really seem mad, he just seemed upset.

"Everything okay?" I asked, with a definite tone of concern in my voice.

"Uh, yeah. I'm sorry I left you down there. This waitress ran right into me and spilled her tray all over me. So I came upstairs to get changed. Uh, I was gonna come back down."

I walked up behind him and placed my arms around his waist. "You scared me. I thought you left me."

He didn't say anything. His eyes met mine in the mirror. "Sorry, Lor. I shouldn't have done that."

Jaxon and I decided we would wait until we got home to discuss our future. We slept in the same bed, but did nothing more than hold each other. It was the most peaceful night's sleep I could ever remember.

Jaxon

I was walking toward the bar when I saw him. The fucking tall cowboy. I had no way of knowing that he was the guy, but I just did. The way he was looking at Lor from across the room. That asshole couldn't take his eyes off of her. I stopped dead in my tracks. He was walking toward her. What the hell was he going to do? An even better question was what was Lor going to do when he got to her? I was stunned. I couldn't take my eyes off of him. He just had this fucking air about him, like he was a god or something.

Stupid bastard was ruining my future. I watched as he got to the table and leaned down to whisper something in her ear. Lor didn't move. I could see her body tense. She turned around and said something to him. Then he said something to her before he grabbed her and pulled her up toward him. She didn't fucking stop him. Maybe she really did have feelings for this asshole.

And then it happened - he kissed her. I couldn't move. I couldn't breathe. How could she let him do that to her? He was pushing her toward the bathroom, kissing her hard. I wanted to kill him. I had never felt that way before, unless you count the time when I almost killed Ratz for what he did to Stacy.

I had to do something, but what? I decided to follow them to the bathroom. I got there just as the door slammed shut and I heard the lock twist. I was losing everything, and it was all my fault. Killing the fucking cowboy wasn't going to change what I had done. I lied to the woman I loved and that lie was gonna cost me my future.

I had to know. I had to know if he was touching her. I had to know if he was screwing her in the bathroom. I stood at the door and listened. I could hear her moaning. Those moans were meant for me, not that bastard. I was sick. I could feel the color drain out of my face. I wanted to go through the fucking door, but instead I just slammed my fist into the wall. I kept listening and finally I heard her speak.

"I don't know what's happening here, but I love him Cade. I can't be with you. Please just stay away from me. If you care about me at all, you will stay away."

Thank god. She loved me. She pushed him away. She made him stop. *She was mine*. But that didn't change the way I was feeling about that fucking cowboy. He needed to stay the hell away from her. She was not his. He had used her for sex, and he was trying to do that again tonight. The fucking cowboy and I were going to have a little "come to Jesus" meeting.

When he walked out of the bathroom, I saw the look on his face. He knew he had lost her. But that didn't matter to me. I needed to explain the situation to him. I walked up behind him as he entered the stairwell. I caught him off guard. This bastard was big, but I had always been strong. I pushed him up against the wall and slammed my elbow across the back of his neck.

"I know what you did to her, cowboy. And I heard what she just said to you. You stay the fuck away from her." I slammed my entire body up against his back. "Because if you don't, I will kill your ass. That's a fucking promise, cowboy."

He didn't fight back. Fucking pansy. I should've known he would be spineless. Anybody who takes advantage of a woman who was obviously going through something, is an asshole.

I had to get the hell out of there. I couldn't see that bastard again. I needed a drink. I made it halfway to the bar when a little blonde waitress slipped around one of the tables and slammed right into me. Her whole tray of drinks spilled down the front of my shirt.

"Oh no! I am so, so sorry, Sir. Please let me help." She tried to clean my shirt off, but it wasn't gonna help.

"It's really fine," I said. I decided to head up to our room. Thank God Lor had given me the key to hold on to. That would give me some time to calm down. I would just go upstairs and change my clothes. Then maybe I could pretend that I hadn't seen what happened. I was gonna give it my best shot. She chose me, not him. I hated him, and one day I would show him exactly how much. But right now I needed to focus on Lor and our future.

Loralei

We decided to get up early and headed home arriving about 10 a.m. I couldn't wait to see my babies. Jaxon went home, and I picked up the twins. We didn't want to admit it to ourselves or each other, but this was a conversation we didn't want to have.

I asked Jaxon to come over after I put the kids to bed, so we could finally get this discussion over with. I probably shouldn't have looked at it that way, but I needed to get everything I was feeling out in the open.

I needed Jaxon to know why I did what I did. Most importantly though I needed to understand how he could've said those horrible things to me.

Tucking my kids into bed had always been the best part of my day. I missed them so much while I was away. It felt like they had been spending a lot of time away recently. We all needed to get back to our regular routine. I read them a story and tucked them in. Once I was sure they were asleep, I called Jaxon and told him it was time for him to come over so we could have that discussion.

"Can I come in?" Jaxon asked through the screen door.

I opened the door and motioned for him to come in. When he got inside, we headed into the living room. I grabbed Jaxon a beer and made some iced tea for me. While I was in the kitchen getting our drinks, Jaxon had sat down on the couch.

I walked in and wasn't really sure where to sit or what to do. If the look on his face was any indication, he felt the same way. He finally motioned for me to sit down next to him, so I did.

"Loralei, you have every right to hate me after the horrible things I said to you. I was just so mad at you for what you did, that I couldn't think straight. You have to know that I didn't mean what I said about Declan." He was so focused on his beer bottle. He was peeling off the label and trying so hard not to look up at me. I could tell he really felt bad about the way he had talked to me. He wouldn't make eye contact and he was all slumped over.

"We both said things we shouldn't have Jaxon. I am so sorry for what I did. You know that I am not that kind of person. You know that I hadn't had sex for ten years when we were together. I was just so upset with you, and I had way too much to drink. You're married. That's something that you should have mentioned before we got close."

"I know I fucked up, Loralei. I know that I should have told you about Stacy and so many other things about my past, but I just couldn't let you know the kind of person I was. I was so happy to be able to be a new person here, without all of my shit hanging over my head," Jaxon said while keeping his gaze on the beer bottle in his hand. He looked so sad.

I reached over and grabbed the beer bottle from Jaxon's hands and placed it on the coffee table. I took his hand in mine and he finally looked up at me. "I want to be with you Jaxon. He meant nothing to me. It was just sex." I could see Jaxon's jaw clench. "I was so pissed off at you. He was there, and I was drunk. It was a mistake, but you are not in the clear on this. I might have committed the act, but you pushed me toward it."

Jaxon's entire body tensed. My words had really struck a nerve. The next words out of his mouth shocked me. "I'm sorry that I drove you toward that fucking cowboy." His entire face changed. He caught my gaze and grabbed me by the back of my neck and pulled me toward him on the couch and kissed me.

He kissed me like we had never kissed before. He kissed me like nothing that happened the past few days had happened. He kissed me like he loved me and at that moment, I knew that I did love Jaxon and now I knew how much he loved me.

He picked me up, and I wrapped my legs around his waist. Without breaking our embrace, he carried me to my bedroom. When he shut the door, I whispered, "Don't forget to lock it." After our incident when Sammy walked in on us, I didn't want to take any chances.

Jaxon was kissing me roughly now. This was unlike him. He was kissing me the way Cade kissed me. All of these thoughts of Cade were flashing through my mind. He was so rough and I loved it. Jaxon bit my lip and I could taste blood. I cried out in pain, "Stop!"

Jaxon looked up at me and said between pants, "Did I hurt you?"

"You kinda did. We don't have to go so fast. You can slow down," I whispered.

Jaxon said, "I thought you liked it that way. I saw the way *he* kissed you." Oh my god. Jaxon did see me with Cade last night.

"What do you mean 'you saw'?" I asked.

"At the banquet, when I went to get our drinks. I saw him kiss you and pull you into the bathroom. I waited to see what you would do and then I followed after you and I heard what you told him about me."

I was completely flabbergasted. I didn't know what to say. Honestly, I didn't know how to feel. Should I have been mad at Jaxon for not saying anything? Should I have been mortified that I didn't tell him what happened? Or should I have been relieved that he heard me profess my love for him to Cade.

All of these thoughts were taking me over, and I swear I started to have a panic attack. I jumped out of bed and ran into the bathroom to splash cold water in my face. Jaxon followed after me.

He put his arms around me, "Loralei, I'm so in love with you. I will do whatever I need to do to prove that to you. If you want me to be rough, I will be. If you want me to be gentle, I can do that too. Just tell me what you want from me. Please, babe."

We locked eyes in the mirror and I could see he was being sincere. "Why didn't you tell me you saw us?" I asked.

"I heard you tell him you loved me. That's all I needed to know. I saw the look on that asshole's face when he was walking toward you. He has strong feelings for you, Lor. It had to break his heart when you told him you love me. I'm not gonna lie to you, I wanted to break his fucking face. But I needed to see if I had lost you. Now I know you're mine. One hundred percent mine. And that's all that matters to me."

I turned around, looking him right in the eyes. "Jaxon, I love you too. And I'm one hundred percent yours. Can you say the same? What is going on with Stacy?"

"She's still in town. We have some things to wrap up, and then she'll be heading back to California." I turned around and Jaxon avoided my gaze in the mirror.

"Are you talking about the divorce? Is she going to fight you on it?" I asked.

He caught my gaze in the mirror as he was sliding his hands down my hips, "We just have some things to figure out. She'll be gone before you know it. I don't want to be with her, Lor, I love you." That last statement was so sincere. I had no doubt in that moment of his love for me.

The look on his face suddenly changed. He slid his hands from my hips up to my breasts. He never took his eyes off of me. He caressed my breasts so gently. God, it felt amazing. Then he reached down and pulled my shirt up over my head. He released the clasp on my bra and it fell to the floor.

Jaxon leaned in and pushed me against the counter. I could feel how excited he was and that amazing piercing. He unbuttoned my jeans and pushed them and my panties down to the floor.

He whispered, "Step out of your jeans, babe." I complied and before I knew what was happening he was pressing into me from behind. He leaned in and nuzzled my neck. Then he nipped my earlobe. "Rough or gentle? Tell me how you want me to love you."

I almost lost it when he asked me that. I said the first thing that came into my mind, "Rough, please Jaxon, love me rough!"

I barely got the words out before he told me to, "Hold on to the counter, baby." He thrust into me so hard that my head almost hit the mirror. He was relentless. He didn't let up. Over and over. Harder and harder. His piercing was rubbing me in all the right places. I looked up and saw our faces in the mirror. Jaxon looked so focused. Like he was trying to prove to me that he loved me and he would do anything for me. I looked like, well, someone getting loved rough. My whole body was shaking and the orgasms wouldn't stop. Apparently, I liked it rough and Jaxon certainly knew what he was doing.

Chapter 10

Cade

Holy fucking shit! What the hell was wrong with me? I hadn't had sex in days, and I didn't even want to. I was sitting in my favorite hole-in-the-wall bar with an ice cold beer in my hand. The gals were hanging all over me. They were begging me to take them home so they could see my big "ranch", but all I could think about was Loralei Harper. What the hell was the deal with that fucking woman? Sure, she was hot as hell, so sweet and shy, with just enough of a wild side to totally get my blood boiling. Oh hell, I had it bad for that woman.

I had to work her out of my system. I surveyed the room trying to cull the herd and pick one of the lucky ladies to go home with me tonight. I had a lot of options, all repeat performances of course, but still great options. Alison was always a fun lay. Or Shannon, that chick was crazy in the sack. Then I remembered I had seen Michelle standing at the bar with her skin-tight jean skirt hanging low on her hips and her tramp-stamp peeking out for all to see.

Michelle was the lucky lady tonight. She was so fucking hot, and it didn't hurt anything that she reminded me of a certain blonde I was jonesing for. I decided it was time for me to make my move. It wouldn't take much.

"Hey babe, let's go." I leaned in and slid my tongue along that special spot behind her ear. I knew she would leave with me. She was always up for a night with me. She nodded and went to get her purse. We headed out toward my truck, and I decided I just needed to get this over with. I grabbed her and pushed her up against the wall, jammed myself between her legs and pushed my hand up her skirt. I found what I was looking for, a nice, warm, wet pussy. So what the hell was wrong with me? Why wasn't "cowboy" excited? Usually by now I would be in and ready to ride. But I wasn't getting hard. *You gotta be fucking kidding me?* What the fuck had Loralei done to "cowboy"? Shit, had she ruined me for all other pussy?

Michelle decided to take matters into her own hands, so to speak. She dropped to her knees, unzipped my pants, grabbed my dick, and had me in her mouth before I could say "holy fuck". That girl could suck the chrome off a bumper, but tonight it just wasn't working. I grabbed her by the hair and pulled her up and told her, "This ain't gonna happen tonight, babe."

"Did I do something wrong, gorgeous? Why aren't you *excited*?"

"No, baby it's not you. I'm just not feeling too good, nothing you did. Thanks for trying - you really did your best," I lied through my teeth. I was fucking feeling fine, I just couldn't get that woman off my mind.

I went home alone to my huge ranch house. House, not a home. I remembered a time when it was the happiest home in the world.

When my mom and dad were still alive, my house felt like a home, now it just felt like a house. My parents passed away a few years back. They were killed in a car accident, hit by a drunk driver. My dad died at the scene, but my mother was in a coma for a few weeks. As the only child, I was expected to take over the ranch, and I did it with everything I had. I don't do anything half-assed and I sure as hell wasn't going to start now with the thing that was most important to my family.

This ranch had been in my family for decades. My dad, Cody Walker, was so proud of the changes he made to make the ranch run more smoothly. When he married my mom, Candy, the whole little town of Dexter, Missouri about flipped shit. She was a dancer, which was code for stripper that my dad met at a bachelor party he attended in Vegas. He came home from that party married to my mom.

By the time I was born, the town had warmed up to her a little. She still liked to wear her short skirts and too much make up, which my dad loved, but it got her strange looks at PTA meetings. I had the best childhood. My mom and dad were so in love. My dad adored my mom and he always told me, "Son, when you find the right one, you'll just know it. Your dick won't pick her, your heart will. Always listen to your heart, because your dick can be a lying bastard!" Yep, my dad was fucking awesome!

So I was sitting in my lonely house worrying about my little lying bastard. I decided that I should have a conversation with him. Wow, I really spent too much time alone. "Cowboy, this shit is unacceptable. If you have warm pussy ready for you, you always take it. I don't care what that woman did to you in Joplin, this shit has to stop. She is not ours, she left with asshat. She loves him and we have to forget about her." Now that my delusional conversation with my dick was over, I decided it was time to go to bed.

When I woke up the next morning, I had a message from George Davidson from the cattle sale. I returned his call and was surprised and excited by his request.

"Mr. Walker, so glad you returned my call so quickly. I'm having a little problem with the cattle we were supposed to deliver out to ya'll. There's been some problems with the herd. They aren't doing too well. We weren't able to save 'em all. I don't expect to make the delivery for about five weeks. Would it be possible for you to meet me at Harper Farms to survey the remaining cattle and then you and Ms. Harper can decide which farm will get which cattle. I'm only asking you to meet me there because it's a little bit closer to me. I'll cut ya'll a hell of a deal and even give you some gas money for the drive." George sounded embarrassed. I kinda got the feeling that he was having some pretty serious issues at his ranch.

"I would be able to see go see Loralei..." was all I heard George say. Fuck yeah I could do it.

I said, "No problem at all, when do I need to be there?"

"The cattle will be delivered five weeks from Monday. I can contact Ms. Harper and let her know what's going on and to expect us."

"No, that's okay, George, I'll let her know I'm coming," I said with a smirk on my face. You bet your ass she'll know when I'm coming.

Five weeks - another five weeks before I could have sex. Damn, I hadn't gone that long without a warm woman, well, since I was a kid. Loralei had apparently ruined me for all other pussy. I was going to have to come up with a plan to win her away from that asshat. And I had five weeks and a lot of pent up sexual energy to do it with!

Chapter 11

Jaxon

It had been two weeks since Stacy and I had the DNA test done on Jaz. I couldn't bring myself to tell Lor about this. I had to make sure Jaz was mine before I said anything to her. I knew that made me a huge asshole, but we were getting so close. Sammy and Mags were really starting to love me. I felt like I was falling in love with them too. I could see myself in this family. I could see Lor and I getting married, raising the twins, and sitting on the porch in our rocking chairs watching the grandkids play. I never dreamed that I would want that kind of life. I had always been a city boy, but this country life with Lor was sounding better and better every day.

Stacy and I had plans to meet that afternoon at the clinic to get the results. I would finally know today. I would know if that sweet little baby girl was mine. And if she was mine, what the hell would I do next? I couldn't stay married to Stacy. I thought I had loved her, but I never felt anything for her like what I'd felt for Lor. If she was mine, I would have to figure out some way to get Stacy to move to Missouri. There was no way I could be that far away from my kid. But that would probably be a moot point. Stacy and I tried for years and couldn't conceive. I really didn't think the little girl was mine.

Loralei

Jaxon had been acting kinda odd for the past week. I wasn't really worried about it because we were getting along so well, and I could tell that he was really trying to make us work.

He was spending most of his free time with me and the kids or just me or just the kids. Seeing him with them really made my heart happy. Mags was his little princess. Sammy was his little man. And they were loving it, especially Sammy. He had already asked Jaxon if, when he turned eighteen, he would take him to get a cool tattoo like his. Jaxon said yes, and then turned to me pretty quick with an "oh crap, I agreed before asking you" look on his face. I smiled to show him it was okay.

But still I could just tell that something wasn't right and my biggest fear was that this had something to do with Stacy. Maybe Jaxon didn't want to divorce her. Maybe he was having second thoughts about everything.

I asked Jaxon to come over for a late lunch at my house, but he told me he couldn't. He said he had something he had to take care of in town. I should've just let it go, but I couldn't.

I had to know what was going on, so I did the only thing I could, I followed him. Not like a stalker. I just went into town before he did and kept an eye out for his truck. That was it. It wasn't like I planned on cowering down in the seat and taking covert pictures of him.

It was a small town, so this was not hard to do. When I finally caught a glimpse of his truck, I noticed he was turning into the medical clinic. That scared me, I thought maybe he was sick.

What happened next made my stomach drop. He pulled in next to a little black Saturn Vue and out popped Stacy. She flung her arms around his neck and hugged him. He didn't look too happy about that, but what were they doing there together?

I sat across the street in the parking lot of the bank and waited for them to come out. Would they come out together? I didn't have to wait long for my answer. Stacy came out first, crying and clutching a piece of paper. Jaxon came out shortly after her. He walked over to her, and said something to her that made her sob harder. He climbed into his truck and started back toward the farm.

I knew that I should have left. Hell, I knew that following him was wrong, but I had to know what was going on. I was afraid that Jaxon would continue to lie to me so I decided to get my answers straight from the bitch's, uh, horse's mouth.

I pulled in next to Stacy, climbed out of the jeep and walked over to her. She was sitting in her car, still sobbing. I knocked on the window, and she rolled it down.

"What the hell do you want? Haven't you taken enough from me? Go the hell away!" she screamed at me and started to roll her window up.

"What is going on? Why are you so upset, and why was Jaxon here with you? Are you sick?" I asked.

"Oh so he didn't tell the little country bumpkin bitch we have a kid huh? We were here getting the results of the DNA test." She sneered at me.

My heart was pounding so fast. Another lie, he had lied to me again. He had a kid with Stacy. He left his wife and kid to go back to the farm. How could he do that? What kind of man was he, really?

"What do you mean, you have a kid?" I screamed back at her.

"Well let me explain it to you, honey. When a man and a woman really love each other, well they fuck like bunnies and make a baby. Ours is a little girl and Jaxon just left us so he could go play house with you. Great man, isn't he? Are you proud of yourself? He's all yours - you won."

I just stared at her. I couldn't speak. This couldn't be true. They have a kid, and Jaxon just left them. Because of me?

I ran back to my jeep, climbed in, and headed home. When I got to my house Jaxon was sitting on my porch, waiting for me. I parked and as I started walking toward the door I noticed how sad he looked. If I hadn't been so mad at him for lying to me, I would've almost felt bad for him.

"What are you doing here?" I asked.

"I was waiting for you; I need to talk to you about something." He looked up at me from under those beautiful long eyelashes.

"Stacy already told me. I know all about *her*." I said while trying to keep a tear from welling up in my eyes. I couldn't look at him. I was on the porch, trying to get in the house without him seeing how bad I was hurting.

"She told you?" he asked.

"Yes, she did. And I think that it's time for you to go home to your family. You belong with Stacy. She's your wife. You need to go home with them," I said in the most unfeeling tone I could muster up.

"She told you everything and you want me to leave? Are you fucking kidding me?" he asked with a weird look on his face, like I had just surprised the shit out of him.

"Yes, I think you need to stay with your wife. I'm fine here. I have my family and my life that I need to get back to. This was fun, but I think we both knew it wouldn't last."

Jaxon stood up and walked toward me. "What the fuck are you saying, Loralei? You just want me to leave? You don't want to give me the chance to explain?"

I turned and faced him. "There is nothing for you to explain. This, whatever the hell this was, is over. You have a family to take care of. So go do it!"

He stomped off toward Jake's truck. When he got in the truck, he slammed his fists down on the steering wheel. He was mad. He was yelling, but I couldn't hear what he was saying. He started the truck up and peeled all the way down the lane.

I watched him drive away. He was angry, but he didn't even put up a fight. No matter how much I didn't want to admit it, I really wished he would've.

I went in the house and called my mom. I asked her if she could please pick the kids up at school and keep them until tomorrow. I lied and told her I felt like I was coming down with something and just needed to rest for a bit. I was sure she didn't believe me, but she agreed anyway.

I ran a hot bath, climbed in, and tried to wash all my worries away. Well, that didn't work so I had to come up with a Plan B. A plan that didn't involve me messing up Jaxon's life. He and Stacy were married and they had a daughter. They needed to be together. Their daughter needed her father.

I was hoping that Jaxon could be a father to the twins, but he needed to take care of his child, and he needed to be with Stacy to do that. I couldn't interfere and ruin their family, no matter how much it hurt me to see him drive away today.

<u>Jaxon</u>

I couldn't understand what was going on. I was so pissed off. But at who? Loralei? Stacy? Or myself? It was a definite toss-up.

Stacy told Loralei about the DNA test and she still wanted me to leave. *God damn it!* She must have felt that this would be an easy way out for her. I was so in love with that woman that I couldn't see straight and she gave up on me. Just like that.

She made the decision that she wanted me to leave. She wanted me to go to my wife and raise a kid that's not mine. How the fuck did I fall in love with her? Apparently, she didn't love me near as much as I loved her.

I had known in my heart the entire time that the DNA test would come back and say I wasn't the father. I knew that I couldn't have kids. Stacy and I had tried for so long and when she told me about Jaz, I just knew she wasn't mine. I knew at that moment, I was the reason why we couldn't have kids.

"Uncle Jake, I think it's time for me to head back to California." I couldn't even look up at him when I said this. I knew that he would know something was wrong. I had moved beyond pissed, now I was hurting.

"Son, what's going on? Did something happen with you and Loralei?" Uncle Jake asked. He was worried about me, but I just didn't want to talk about this right now.

"Stacy came back, and she has a kid. Her name is Jaz." The look on Uncle Jake's face looked like something out of a bad movie.

"What do you mean *she* has a kid? Is it yours? Does she look like ya, son?"

"That doesn't matter, Stacy's my wife and I need to do the right thing by her and our family. I am taking her back home. I just want you to know how much I appreciate you letting me come stay with you. I really needed to get away, and you made me feel at home here. I can't thank you enough for that."

I grabbed Uncle Jake and pulled him into a man hug. Trying not to let him see how much it was hurting me to leave Loralei.

But this was her decision and I had to abide by it, because I loved her.

Chapter 12

Cade

These past five weeks had passed like molasses. I hadn't had sex for almost two months. I was so horny I could explode, literally. I planned to leave for Harper Farms tomorrow. I was taking my cousin Clay with me to help me with the cattle. He wasn't too much of a worker, but I had to get his ass out of town before he got himself killed.

That boy needed to learn to keep it in his pants, or at least pick his partners from a higher breed of women. He was twenty-one years old, and he definitely inherited our family's good looks and charm. We were a sexy-ass bunch of cowboys. The last gal he was with told her brother about some of the things he did, like when she caught him in bed with their mother, and he threatened to shoot him. I'm pretty sure he would've if I hadn't intervened. Goddamned family, can't live with 'em, and it's illegal to shoot 'em.

Tomorrow I would get to see Loralei again. I missed her so much. I told Mr. Davidson not to tell her I was coming. I wanted to surprise her - boy would she be surprised. I really wanted her to be happy to see me. I really hoped that asshat was out of the picture. A guy could dream right?

I didn't sleep a wink that night. I was like a kid waiting for the carnival to come to town. I was too damn excited to sleep.

"Wake the hell up!" I screamed at Clay from down the hall. "I got shit to do today, and you ain't holding me up."

"Hold your fucking horses. I'm awake!" he screamed back at me.

We were in the car and headed to Harper Farms before six o'clock a.m. I had my thermos of black coffee, and I grabbed a pop-tart on the way out the door. Clay was asleep before we hit the end of the lane. That was fine by me. I didn't need to hear him whine all the way to Kipton. We had about a four hour drive ahead of us, and I was hoping he would sleep for most of it.

I stopped in Joplin for gas and to grab some actual food. Clay woke up long enough to use the facilities and scarf down some biscuits and gravy. I was getting kinda nervous, or maybe I was excited, or maybe it was a little bit of both. I needed this woman, but what if she didn't want to see me. I couldn't understand what the hell it was about her. I just needed to be with her. She was the only damn thing I could think about.

Well? I'd had weeks to think about this, and I had a couple of ideas on how to make her mine. I couldn't wait to get there and see her beautiful face and that amazing ass. Oh my god, I had missed that ass. Just thinking about it was getting "cowboy" all excited.

"What the hell, man?" Clay yelled as he smacked me across the back of the head. "You gonna take care of that shit in the truck? Man, I'm sitting right here. That is fucking sick!"

That's when I realized I was kinda playing with "cowboy" through my jeans. Oh man, this shit had to stop. I had to have

Loralei. I had to make her mine again and hear her scream my name.

All of these thoughts weren't helping my current situation. They just caused Clay to smack me upside the head again. "Seriously, man. Pull the hell over and let me out of the truck!" I started thinking about chickens and cattle and anything else that would make my dick calm the hell down.

We were almost there and "cowboy" had finally calmed down. Clay only had to smack me on the back of my head a couple more times on the way there.

When we pulled onto the Harper Farms property, I immediately felt like I knew Loralei a little bit better than I had. This was her farm. I had my ranch and I knew what it meant to me. And I knew that she felt the same way about hers. I could tell she put her heart and soul into this farm. There wasn't a thing out of place. The fence was perfect. The lanes were all tree lined. The farm definitely had felt a woman's touch. My Loralei's touch. I couldn't wait to feel that touch again.

We were slowly driving down the lane when I looked over to the stables and saw her. Her beautiful blonde hair was pulled up in a ponytail, she had on a blue flannel shirt and those amazing, "huggin' her in all the right places" jeans. She had on her old work boots. She was brushing out one of the horses and finally she heard my truck, stopped what she was doing and made eye contact with me. That's when I noticed she wasn't wearing any make-up and she looked even more beautiful than I remembered.

Loralei

What the hell was he doing here? No way - why was this happening? Cade, goddamn Cade was here. He was at my farm. *Shit!*

He got out of the truck and started to walk over toward me. He was so amazingly sexy. Why did he have to be so incredibly sexy? He didn't walk, he sauntered. Never losing that sexy sideways smirk. He was wearing his skin-tight wranglers, cowboy boots, ten-gallon hat, and a green button-up shirt that made his green eyes shine even brighter.

"What the hell are you doing here?" I asked before he made his way all the way to me.

"Well, hello to you too, hon," he said with that sexy southern drawl.

"Seriously, Cade, why are you here?"

"Didn't George tell ya? There was a problem with his herd. He said we would need to check the cattle out and decide who gets what. I really thought he would've called ya."

There was something about the way he said that. It made me think that he had known all along that George hadn't called me about the cattle.

"I had no idea you were coming. I got a call this morning that the cattle delivery has been postponed until next Monday. I find it a little odd that they didn't mention you to me when they called this morning." I leaned up against the barn. I hadn't really noticed until just then. But I guess the entire time we were talking, Cade was getting closer and closer to me. By the time I realized it, I felt the barn behind me.

"Where's asshat? He around here somewhere? Will he see me if I kiss ya right now?" Cade asked, as he leaned in closer to my face. I could feel his breath on my face. It felt pretty nice.

"Mom! Who's the cowboy? Is he tryin' to kiss you? MOM!" I heard Sammy yelling this from across the field. Cade jumped back away from me. The look in his eyes was almost sinful. He looked like he wanted to eat me alive. And I think he really did.

"Mom! There's another big cowboy over by that truck, Mom. I'll kick their butts! Don't you touch my mommy, you asshat cowboys!" Sammy yelled as he ran across the field.

"Honey, mommy is fine. I know this cowboy. His name is Cade. Come and say hello. And watch your language."

"Hello, cowboy Cade. Who's the other cowboy?" Sammy asked, huffing and puffing, trying to catch his breath. About that time the other cowboy came out from behind the truck. He looked like a carbon copy of Cade, except smaller. Cade was so big and muscular. This guy looked like he didn't work quite as hard as Cade.

"This is my cousin, Clay. Clay, say hello to these nice people," Cade said.

"Hello, nice people." Clay tipped his hat, using that same sexy southern drawl his cousin had.

"Nice to meet ya, Clay. I'm still a little confused about why ya'll are here, though."

"Mommy, I'm hungry. What's for lunch?" My little Sammy was always starving.

"I was just going to make some sandwiches. We'll eat in a bit, okay babe?" Sammy skulked off toward the barn.

Cade walked over towards Sammy, and said, "A sandwich sounds great, buddy. Maybe your mom will make one for me too?" Cade looked up at winked at me. Damn it, now I was going to have to invite them in for lunch. My mom did not raise me to be impolite.

I shrugged my shoulders and wrinkled my eyebrows, "Sure. We would love for ya'll to come have lunch with us. Sammy, go get your sister." Sammy headed off to get Mags.

When the kids got there, I had Cade and Clay follow us to our house. On the drive there I couldn't help but think about the time I had spent with Cade. The things we had done together. The things he had done to me. I could feel the color draining from my face. I felt a little hand on my cheek.

"Mommy, are you okay?" Mags asked with a raised eyebrow and her little eyes squinting at me.

"Oh, sweetie, Mommy's fine. Just thinking about stuff. Don't worry about me." I put a smile on my face for Mags, but when I looked in the rearview mirror and caught a glimpse of Cade that smile quickly faded.

We pulled down our drive and Cade pulled right up beside us. The kids jumped out of the jeep and ran in the house. I nodded to Clay and had them follow us in.

"Nice place ya got here, Loralei," I heard Cade say as we were walking in the house.

I kept walking, "Thanks, we like it."

After they removed their hats at the door and hung them on the rack on the wall, I led Clay and Cade into the kitchen. They had a seat at the table. Sammy and Mags were already getting in the fridge and pulling out the sandwich fixings. The table was covered with lunch meat, cheese, lettuce, tomatoes, olives, pickles, mayo, mustard, and bread.

"Boy, when ya'll say sandwich, you mean sandwich." Clay sounded in awe of our sandwich fixings.

Mags said, "Sammy, throw me the bread." Sammy picked up the loaf and threw it at Mags head.

Cade jumped up and caught it in the air. He passed it to Mags. "Here ya go, sweetie."

She blushed and smiled, "Thanks."

We sat around the table and ate. Clay and Cade were pretty funny.

"Knock knock," Clay said to the kids.

Sammy said, "Who's there?"

"Yah."

"Yah who?"

Clay started cracking up, "Yah HOO, ride 'em cowboy!"

Cade said, "I've got one. "What did the horse say when it fell?"

Sammy and Mags were really thinking about it. Finally, Sammy looked at Mags. "We give up. What did it say?"

"I've fallen and I can't giddy-up," Cade was laughing so hard he was shaking. Even though the joke wasn't that funny, his laughter was contagious. Before I knew it, we were all doubled over laughing.

Then Cade smacked Clay upside the head. "Get your elbows off the table. Your momma raised you better than that."

Clay smacked him back. "Don't hit me in front of the kids."

"Didn't you just hit me?"

"I was protectin' myself."

Then Cade smacked Clay on the back of the head again. "What the hell, man?" Clay whined.

"I said get your elbows off the damn table."

Clay jabbed his elbow into Cade's ribs. Cade screamed out, grabbed Clay by the back of the head and body slammed him on the ground. Clay was laughing as Cade had him flat on his back. "You said get 'em off the table. You didn't tell me where to put 'em."

The kids and I were watching, not really knowing if we should intervene or not.

Mags said, "Mommy, what's wrong with these cowboys?"

I grinned at Mags "Honey, you'll learn this soon enough. Cowboys are all a little silly."

Cade and Clay looked up at me and laughed. We spent the rest of the lunch laughing. It was nice to not think about Jaxon for a bit. I wasn't the only one who missed him. The kids had been asking about him ever since he left. That was what I had been afraid of when I opened my heart up to him. I couldn't stand to see the kids hurt. This was the first time since he had left weeks ago that we were all laughing and having a good time.

When lunch was over the kids ran outside to play, and Clay went out to the truck to make a phone call. Cade and I were sitting in my living room.

"Well this isn't weird at all, is it?" He ran his hands through his hair. Messing up that already messed up blonde head of hair.

"Why are you really here, Cade? There's no future for us, you understand that, right?"

Cade was trying to look innocent. He had on his best "good little country boy" face. "I do, I'm just here for the cattle. I thought it was going to be here today. George said it was. I had no idea the shipment had been put off."

"I am still not quite sure why you need to be here for the delivery."

"George called and there have been some problems with the cattle. A whole bunch of 'em came down with something pretty bad. He said we would need to decide which ones we each wanted to keep. He said he would work out the money stuff later. Said he'd give us a hell of a deal next year."

"Okay, guess that makes sense. Well since the delivery isn't going to be here until Monday, you and Clay are welcome to stay here at the ranch. We have an old log cabin down by the pond. It's all set up. You can eat in the barn office with the farmhands."

Cade gave me a little sheepish grin, "Well, that's mighty thoughtful of ya, Loralei. I would hate to impose, but since you're offering we'll take ya up on it."

I had Cade and Clay follow me to the cabin. I showed them around the cabin and helped them get settled in. I told them about the diner in town so they could grab some dinner. And I let them know that breakfast would be served in the barn office at 6:00 a.m. I headed home with the understanding that I would see them at breakfast.

Cade

I didn't sleep an hour last night. I couldn't believe I was finally here. Finally this close to her, and I couldn't touch her. I couldn't kiss her. I couldn't be with her. I needed this woman. She had gotten under my skin like no other woman ever had. I didn't just want her, which I did more than anything, I needed her.

I was up showered, shaved, and ready for breakfast before Clay even crawled his lazy ass out of bed. "If you wanna eat breakfast, you better get your ass in gear, boy."

"I'm coming. Don't get your panties in a wad, Cade."

Little bastard. I should've left him at home and let that dude kick his ass. He needed to be taught a lesson. But of course I couldn't do that to him. I happened to love the little bastard.

We got in the truck and headed to the barn office. When we got there I noticed about eight guys walking with Loralei toward the office. Damn that woman was spectacular. I could spend an entire lifetime just looking at her. Taking her all in. All day, every damn day. I was afraid if I wasn't with her soon, "cowboy" would never work right again.

All the guys were hanging on every word she said. Not like in a sexual way, like in a respectful way. That woman had the power over those men. They definitely knew who the boss was. Damn, I couldn't wait to find out everything about this woman that was takin' over my every thought. Just from what little I knew, I didn't think she could be any more perfect.

She caught a glimpse of us pulling in, and I could tell she wasn't real happy to see me. That was killing me. I wanted her to feel somethin' for me, but not hate. I wanted her to want me the way I wanted her.

Clay and I parked and headed into the barn office. Loralei was already sitting at the big round table in the middle of the great room. This barn was huge. I could tell she had put some work into this place. It looked like we walked into a banquet hall instead of a barn. The great room was surrounded on the right with several offices. And on the left with restrooms, a kitchen, and a couple of sleeping quarters, I assumed they were for the farmhands who had to work overnight during birthing season.

This barn was almost identical to mine. I wondered if we had the same guy work on our remodels. I thought I might ask her about that after we had sex again. Definitely not before. Priorities.

I walked over to Loralei, dragging Clay's tired ass behind me. "Good mornin', Loralei." I tipped my hat.

Without looking up at me, she said, "Good morning, Cade. I assume ya'll slept well?"

I wanted to be honest with her and tell her *hell no*, I didn't sleep well. I didn't sleep a fucking hour because all I could think about was burying myself as deep in her as I could get. I thought that might scare her, so I told her, "Yes, ma'am. Thanks for askin'."

"Well, ya'll can grab some breakfast and then you're more than welcome to get your hands dirty out on the farm. Jake will show ya around, and put you both to work, I assume."

An older gray haired man was sitting next to Loralei, just laughed, and nodded his head at me. "I assume we could find something to keep ya'll busy."

I sure as hell didn't come here to work, but I wasn't above gettin' my hands dirty either. "Sounds like a mighty fine idea. You just tell us what to do and we'll do it."

Clay looked like he was gonna hit me. He didn't like to work on my farm and I paid him, he sure wasn't happy about working for free.

Loralei

I was having a hard time focusing today. I hadn't been feeling real good and with Cade being here, I just felt out of sorts. He had been here less than a day, and he was already turning my life upside down. If I was being honest with myself, I would have to admit, I missed Jaxon. I knew I had sent him away, but the thought of never seeing him again was tearing me up inside. He needed to be with *his* family. As much as I wanted that family to include me and the twins, it just didn't. I was going to have to get over him. But I wasn't sure how to go about doing that.

I walked down to the horse barn to see if the guys needed any help, when I saw him. Cade. He was standing in one of the stalls. He had his shirt off, and he was bent over mucking out the stall. Holy hell, that man was built. And so tall. His blonde hair was slick with sweat. His Wranglers were hugging him in all the right places. He had on his boots, but his hat was hanging on the door of the stall.

He turned around to shovel some crap out of the stall and our eyes met. Not real romantic, you know, with the crap and all. But his eyes - he looked so happy to see me. His eyes were smiling. I know that sounds weird, but that's the only way to describe it. He really was happy to see me.

Why did I hate him so much? He hadn't taken advantage of me. I had started everything with him. Any guy would've done the same thing. He really did do things to me, things that I had never dreamed of another man doing to me.

"Well, hello hon. Come to help the men work?" He smirked.

I walked toward him and crossed my arms over my chest, "No, I think I'll leave the shit shoveling to ya'll. Men seem to be pretty good at that."

He just laughed at me, that deep belly laugh that I remembered from our dinner together. I turned around to start out of the stall when I lost my balance and started to fall. Before I knew what was happening, I was in Cade's arms and he was lowering me to the ground. He was cradling my head and I felt like I was going to pass out. I was really weak and shaking all over. I realized I broke out in a sweat.

"Hon, are you okay? What can I do?" Cade looked really scared. He was white as a ghost.

"I'm fine, Cade. Just help me stand up will ya?"

With that Cade lifted me and then sat me down on my wobbly legs. I couldn't get my balance and then everything went black.

Chapter 13

Loralei

I was so comfortable. I hadn't been this relaxed in years. I opened my eyes, and I was in a very familiar place. I looked all around the room. Declan's room. I was lying in his bed. I could feel someone nuzzled up to my side. I turned and looked down and was staring into the most beautiful crystal blue eyes I had ever seen. Declan's eyes. I reached out and touched his face. How was this happening? This couldn't be real. Declan had been gone for so long.

"*Declan, sweetie, is that really you?*"

In that sexy southern drawl I had missed so much, he said, "Good mornin' sweetheart. How ya feelin'?" Then he gave me that smirk. Oh my god, how I had missed that smirk. I couldn't help it, I broke into tears. He leaned up and kissed my cheek, kissing my tears away. "Lor, please don't cry. I love you so much - I always loved you. What happened to me was not your fault. It wasn't anybody's fault. I'm so proud of the woman you've become. I'm so sorry that I haven't been there for you and our babies, Lor. You have no idea how much I wanted to grow old with you. How I wanted that destiny we had always dreamed of. The two kids, the big front porch to sit on and watch our grandkids play. I wanted all of that with you Lor, but sometimes your destiny has to change. Sometimes life gets in the way, and you have to change your plans.

But you rolled with the punches, and you became the amazing, strong woman that is here today."

I turned over to where we were lying face to face. I reached up and placed my hand on his cheek and just stared into his eyes. I didn't want to look away. I didn't want this dream to end. "Dec, what's going on? Why am I here like this? Oh my god, did I die? Where are my babies?"

Declan wrapped me in his arms. "You are not dead baby, but I am. You can't live another minute for me. This life is yours, and you have to start living it. I want you to be happy. Do you hear me, Lor? You deserve to be happy. Do you think Jaxon would make you happy?"

I didn't know how to answer that question. I believed that I did love Jaxon, but after everything that happened, I just didn't know anymore. "I don't know, Dec. I just don't know."

"Would Cade make you happy?" He tucked my hair behind my ear.

"No Declan, I don't think he would. I don't feel for him the way I felt about you. I've never felt that way about anyone."

Declan looked down at me, piercing me with those beautiful crystal blue eyes that I had missed so much. "Does Jaxon make you smile, Lor? When he looks at you, does your heart skip a beat? Does he give you those butterflies deep in your belly?"

I knew the answer - he did, he did all of that. "Yes, he does Declan, he really does. But so much has happened. I don't know how to fix it."

"Lor, if you love each other, ya'll will find a way. You need to make it work. There is nothing I want more for you than happiness."

I couldn't stop crying. I knew this was gonna end. I didn't want him to leave. I didn't want to wake up. I wanted to stay here like this forever.

"Dec, you know how much I loved you, right?"

He nodded, and kissed my hand that he was holding. "Sammy looks just like you. He is such a handful, but he has such a big heart. Your mom has a really hard time watching him play sometimes. I know it's because he reminds her so much of you. He looks and acts just like you. Mags is my little princess. She's perfect, Dec. She's got your eyes, but otherwise she looks like me. She is a sweetheart. She's a little shy, but I think she'll come into her own soon."

He said, "Sounds like she's a lot like her mom. Beautiful, shy, and my sweetheart."

"Lor, it's time for you to wake up. Always remember I loved you more than anything. You were my heart. Now let me go, but never lose the memories from the times we shared. Promise me, Lor, promise me you'll move on and do everything to be happy. For you and for the kids. Promise me." He placed a soft kiss on my lips.

"I promise you, Declan. I promise."

Opening my eyes slowly, I looked all around the small, bright room. The fluorescent lights were shining down brighter than the sun. I quickly shut my eyes, and then tried to squint to see who that was sitting in the chair beside me. I tried to turn my head to get a better look at them, but my head hurt. Really, really hurt. It felt like someone was using a jackhammer on the back of my head.

What had happened to me? Obviously, I was in the hospital, but why? I guess I hadn't been feeling well for a bit. I came to the conclusion that I was probably dehydrated and they just needed to give me some IV fluids before they sent me home. That sounded reasonable.

In my peripheral vision, I saw movement to the left of me. The person stood up. I looked up, way up, and saw that it was Cade. After my dream with Declan, I really hoped to wake up and find Jaxon here. But that was just a dream. A dream that I was going to somehow make a reality. I promised Declan that I would move on. I had to talk to Jaxon and find out if he still loved me. I had to know what we needed do to move forward. I just hoped it wasn't too late.

"How's your head, hon'?" Cade whispered. He looked liked he hadn't slept for days. His shirt was a wrinkled mess and his hair was all over his head.

"It's okay. How are you? You look like somethin' the cat dragged in."

He let out one of those deep belly laughs, "Thank God, you're back, hon'. I was gettin' mighty worried about ya." He leaned in and lightly kissed my cheek. About that time a doctor walked into the room.

"Ms. Harper, glad to see you're awake. My name is Dr. Cotter. How are you feeling?"

I was still trying to get my eyes to focus. "I'm feeling okay, but boy-oh-boy, my head really hurts. And I'm kinda having a hard time focusing my eyes."

The doctor got out his little light pen and flashed it in my eyes. "I think the issue with focusing is just because you have been out for a while. You hit your head pretty hard when you fell. Mr. Walker brought you in, and we've been waiting for you to wake up." I didn't even realize I had hit my head. I guess Cade didn't get to me quite as fast as I thought.

The doctor read over my chart. "Well, I do have some good news for you. Congratulations, Ms. Harper you're expecting."

My head started spinning. What did he just say? No. No. No. There was no way. I couldn't be pregnant. Could I? Well, I mean I *could* be, but was I really? I looked up and Cade had the biggest smile on his face. And then it hit me. He thought the baby was his. Oh my god, it could be his. But, no we used protection both times. It couldn't be his. It had to be Jaxon's. Didn't it? I never thought I would have this kind of dilemma. Trying to figure out who my baby-daddy was.

Dr. Cotter continued, "We believe you're about seven weeks along. You will need to make an appointment with an OB/GYN. If you don't have one, I can set up an appointment for you."

"Um, I have one. I'll use Dr. Grubbs again. She delivered my twins."

Dr. Cotter started making notes in my chart. "I would recommend you get an appointment scheduled as soon as possible."

I looked over at Cade and he was still grinning from ear to ear. Then I asked Dr. Cotter, "How long before I can have a DNA test? I need to know who the father is." I couldn't look up at Cade. I knew he had been so thrilled at the thought of this baby being his. But I had to have proof that it was Jaxon's.

Dr. Cotter responded, "A DNA test can be done via an amniocentesis at the end of your first trimester, which would be in about six weeks. If our calculations are correct. You will need to discuss that with Dr. Grubbs. She will be able to schedule that for you."

I had to get out this room. I had to get home. I needed to see my kids. I couldn't handle this news right now. After that dream with Declan and now this. I was going to have a baby. A baby. I was scared, excited, and nervous all wrapped into one. I tried to get up out of bed by myself, but I was still a little woozie.

Cade grabbed me and had me lay back down. "Take it easy, hon. We aren't in a hurry. Let me help you get dressed."

Cade and I had been very intimate, but the thought of him getting me dressed, just felt wrong. "That's okay, I can do it."

He took the hint and pulled the curtain closed around me. He placed my clothes on the edge of the bed, and then stepped out of the room.

I very slowly stood up, still holding on to the side of the bed. I stood there and got my bearings. I finally slipped my shirt over my head. I didn't bother with my bra, too much work. I sat down on the bed and slid my jeans on.

About that time I heard Cade, "How ya doin' in there, hon? Need help?"

I actually could use some help with my boots. "Yeah, could you help me put my boots on?"

Cade stepped around the curtain, "No problem, hon. Here lift your foot up a little." He helped me get both boots on and then we waited for the nurse with the discharge papers to arrive. We sat in silence. Cade was in the chair across from me, while I sat on the bed.

I had to talk to Jaxon. The sooner the better.

Cade

How could I go from being over the moon happy to feeling lower than the mud on the bottom of someone's boot in less than sixty seconds? Loralei Harper, that's how. That woman just broke my heart. I had always dreamed of bein' a daddy. I wanted that so bad. Ever since my parents died, I had wanted a family. I had my cousins, but I'd always wanted a kid. And for less than a minute, I had it. But of course she thinks it's asshat's baby.

We had used protection when we were together, but I just wanted this so damn bad. I really hoped it would be mine. I guess I would have to hang around a few weeks to find out. If that baby was mine, there was no fucking way Loralei Harper wouldn't become mine too.

Loralei

"Cade, I really don't want to talk about this right now." We were on our way to my house from the hospital. My parents had the kids and were waiting for me at home.

"Hon, we need to talk about this now. I'm not leaving here until I know if that baby in your belly is mine. I know you keep tellin' me you don't feel a spark with me, but by God I feel one with you. I haven't slept a wink since we parted in Joplin. I have been hurtin', physically hurtin', for you. You can't tell me that you didn't have a good time with me, hon. I know you did. And where the hell is asshat anyway? Why wasn't he here for you when you needed him? Sure as hell wasn't him driving you to the hospital. Or sitting up all night watching you sleep, just to make sure you were breathing okay. Where was he, huh, Loralei?"

I couldn't even look at him. He was right. He was there for me when I needed him. And this baby could be his. But in my heart, I knew it was Jaxon's. There wasn't a question in my mind. No matter what had happened, I loved Jaxon, not Cade. And I had to tell him.

"Cade, you did make me happy. You were exactly what I needed at that point. But you are not my future. I'm so sorry, but I don't love you. And I don't believe that you love me either. I really think I'm more of a game to you. Something you can't have, so you want it even more. I love him, Cade. And no matter what's happened between he and I, that hasn't changed. We may not end up together, but I will never feel for you, what I feel for him."

We rode the rest of the way home in silence. Every once in awhile I would glance over at Cade, but he never took his eyes off the road. He had this look on his face. I had only seen it a couple of times before. He was fiercely determined. That look scared the hell out of me. He wasn't going to go anywhere until we knew who the father was. *Oh my god!* How was I going to tell my parents I was pregnant? Oh, and I would have to tell them I wasn't sure who the father was. Wow, who'd have thought my life would come to this?

I broke the silence when we started down the drive to my house. "Cade, I don't want to tell anyone about the baby yet."

He didn't even look at me. "I'll do whatever you want, hon. You just tell me, and it's done. You don't want anybody to know. I won't tell a soul. But I'm not leaving here until I know if that baby is mine." He finally looked up at me, with his green eyes burning. "And if that baby in your belly is mine, *you* will be mine too. That's a guarantee." He finally looked away from me when my dad opened my door.

"Darlin', we were so worried about you. We took good care of the kids, while Cade took you to the hospital. Thanks again for that, Cade. I can't tell you how much I appreciate ya takin' care of my baby."

Cade tipped his hat at my dad. "The pleasure was all mine, Mr. Harper, I assure you." He glanced over at me. "Looks like ya'll could use a couple of extra hands with the new cattle comin' in and all. Why don't Clay and I stay here with ya for a bit? Mr. Davidson will be here tomorrow with the cattle from the sale. Since it's doin' poorly, probably wouldn't be a bad idea, to keep 'em all together for a while. Then we can cull the herd and go our separate ways in a few weeks probably."

My dad looked at me, waiting for me to respond to Cade. "Uh, I guess that'd be okay. You can stay in the old cabin as long as ya need to. But we don't want to keep you from anything at your ranch. If you need to get back, *everything* here will be just fine."

Cade was getting mad. He was glaring at me. "No, hon, right here is where I need to be. I'll send Clay to the ranch to pick up some stuff for us and we'll see ya'll tomorrow. Mr. Davidson is plannin' on gettin' here around lunchtime right?"

I nodded and my dad helped me down out of the truck. He tipped his hat at Cade. Cade drove away toward the cabin.

We went into the house and my mom came running over toward me. "Loralei Harper, this is what you get for not listening to your mother. I told you, you need to eat healthier. You don't eat right, sweetie. It's not good for you. And you aren't setting a good example for the kids."

I really couldn't handle this right now. "So, mom, if you're done yelling at me about my eating habits, could you maybe tell me where my kids are?"

My mom glared at me. "You know you're never too old to bend over my knee ma'am."

Seriously, she was going to do this now?

"Mom, I am suffering from a head injury, I cannot handle this right now. Where are my babies?"

My mom pointed toward the back hall that led to the kid's playroom. I walked in and Mags had Sammy pinned to the floor in a chokehold. God, I loved that girl. "Whatcha doin' there Mags?"

She looked at me with that sweet, innocent expression on her face. The one she always got when she was doing something to Sammy that she shouldn't be doing. "Mom, I'm trying to teach your son a lesson. He keeps telling me that girls aren't as tough as boys. But look, Mommy, he can't get up. So, who's stronger now, Sammy? Huh, huh? Is it you?"

Sammy grunted, "No."

Mags won. She was thrilled. "See, was that so hard? You shoulda just agreed with me. Boys are not stronger than girls."

Sammy ran over to me and threw his little arms around my waist. He gave me the biggest hug and looked up at me through those long black eyelashes, with his daddy's eyes. "I love you,

Mommy." Then he whispered, "I'm so glad you got here, Mommy. I think Mags was gonna kill me."

I had to laugh at that. "Sweetie, your sister wasn't gonna kill you. But remember all little boys were made by mommies. So mommies must be pretty strong girls, huh?"

Sammy thought about that for a minute and then he said, "You're right, Mommy. You're a very strong girl." And then he pulled my head down closer to him. "Mags is pretty strong too. But don't tell her I think she is, okay. Can it be our secret?"

I shook my head at him and told them to go get washed up for dinner.

I had things I needed to start working on now. I made a promise to Declan and I intended to keep it.

Chapter 14

Cade

Clay and I had been working on the farm for a few weeks now. He went to my place the day after Lor was released from the hospital, and picked us up enough supplies to last for the entire time that we needed to stay here to wait for the DNA test.

Loralei was doing her damnedest to avoid me. In the morning, when we went to the office for breakfast, she would always be already sitting with Jake or some of the other guys. I didn't know if she told them something about me, or if they just didn't trust me. But they watched both of us like a hawk. If it hadn't been me that they were keepin' away from her, I woulda appreciated them takin' such good care of her.

When we were out working in the field, she would make sure to keep a field's distance between us. Every time I saw her, I couldn't take my eyes off of her. I couldn't put my finger on it, but there was something about this woman that made me lose all sense.

I finally caught her alone out beside the barn. I walked up behind her and put my hands over her eyes. "Guess who?"

She said, "Cade, back off. You're too close."

Well, I felt like I needed to be a hell of a lot closer. Like inside her, and that wouldn't even have been close enough. "Hon, I could never be too close to you," I said as I gently pressed my body up against her backside.

She jumped away from me. "I'm serious, damn it. Back off!"

"Okay, okay. Goodness, I was just playin' around. It seems like you've been ignorin' me. I haven't had a minute alone with you since the truck on the way home from the hospital. I miss ya. How have ya been feelin'? Everything okay with the baby?"

That pissed her off. The look on her cute little face said she wanted to pull my head off and feed it to the coyotes. I had no idea what I had done to piss her off, but I had a feelin' I was gonna hear about it real soon.

"Damn it, Cade! I told you I don't want anybody to know about the baby! Don't say a word about it, someone will hear you!"

I hated that she wasn't excited about our baby. I wanted to shout it to anyone that would listen, but she wanted no part of that. I was so fuckin' excited, I couldn't stand it. I didn't think the smile had left my face since I found out she was pregnant. That damn test was unnecessary, that baby in her belly was mine. I had wanted to have a family for so long. This had to be God's way of helping me out. I was finally gonna have a family. I couldn't fuckin' wait!

I rubbed my hands up and down her arms and then slid them down to her hands. I grabbed her hands and held them in mine. I pulled them up to my mouth for a quick kiss. I loved it when I made her shudder. She was as affected by my touch as I was by hers.

God, I wanted this damn woman more than anything. "I'm sorry, hon. I won't mention it again. I'll wait until you're ready." I leaned in and whispered in her ear, "But I hope we don't wait too long, because I'm so excited to be a daddy. You have no idea." I kissed her ear and just as I was about to suck her earlobe into my mouth, her dad walked around the corner.

He cleared his throat. "Loralei, what the hell is going on here?" He asked with a look of serious disdain. When I turned toward him he had his eyebrow raised and was staring at me like he wanted to brand me with that branding iron he was holdin'.

Loralei said, "Nothing, Dad. Not a thing. Cade was just heading inside, and he was checking to see how I was feeling, that's all."

Her dad looked me up and down, with his eyebrow still raised. "Sure as hell didn't look like nothin' to me. But you're a grown woman and I got no say in your business. So, I'm just gonna get the hell out of here, and not mention a word of what I just saw to your momma."

"Guess that was a close one, huh?" I whispered as I leaned in to kiss Lor.

She placed her hands on my chest and pushed me away. "Cade, I can't, I just can't. I'm sorry." She ran off toward her jeep, climbed in and drove away.

I needed those test results. As soon as she knew the baby was mine, she would wanna plan a future with me. My God, I prayed, please let that baby be mine.

Jaxon

I had been back in Richmond for only a few weeks, but it felt like forever. My mom agreed to let us stay with her until we could find a place of our own. To be honest, I wasn't really out looking too much. I was trying to live with Stacy and Jaz as a family.

Jaz wasn't my daughter, but I was trying so hard to pretend. I held her, I helped Stacy feed her, bathe her, and I played with her. I was trying so hard to be a daddy to her, but the more I looked at her, the more I realized what I had lost. All I had wanted was to become a family with Lor and the twins. Grow old with her on the farm. I still couldn't understand why she was so quick to let me leave. I was so pissed off at her that day. I didn't even put up a fight. I was such a dick. I thought she felt the same way for me, as I felt for her, but apparently I was wrong. Those weeks we were together will always be the best weeks of my life. This just proved to me that I was a total fuck-up.

Stacy was giving Jaz a bath. "Jaxon, come get her for me."

I walked over to Stacy and took Jaz out of her arms. She was all wrapped up in her little pink princess towel. It had a hood that looked like a crown. That hood was covering up her beautiful blonde curls.

She had the biggest blue eyes. She was beautiful, just like her mommy. Why couldn't she be mine? Why couldn't we have had her, when we were trying so hard? When we were happy? Maybe if we had, things would be different. Back then I thought that Stacy was my future. Meeting Loralei changed all of that. It changed me.

I took Jaz into the spare bedroom we were staying in at Mom's. She put her head on my shoulder and snuggled down into the crook of my neck. I just couldn't understand why things had to be this way. If she had been here a couple of years ago, my fucking life would've been so different. But that's not how it happened.

Even though she looked just like Stacy, I could see Ratz every time I looked at her. I just knew he was her dad. How could an asshole like that make something so perfect? Something that he would never appreciate? Something he couldn't take the time to be bothered with?

She smelled so good. I could've sat there and snuggled with her forever. But Stacy came and took her out of my arms and started to get her ready for bed. I went downstairs. My mom was in the kitchen on the phone. I started through the doorway when I heard:

"He's just not himself, Jake. He misses her. He hasn't said anything to me, but I know that's what it is. He's tryin' so hard to love this baby girl. But he won't ever love her Momma again."

"I know. I feel the same way. I just don't know what to do. He has to be a man. After what his daddy did to us, he won't ever leave her, Jake, You know that."

"I don't think I can stand to watch him hurtin' like this much longer. I know. I love you too. Talk soon."

I stepped into the kitchen. "Hey, Mom, who was on the phone?"

She shrugged her shoulders. "Oh, just somebody tryin' to sell me somethin'. You know how that goes..."

I hated that she felt she had to lie to me about talking to Uncle Jake. He knew I had to do this. They both knew that it would be hard for me to abandon Jaz. Especially, after I became attached. Stacy needed me to help her with the baby. There was no way she could raise a kid by herself. And we were married. I just needed to forget about my fucking fantasy future, and live in the here and now.

"Yeah, Mom, I know. I promise we will get out of your hair soon. I don't wanna cause a burden for you. I really appreciate you letting us stay."

Mom motioned for us to sit down at the table. "Son, I need to know what you're gonna do about that girl in Missouri. I know you mean to do the right thing by that sweet baby girl upstairs. But what about those kids in Missouri? There as much yours as Jaz is."

"What the hell are you talking about, Mom? The twins aren't mine."

"And neither is she. You can't lie to me, Jaxon. I know that baby isn't yours. A mom always knows this stuff. Now tell me why you're lyin'."

Wow, this woman was truly amazing. I was so relieved to get this out. "You're right. We had a test done and she isn't mine. But mom, she needs me. Stacy can't raise a kid on her own. As it stands, she's got one foot in a crack house. If I leave her, it won't do either one of 'em any good."

Mom leaned across the table and took my hands in hers. "Jaxon, I raised you to be a good man, a man that does the right thing. This is not the right thing for you. You can't do this for them. You have to live your life for you, son. You love Loralei, don't you?"

I squeezed mom's hands in mine. "Mom, I love her more than anything. She's what I want and what I see when I imagine my future."

About the time those words came out my mouth, Stacy came through the doorway. "So, you're just gonna leave us? Just like that. Is that little country bitch really what you want? You'd give up a life with me and Jaz for *her*?" The way she referred to Loralei made my stomach churn.

I let go of mom's hands and stood up from the table. I never broke eye contact with Stacy. I slowly walked to where she was standing. "I didn't give up our life together, Stacy that was you. That little girl is not mine. We both know who her father is. Maybe you should give him a call and see if he'll take you in. I can't be your husband when I am in love with someone else."

Stacy started sobbing, grabbing at my shirt, begging, "Please don't do this, Jaxon. Please don't leave us. I need you. God, how I need you. I can't raise her by myself. You know Ratz won't be there for us. I don't have anyone but you."

I tore her hands away from my shirt. "Stacy, you don't have me. I am not yours. I don't love you. Now get your hands off of me. And it sounds to me like you know damn well who her dad is. I'm sure you knew it the whole fucking time."

Stacy stepped back from me. "Well, she sure as hell wasn't yours. You weren't even man enough to do that. Let's see how much your little country bitch loves you when you can't even give her a baby." Her true colors were finally showing. I put my hand on her shoulder and gently pushed her aside, so I could step through the door.

Stacy started sobbing again. "What the fuck am I supposed to do Jaxon? Where am I supposed to go? I can't go home. You know how my mom treated me after rehab." She had a point. Her mom had written her off when she found out she was using drugs. But I had lost all sympathy toward her. Of course I wanted Jaz to be taken care of, but she was her responsibility. And she was going to have to grow up and take care of her.

"I don't know what you're gonna do, Stacy, but you're gonna have to figure your own shit out. Get a job. Get on welfare. Do whatever you have to do to make a home for Jaz. She deserves that. She deserves a good childhood, Stacy. And you're the one who is gonna have to provide that for her."

I went upstairs and started packing my shit. I was ready to get back to Missouri and back to Loralei Harper...my future.

Cade

Finally, I got into the great room early, she was standing at the counter making herself a plate of fruit. I walked up behind her, got as close to her as I could, and whispered in her ear, "Mornin' hon."

Her breath hitched, and I could tell she was happy to have me so close.

I chuckled, "Well, good to know I haven't lost my touch. It's been too long."

I was still leaning into her and whispering in her ear. I loved to watch her breathing speed up when I was close to her. She was wearing blue jeans, a black faded Hank Jr. t-shirt, and her old brown work boots. I reached up and rubbed my hand down her arm. Then I turned her to where she was facing me. Her eyes were closed, and her lips were parted. I could tell she was really concentrating on something.

How could I not use this opportunity to my advantage? I leaned in and kissed her hard. I slammed my tongue into her mouth, pushed her up against the counter, settled myself between her legs, and before I knew it she had her legs wrapped around my waist, and I had her sitting on the counter. The kiss was intense, and it wasn't slowin' down. She was meeting my tongue with every stroke. She ran her hand up my chest, my neck, through my hair. I barely even noticed when my cowboy hat fell to the floor.

I reached down and unzipped her jeans. I slid my hand down the back of her jeans and cupped her ass. This ass had been fucking with my mind for weeks. Finally, I had it in my hands again. I wanted inside her so bad.

Just as I started to slide my hand down the front of her jeans, I heard, "What the fuck is going on in here?" I turned toward the door and saw him. That fucking asshat. He had on fucking fancy jeans, and a damn AC/DC t-shirt. His arms were covered in tattoos, and what the fuck was on his face? A damn ring? I didn't notice that when I saw him at the banquet. But it's not like I gave a shit about him that night. Before I could say anything he had me by the throat. He pushed me up against the wall.

I could hear Loralei yellin', "Jaxon, get off of him. What the hell are you doing?"

This shit wasn't working for me. I hit that bastard with all my power, right in the jaw. He fell back to the ground. His eyes looked fucking crazed. "What the fuck is wrong with you?" I growled at him.

He jumped up at me. "Why can't you stay the hell away from her? Haven't you done enough to us?"

He was coming at me again, when I heard Loralei say, "Us? There is no us, remember? What the hell are you doing here, Jaxon?"

He stopped and leaned closer like he was going to hit me. "Stay the fuck away from her, or the next time I'll kill you. Do. You. Fucking. Understand?"

I couldn't help but laugh at the bastard. "Hey, asshat. I don't know who taught you how to fight. But when you get knocked down, ya know, like I just did to you. That means you didn't win." I took a step toward him and whispered, "If you are here to hurt her again, I will fucking kill you. And the difference between you and me, boy, is I'm actually capable of it." I lunged a little at him, just to scare him. He didn't flinch, but I was pretty sure he about pissed his pants.

Loralei

What the hell just happened here? I was looking over at Cade up against the wall and Jaxon trying to pick himself up off the floor. Jaxon leaned over and said something to Cade. Then Cade lunged at Jaxon and shouted at him.

Cade made his way over to me. "You okay, hon?"

Was I? I didn't know what the hell was going on. One minute I was kissing Cade and trying hard not to think about Jaxon. The next minute, Jaxon was here pushing Cade up against the wall. I did what I had wanted to do ever since he walked in...I ran over to Jaxon. "Are you okay? Did he hurt you?"

Jaxon was wiping the blood from his lip. "I'm fine. That fucking cowboy can't even punch like a man."

Cade walked over to me and leaned toward Jaxon. "Really, asshat? You wanna talk about being a man? I don't think you wanna have that fuckin' conversation with me."

Jaxon lunged at Cade again. I jumped in between them and felt this excruciating pain in my face. It didn't take me long to realize what had happened. Jaxon tried to hit Cade and punched me in the eye instead. I fell back to the ground. *Holy hell,* that man could hit. I felt like I had been hit by a mack-truck. Cade jumped to catch me, but he wasn't quite fast enough. My body hit the floor...hard. Cade was on the ground beside me, trying to help me set up. Jaxon came over and kneeled in front of me. He tried to take my hand.

Cade said, "You get your fucking hands off of her, asshat." Cade was pissed. "Lor, are you okay?" His hand automatically shot to my stomach. "Everything okay, hon?" I looked up and saw Jaxon staring at Cade's hand. The realization hit him. It was written all over his face.

He raised an eyebrow at me. "You're pregnant?"

I wanted to jump up and hug him and tell him I was pregnant. Tell him he was going to be a daddy to our child. But I couldn't do that, because I knew it might be Cade's. And I didn't want to be the reason why Jaxon left his family. I couldn't take him away from his daughter, especially without knowing if my baby was his.

Cade was holding me up and had his arms around me. I couldn't look Jaxon in the eye. I looked down at my legs stretched out in front of me on the ground. "Yes. I am, Jaxon."

Chapter 15

Loralei

The look on Jaxon's face broke my heart. He looked completely defeated. His eyes went blank. It was like he was looking right through me, as he stared at Cade's hand on my stomach.

Jaxon stepped back. "I'm sorry, Lor. I, uh, I shouldn't have come here. I won't do anything else to hurt you." He turned around and walked outside.

Cade was still holding me up with his hand placed protectively over my stomach. He helped me stand up and steady myself. "I'm sorry you had to witness that, hon'. But he deserved everything I gave him. We're havin' a baby. Now that he knows that, we can start plannin' our future." Cade leaned in to kiss me, and I placed both of my hands on his chest and pushed him away. I felt horrible, but I had to be honest with him.

"Cade, I don't know what the hell was happening when Jaxon got here, but I don't have feelings for you. If this baby is yours, we will raise it. I want you to be a part of the baby's life. But I don't see a future with you."

Cade cupped my face in his hands. "But hon, that kiss. You kissed me back. I know you feel what I feel when I kiss you." He leaned toward me and pressed his lips to mine again.

I couldn't do it. I couldn't let him kiss me again. "Stop. When you were kissing me, all I could think about was him. It's always been him. I love him, Cade."

He was still holding my face in his hands. "I don't fuckin' believe you." Then he smashed his lips into mine and pushed me up against the counter. He lifted me up onto the counter and worked his way in between my legs. I wasn't kissing him back, I was pushing him with all my strength.

I finally broke away from his lips. "Cade, no. Don't do this. I don't want this with you. Please, stop."

He pulled his mouth from mine and started kissing a trail down my neck. All the while I was pushing his chest and trying to get him off of me. "You feel it, Lor. I know you fuckin' feel it," he said as he continued down my chest.

The next thing I knew Cade was flying across the room.

Jaxon was screaming, "Get the fuck off of her. What the hell is wrong with you?" Jaxon jumped onto Cade, who was lying on the floor trying to catch his breath. Jaxon laid into him, hitting him over and over and over again. Cade didn't hit him back. He just took it all. His eyes met my mine, and I could see the sadness. He really had feelings for me, and it was killing me to see him hurt like that.

"Jaxon, stop! Let him go."

Jaxon dropped Cade's collar and let him fall to the ground. "If you ever lay another hand on her, I promise you, you will not live to see another goddamn day." He climbed off of him and started toward me.

He leaned in and placed his hand on my cheek. "Are you okay, Lor? Did he hurt you?" He was being so gentle with me, after just beating the shit out of Cade. I loved this man so much. When I looked at him I saw my future. I wished it was that easy. I wished that we could just forget all about Stacy and Jaz. But we just couldn't do that.

"Babe, are you okay? Is the baby okay?" he asked when I didn't answer him.

"Yeah, Jaxon, I'm fine. He wouldn't hurt me."

Jaxon dropped his hand from my cheek and crossed his arms in front of his chest.

I looked him in the eye. "I think we need to talk."

He nodded in agreement and I said, "I need to talk to Cade for a minute. I'll meet you at my house, okay?" He agreed and started out to his motorcycle.

I walked over to Cade, who had sat up and was leaning against the wall. His head was up against the wall, and he was rubbing his hand over his cheek. It looked like he was trying to rub the pain away.

I scooted down the wall and sat down next to him. "Why didn't you fight him, Cade? Why'd you let him hurt you?"

He gave me that belly laugh, "I got no reason to kick his ass, Lor. He won fair and square. You love him. You never loved me. I shouldn't have been touching ya like that. Kissin' ya that way. The man had every right to kick my ass."

I reached down and grabbed his right hand and laced my fingers through his. "Cade, you have been a great experience for me."

He laughed again, "An experience, huh, hon?"

I smiled at him. "Yes, sir. You have been quite the experience. You were what I needed. You showed me what I want my future to be."

"Lor, if that baby in your belly is mine, I ain't goin' away. I will take care of it and its momma."

I placed my hand on his cheek. "Cade, if this baby is yours, I will not keep you away from it. I want you to have a relationship with him or her."

"Her, it's definitely a her." He said with a smirk on his face. "I always wanted a little cowgirl of my own. Lor, I will always be here for you and the baby. Even if it's not mine. I'm just sorry you don't get those damn butterflies in your belly for me. I saw the way you looked at him. He's your future. As much as it's killing me. Deep down inside, really deep down, because you know I hate that asshat."

I chuckled at him, and he said, "You belong together. Do whatever you need to do to make that happen. Just know that I will be here for that baby, no matter what. Even if she ain't mine. I won't let him hurt you ever again. You understand me, Lor?"

I removed my hand from his cheek and placed it in his. "I understand you, Cade. And I wish things were different. I wish...I just want you to be happy. Promise me, okay?"

"Hon', you can't ask me to make a promise like that right now while you're breakin' my heart. Damn, woman, you're cold." He laughed that big belly laugh at me and started to stand up. He was a little unsteady on his feet, but he got up and wiped the blood from his lip. He started toward his truck. "I'm gonna need a day or two to lick my wounds. If ya need me, ya know where to find me, okay?"

I answered as we were walking outside, "Yes, sir, I sure do. And Cade, thanks for..."

He finished my sentence, "The most amazing sex of your life? You're welcome, hon." And there was that big belly laugh again, but it was followed by a really sad smile. It was killing me to hurt him like this, but I had to be with Jaxon. He was my future. I had made a promise to Declan, and I intended to keep it.

<u>Jaxon</u>

As I headed to Lor's house, I couldn't stop thinking about the baby. She was gonna have a baby. I knew it wasn't mine. She was having *his* baby. I loved her. How was I going to handle this? I didn't know the answer to that, but I did know that I loved that woman more than anything in this world. She was my future, and like hell if I would let that fucking cowboy ruin it for me. I would love that baby, just like I loved the twins. We would be a family no matter what, if she would have me.

I had to fix this. This whole thing was my fault. How could I have been so fucking stupid? If I had been honest with her from the beginning, none of this would have happened. She never would've met that fucking cowboy. We would be together now. She wouldn't be pregnant though, and I would never take that away from her.

I pulled down the drive and parked in front of her house. It felt like home, like I belonged here. I wanted that perfect postcard family life. I wanted that with Lor. I had to fucking fix this. I just had to.

I walked up and sat down on the front porch in one of the white rocking chairs. I decided to sit there and think about what I was going to say to Lor. I had been practicing what I would say ever since I left Richmond, but things had changed. The baby was a new hurdle, but not really. I wouldn't treat it like anything other than mine. The same way I planned to treat the twins. I wanted this family, and right now all I could do was wait for Lor to get here.

Loralei

On the short drive to my house all I could think about was the look on Jaxon's face when he realized I was pregnant. He didn't look like a guy who thought he was going to be a dad. He looked like a guy who had been sucker punched. We hadn't used protection when we had sex. I really thought he would be happy when he found out. Maybe I was just delusional. I didn't know. We had to talk this out. We had to do what was best for all of us...and that included his family back in Richmond.

What made him come here? Did he miss me? Did he realize he couldn't live without me? Or did he think we needed a real goodbye? I didn't know, but I couldn't wait to find out.

I pulled up and parked next to Jaxon's bike. I was hesitant to go to him. I didn't know why. I wanted him with everything in me. But I think I was scared. What if he wasn't here because he loved me?

Oh my God, Loralei Harper, get your ass out of the jeep and go talk to that man.

I got out of the jeep and started walking toward the front porch. His gaze met mine, and I couldn't look away. Those beautiful brown eyes with the golden flecks were mesmerizing. I took a seat in the rocking chair facing him. We both started talking at the same time.

He said, "Lor, let me explain, please?" He took my hands in his and started rubbing circles with his thumbs on my palms. "I never should've left here. Never. I don't know what the hell came over me. I couldn't believe that Stacy told you Jaz wasn't mine and you still wanted me to leave."

I couldn't believe those words came from his mouth. I pulled my hands away from his and jumped out of my chair. "What the hell do you mean, she isn't yours? Stacy told me the test came back and you were the dad."

He stood up, stepped toward me, and grabbed my hands again. "She is a lying bitch, Loralei. Jaz isn't mine. I thought you wanted me to be with them. I couldn't understand why, but I thought that was why you were telling me to leave. Stacy and I tried for years to have a baby and it never happened. We don't need the DNA test. Your baby can't be mine. But I will raise it like it is."

This was all too much for me. I fell back in the rocking chair. Jaxon was still holding my hands and he dropped to his knees in front of me. I said, "So, this baby can't be yours? Are you sure?"

Jaxon looked down to the ground. After a long silence he looked up at me with a tear in his eye. "You have no idea how much I want that baby to be mine. But no, it's *his*."

Both of my hands immediately flew to my belly. I was having Cade's baby. But I loved Jaxon. I couldn't be with Cade. He said he understood, but would he really, after the baby came. Cade was going to be a part of our lives forever. Could I handle that? I didn't know the answer to that yet.

"I still want the test Jaxon. I want to know for sure. I can have it in a couple of weeks. What is happening with Stacy and Jaz?"

He stood up and took a seat in the rocking chair he had been sitting in. "She signed the divorce papers. My mom is letting her stay there until she gets on her feet. My mom fell in love with Jaz, so no matter how she feels about Stacy, she will make sure that little girl is taken care of. Stacy is out of my life Lor, and Jaz is not my daughter. I want that future that we talked about. I want us to grow old together. Will you have me? Can we please try again?"

I wanted that more than anything. But I was having another man's baby? I didn't know what that would do to Jaxon and I. Jaxon may have said it wouldn't change anything, but that would all change when Cade started hanging around all the time to be with the baby.

"Jaxon, we have been through so much. I just...I just don't know. I want to be with you, but I'm so scared that some other secret will come out. Is there anything else I need to know? Please don't tell me you have another wife somewhere else, or that you're wanted by the law. I really don't think I could handle it!" He hugged me and we laughed together. It felt so good being in his arms. I had missed him so much.

Chapter 16

Loralei

Jaxon and I decided it would be best for him to stay with Uncle Jake until we could figure things out. We loved each other and wanted to spend our future together. Now we needed to figure out how to do that.

I told him we needed to sit the kids down and talk to them about what was going on. We didn't need to mention the baby yet, but we needed to let them know that Jaxon was back and here to stay. I didn't want them to be surprised when they saw him around the farm. And I hoped to be spending time with him, lots of time, and I didn't want that to upset them.

We decided Jaxon should come over for dinner, so we could have this conversation with the kids. Why was I so nervous? This was crazy. This part shouldn't be so hard...should it? The kids loved Jaxon. But they knew how hurt I had been over the past few weeks. They could tell how much I missed him and I knew they missed him too.

When Jaxon got there and walked up to the door, my heart melted. He was the most beautiful man I had ever seen. That shaggy brown hair, those beautiful brown eyes with the golden flecks, he was wearing black jeans, boots, and a button-up white dress shirt. He had the sleeves rolled up to showcase his tattoos. When our eyes met, neither one of us could look away. It was like an electric current was pulling us toward each other. He opened the screen door and stepped inside. I touched his cheek, and he did the same to me.

"I missed you, Lor. I can't stand to be away from you. Even just for the night. Did you miss me, too?"

I was lost in his eyes. "I missed you so much, Jaxon."

He leaned in to kiss me, but as soon as his lips touched mine, we heard voices. "Jaxon!" The twins crashed into him. They threw their arms around him and Sammy said, "You're back. Are you really back? You won't leave again, right?"

Jaxon looked up at me. "I'm here for as long as your mom will have me, little man. And I missed you guys too." The kids wouldn't let go of him and Jaxon didn't seem to want to let them go either.

We finally pried the kids off of him and walked into the kitchen. The kids sat down at the table and Jaxon said, "Need any help, babe?" I loved hearing him call me that. I had missed that so much.

"No, I think I can put the pizza and salad on the table." He laughed and sat down with the kids. We enjoyed the meal so much. It took me back to the last time we had all sat at this same table and ate pizza. Back before everything changed. Before I learned about Stacy and Jaz. Before Cade. Cade, God, I felt so bad for hurting him. He was not the kinda guy to have feelings for someone, but he definitely had feelings for me.

The baby. His baby? In my mind and my heart, it was Jaxon's baby. But my brain understood that it could be Cade's. Cade was a good guy and he would love this baby more than anything. I could see that in his eyes every time he had mentioned *her.* He thought the baby was a girl, his little cowgirl. We needed this test. I had to know.

When we finished eating, Jaxon got up and helped Mags clear the dishes. She was so happy he was back. She hadn't smiled this much in weeks. That made my heart smile. They loaded the dishwasher, and Sammy and I walked into the living room and sat down on the couch.

He snuggled up beside me and said, "Mommy, I missed Jaxon so much. Is he gonna stay this time? He's not gonna leave us again, is he?" He put his little hand on my cheek and pulled my head down toward him, and whispered, "He loves us, right Mommy? Like we love him."

I felt a hand on my shoulder. Jaxon reached over and picked Sammy up. Pulling him into his arms, he said, "Little man, I never stopped loving you. Not for a minute. I love you, Mags, and your Mommy more than anything. I'm not going anywhere, okay?"

Sammy nodded and grabbed Jaxon around the neck in a big ole bear hug. Jaxon was looking down at me with the biggest smile on his face. Mags walked in and sat down by me on the couch. She was smiling too. Everyone was so happy. We needed this to last. We all deserved to be happy.

Jaxon

After dinner at Lor's place, we kissed goodbye. It was really gentle and sweet. We were trying to get back to where we had been. As much as I wanted to tear her clothes off and carry her upstairs caveman-style, I couldn't do that. We had things to work through first. I called her the next morning and asked her out that night. I wanted to do something special with her. She accepted, and I told her I would pick her up at seven o'clock.

I was so damn nervous all day. This shit was killing me. I couldn't stand being that close to her, but not being able to be with her. I decided I would go down to the barn and help Uncle Jake out a little bit. It never entered my mind that the fucking cowboy would be doing the same thing. When I got around to the side of the barn, there he was. That cocky asshole. The man didn't walk, he strutted. It fucking killed me that I pushed Lor toward him.

I hollered at Uncle Jake, "Need some help?" Cade's eyes locked with mine. Neither one of us was gonna back down.

Uncle Jake walked over toward me. "Don't stir anything up, Jaxon. He's helping us out. We don't need any shit here."

I broke the eye contact. I looked down at Uncle Jake. "No problem. I think I'll just head back to the house." I couldn't work with him. I decided to just go back the house and wait until I could pick Lor up. I had to hear her voice, so I decided to call her.

"Hi, Jaxon."

"Hi, babe. What are you wearing?" I loved to ask her that, it always made her laugh.

She giggled, "A smile?"

God, I loved that woman. "I miss ya. God, I really miss ya. Are the kids home?" I knew they were probably at school, but I needed to make sure.

"They're at school, why?"

"Can I come over? Please? I really need to see you." I was almost pleading, I needed to see her.

"Uh, sure. I've been cleaning house, so I'm kinda stinky."

"That's perfect. I'll be there soon." Thank God she was letting me come over. I started my bike up and headed to her house.

I couldn't get parked and inside the house quick enough. When I made it to the door, she was standing there, waiting for me. She had shorts on and was wearing my blue Elvis t-shirt. She had it tied up in a knot on the side. I wondered where that shirt had gone. She looked so hot! I guess what they said about pregnant women was true. She was glowing. Even standing in front of me all sweaty with her hair pulled up in a messy bun, she looked perfect. And I wanted her so bad.

I wouldn't attack her. I couldn't do that to her. I had to go slow after what I had pulled. She opened the screen door and just about knocked me over. She jumped up into my arms, wrapped her legs around my waist, and she made me fall up against the wall. She wanted me.

Her eyes were locked with mine, and she had this sexy smirk on her face. "Are you gonna kiss me or not?"

That was all it took. I smashed my lips to hers. I turned us around and pushed her up against the wall. I couldn't control myself. I wanted her too bad. We were kissing each other so hard. She was rubbing my chest and pulling on my jeans.

She whispered, "Inside, now." I started to unzip my jeans, she shuddered. She looked horrified, "Oh my God, no, inside the house, now. You damn pervert."

I laughed at her and carried her upstairs to her bedroom, gently laying her down on the bed.

"Are you sure, Lor? We don't have to do this." I really didn't want to push her into anything, but she had just about attacked me on the porch. She pulled her shirt over her head, took off her bra, and started to slide her shorts down.

"I want you, Jaxon. I've missed you so much. Please, make love to me."

I pulled my shirt off and took my jeans off. I was standing in front of her in my boxers. She stood up and stepped toward me. "Let me, please?" I nodded and she kneeled in front of me. She pulled my boxers down. When her breath hit my piercing, I couldn't think. I needed this...I needed her. This was beyond physical. This was my heart, my soul, my everything. They all resided in this beautiful woman, who no matter what happened, would do everything she could to make me happy.

She looked up at me through those long eyelashes. "I've never done this before Jaxon. Tell me if I do it wrong, okay?" She was worried about doing something wrong after everything I had done to her?

"You are amazing, Lor. Nothing you do could be wrong." When I said that, she licked the tip of my erection around my piercing and I almost collapsed to the ground. I was literally shaking. She felt so good. When she sucked the tip into her mouth and flicked my piercing, I grabbed her hair. I really tried to be gentle, but I couldn't do it. I tugged and pushed further into her mouth. I went a little too far and she gagged. "Shit, I'm sorry, Lor." She looked up at me and sucked in my entire length. She was using her hand around the base and pulling and sucking and I was so close. She didn't stop, she sped up. I saw stars as I came so damn hard.

She stood up and kissed me. "Did I do okay?" She asked with a giggle. I pushed her back onto the bed and settled between her legs.

"Yeah, babe...you did really okay." I nipped on one nipple, while I massaged the other with my fingers. She was arching her back and she had her hands in my hair. I kissed a trail between her breasts. When I got to her belly, I gently kissed it and caressed it. I looked up into her eyes and she was smiling at me.

"I know the baby is yours Jaxon. In my heart I know it." I couldn't think about it right now. I couldn't get my hopes up, but that would make me the happiest fucking man alive.

I sat up on my knees and started to pull her panties down. She took a deep breath. "You, okay?" I asked. She gave me that look that I had missed so much. The look that said I love you and I trust you.

Then she said, "I'm wonderful, Jaxon. Really, really wonderful."

I finished pulling her panties off and threw them onto the floor. I crawled up her body, placing light kisses all the way up to her lips.

When I got to her lips, I kissed her, "I'm gonna love you gentle, okay?"

She nodded and I started to press into her. Our eyes were locked. Those beautiful brown eyes were melting my heart. I moved very slowly. I was making love to her. This wasn't sex...this was love. We both needed this. We made love all afternoon. So sweet and gentle. Both of us so happy. I never wanted the afternoon to end.

Loralei

I was so happy after our afternoon together. I couldn't wait for Jaxon to pick me up for our date tonight. I took a shower and put on some jeans and a white lacey blouse. I left my hair down and was ready to go, when I heard a knock at the door.

"What are you doing here?" I asked Eric, who was standing at my door.

"I need to talk to you, Lor. I've got some apologizing to do."

I motioned for him to come in and he took a seat on the couch. I walked over and sat down on the opposite side of the couch. Eric was looking down at his boots and wringing his hands.

"I'm so sorry, Lor. I'm so damn sorry for everything." He said with a tear streaming down his cheek.

I reached over and placed my hand on his arm. I had known Eric my whole life. He had always been like a brother to me. I couldn't stand to see him hurting.

"What's going on, Eric? What are you sorry for?"

He looked up at me and said, "I'm sorry for the way I treated Jaxon. Emma told me he was back in town. I just want you to know how wrong I was to butt into your life like that. You are one of the smartest, strongest women I know. So if you say he's good enough for you, then by God he is. I shouldn't have said a damn word about him."

"What else is going on, Eric? It has to be more than that." I asked as I brushed a tear from his cheek.

He was sobbing as he said, "I'm so sorry for that night, Lor. I'm so sorry for making ya'll come back and get me. I'm so sorry for being drunk and gettin' my best friend killed. My best friend, Lor." I leaned over and hugged him, crying right along with him.

"Dec was like my family. And ya'll were so happy and I ruined your happiness. Lor, I tried so damn hard to be like a father to the twins. I tried to make up for the horrible pain I caused ya'll, but I could never do enough. I could never fix what I did."

"Eric, it was an accident. It was just a terrible accident. If anyone is to blame, it's me. I was driving, not you." We were both sobbing and holding each other.

We let go and Eric said, "Lor, I never told you this. I couldn't bring myself to do it. Right after the accident, I pulled Dec out of the truck. He was still alive, Lor. He said something to me. He had me make a promise and I've screwed it up, so bad."

"What? He was alive? Why didn't you tell me? Why didn't you say anything to me, Eric? What did he say?" I was pleading.

"He asked me to take care of you and keep you safe. He asked me to make sure you found someone to love. He asked me to make sure you weren't sad for him. Dec knew he wasn't gonna make it, Lor. He knew what was happening. I promised him. And the way I treated you over Jaxon, I am ashamed. You deserve to be happy. That's what Declan wanted."

"I loved him with everything I had, Eric. He was my whole life and those babies were the only things that kept me going after the accident. Accidents happen. It wasn't your fault, or mine. It was just life. He wasn't meant to live past seventeen. I haven't lived in so many years, Eric. I have been so lonely. And I've found someone who makes me happy and makes the kids happy. I love him, Eric."

Eric grabbed my hand in his and said, "That's why I'm here, Lor. I wanted to tell you I was an asshole. If he makes you happy, that's all that matters. I love you and I love the kids. I will always be here for all of you."

"Eric, you and Emma are my family and you always will be."

"Dec wanted you to be happy, Lor. You do what you need to do to make sure you are. I will support you always. But if he hurts you again, I will have to kick his ass." We laughed together, through our tears.

After that we sat for a long time sharing some of our favorite Declan memories. It was sad and happy at the same time. We both loved him so much. We needed this.

With everything that had just happened, I forgot all about my date with Jaxon, until I heard a knock at the door. I answered it and Jaxon wrapped me in his arms. Eric walked up behind us and Jaxon let go of me and stepped back.

Eric reached his hand out to Jaxon and said, "I was an asshole. Can we try to forget it or forgive?"

Jaxon looked at me and then back at Eric. He shook his hand. "I know you were just looking out for her. I just want you to know, I love her and the kids. I'm not going anywhere."

Eric looked at me and said, "I know ya'll love each other. I'm happy that you make her happy." He leaned toward Jaxon and whispered, "But if you ever hurt her again, they'll never find your body." He slapped Jaxon on the back, gave me a hug, and said his goodbyes.

Jaxon said, "Well, that was interesting."

"We needed to work some stuff out. This was never about you, Jaxon. He had a lot of guilt about Declan. We talked it out and I think he's okay now."

"I'm glad ya'll talked about Declan. I think you both needed that."

I wrapped my arms around him and said, "I love you, Jaxon. Thank you for loving me." I leaned up and kissed him before we headed out to the truck.

He drove Uncle Jake's truck since we were going out to the pond. He held my hand all the way there. I was sitting right next to him, but I felt like I couldn't get close enough. I leaned in and kissed his neck.

"Now, don't start that, or we won't make it to the pond." He gave me a sexy grin.

I started to scoot away. "Yes, sir."

He grabbed my leg and pulled me back next to him. "I didn't tell you to move, I just said stop kissing me."

When we got to the pond he got out of the truck. "Wait here a sec, I have a little surprise planned."

He walked around toward the back of the truck. I felt him jump up in the truck bed. I turned to watch him. "You just keep those pretty little eyes looking straight ahead. What part of surprise did you not understand?"

I laughed and turned back around.

I felt him jump out of the truck and then he was opening the truck door. He extended his hand out to me. "Your surprise is ready."

I put my hand in his and he grabbed me in a big hug. We started back to the back of the truck. He jumped up and put his arms out to pull me up. He had laid tons of quilts and pillows all over the back of the truck. He had lit candles and placed them up on the roof of the cab of the truck. Those with the moonlight were all the lighting we needed. He sat down and had me sit down beside him. "Your mom packed dinner for us. She really wanted to help me out." He opened up a box my mom had given him. She had made my favorite meal...fried chicken, potato salad, and her delicious homemade rolls. She had also packed diet coke...my go-to drink.

"Have I told you lately, how much I love your Mom?" Jaxon asked as he was getting out the plates and silverware.

"She is pretty awesome. If it wasn't for her, this might not have happened. If she hadn't tricked me into going into town with you that Sunday, we might not have fallen in love."

He stopped what he was doing and grabbed my hands in his.

"I thank your mom for pushing you that day, but I wouldn't have been able to stay away from you. The minute I saw you out in the field, I knew I wanted you. It was like they write about in those romance novels...it was like a current zapping through me. I just felt like...well, it was you. You were what I had been waiting for. And, honestly, it scared the hell out of me."

I couldn't stop giggling, these pregnancy hormones had my mood all over the place.

"You know how I feel about you laughing at me," he said, and I broke out into full-blown laughter.

He looked so confused, he had his eyebrow raised at me. "What is so damn funny? I just laid everything out for you and you're cracking up."

I tried so hard to stop laughing. I gained enough composure to say, "You just told me you read romance novels." And then the laughter started again. Was he blushing? It sure looked like he was.

"Where do you think I learn all those amazing things that I do to you? I didn't hear you complaining about it earlier today."

Well, that changed everything. My laughter stopped and I caught his gaze. His eyes were smoldering.

I licked my lips. "Maybe we can eat *later*?" He nodded and kissed me. We made love, and it was amazing. I was so glad that he read romance novels.

Chapter 17

Cade

I'm not gonna lie, the past two weeks had been torture. Seeing her with him, knowing she was pregnant with my baby. The baby I had dreamed about for years. The baby inside the woman that I had fallen so damn hard for. It was fucking tearing me up inside. And there wasn't a damn thing I could do about it. He had won. She had always been his. I was just here. I was the distraction she needed to realize how much she loved the asshat.

I had stayed at Harper Farms, but I was spendin' most of my time out workin'. I had ventured into town a couple of times. Even spent a little time gettin' to know some lovely ladies at the tavern in town. I had met this chick named Mare, yeah, just like a horse. *Damn she was hot.* Right then and there, she asked me to take her up against the wall in the back of the bar. I couldn't fuckin' do it...but damn she was temptin'.

Lor was havin' the test done tomorrow and they had said we would know in a couple of days. I wanted that baby to be mine more than anything in this world. I had always dreamed about having a family. A sweet little toe-head girl following me around on the ranch. Teaching her everything I knew about horses and workin' the farm. I wanted that, damn I wanted that. And I wanted it with Lor. I knew that wasn't happenin', but a man could dream, right?

Loralei

Tomorrow was the day. It was the day that I would have the test to find out if the baby I was carrying was Jaxon's. Jaxon and I had been spending all of our time together since the date at the pond.

We were living as a family, mostly. Jaxon wasn't spending the night, but he was eating dinner with us almost every night.

While Cade was here, we agreed that it would be better if he didn't work on the farm. So he would come by in the morning and tell the kids good morning before they went to school. Some days we would have lunch together at my house or Jake's.

I was spending a lot of time trying to avoid Cade. I didn't want to see him, until I knew if he was the father. We had some awkward run-ins when Jaxon came to visit me in my office, but we had survived.

I was out in the field, checking out the new cattle we had received, when I saw him. Cade was walking right toward me. "Hey, hon. How ya feeling?" He placed his hand on my upper arm.

"I'm feelin' real good. No morning sickness or anything. I had it so bad with the twins. I was pretty worried about it this time, but so far, so good."

He looked down at his boots while he was kicking the dirt around. "Uh, can I go with ya for the test tomorrow?"

That really surprised me. "You really don't need to Cade. Jax...uh, I mean, I won't be alone."

He looked up and his eyes met mine. He looked so sad. "I know he'll be with ya. I just kinda hoped I could be there too."

I couldn't really tell him no, he had every right to be there. "Sure, if you want to be there, I don't have a problem with it. My appointment is at two o'clock. Do you wanna meet us at the clinic in town?"

He gave me a little sideways smile. "Yeah, hon, that would be great. Thanks."

Jaxon

This morning I had gotten up and gone to Lor's to help her see the kids off to school, like I had been doing for the past couple of weeks. I hadn't spent the night yet, but Lor and I had decided it would be best to not do that for awhile. We needed the kids to be used to me being there for a bit longer.

"Your appointment is at two o'clock, right babe?" I asked Lor as she walked into the living room and sat down on the couch beside me.

"About that, are you sure you wanna go with me? You really don't have to."

"How could you ask me that? After the past couple of weeks. I thought we were in this together. I thought you realized how much you mean to me? I will always be here for you and the baby, no matter what."

"We are in this together, but Cade asked me yesterday if he could go with me."

"And you don't want me to go, but you want him to take you? Seriously?" I couldn't believe she didn't want me there. It hit me hard. I thought we were in this together. Maybe she was having second thoughts about me and the type of father I could be to the baby. Maybe she wanted Cade.

"No, Jaxon. That's not what I'm saying at all. Of course, I want you there with me. I just know it will be awkward for both of you to be there. And honestly, it's just a test. A little needle...not a big deal."

"I'm going to be there with you. If *he* is there, I won't have a problem with it. He might though."

"He knows you'll be there. He will meet us at the clinic." She said this as she stood up and started to walk away.

I grabbed her around the waist and pulled her onto my lap. "Do you have to work today? Or can you stay in with me until it's time for the appointment?"

She smiled that beautiful smile. "That's the beauty of being the boss. I don't have to work if something better comes up." She shifted around on my lap.

"Something better is definitely coming up, babe." We spent the rest of the morning making out like teenagers on the couch. It was one of the best mornings of my life.

Loralei

Jaxon and I made it to the clinic a little before two o'clock. Cade was waiting for us in the parking lot. We got out of the jeep and he walked over toward us. He never said a word, just tipped his hat, and gestured for us to walk ahead of him. Needless to say, it was a little awkward walking into the clinic with Jaxon and Cade. I believe it was pretty clear to everyone, why I was there. Most women didn't bring two guys with them to see their OB/GYN.

The appointment went by without incident. Jaxon and Cade shared a few intense stare downs, but basically it all went pretty well.

The doctor told me we should have the results in about three days. These were going to be the longest three days of my life...

Three days later

My phone was ringing off the wall. I ran to answer it, a little out of breath, "Uh, hello."

It was the nurse from the clinic. "Ms. Harper, we have the results of your test. We don't normally do this over the phone. Can you come in and pick them up?"

Really? Did she have to ask? "Of course, I'm on my way."

The kids were already off to school, so I jumped in the jeep and headed to the clinic. I decided to do this alone. I didn't need Jaxon or Cade with me. I needed to find this out on my own. It would be difficult, but I needed to tell the father myself.

I was almost sick by the time I got to the clinic. I hadn't had morning sickness the entire pregnancy, but right then I was so nauseous. I just knew I would puke before I could read the results. I went into the clinic and the nurse handed me a plain white envelope with BABY HARPER typed on the front of it.

I walked out to the jeep holding the envelope. I heard my cell chirping and saw that Jaxon had been calling me. I couldn't talk to him right now. I had to see what the results said.
I opened the envelope and tried to read the results.

The first two pages were a bunch of graphs and numbers. The grid was titled: "A" and "B". I read on and realized that Jaxon was "A" and Cade was "B". Thank God there was a title on the second page that spelled that out. I got to the last page and it said: Paternity Verified, and that was followed by a letter. I finally knew who the father was.

Cade

The past three days had about killed me. I couldn't eat, sleep, nothin'. Today should be the day that we find out. I just needed to know. I needed to get back to my life either way. I had been neglecting everything and that just wasn't somethin' I did.

Since my parents had died, that ranch was my life. Clay and I had been away for too long. If the baby was mine we were goin' to have to figure somethin' out. I didn't know how we were gonna do it, but I wouldn't be away from my kid.

When I heard the knock on the door, I about jumped outta my hide. I got up and headed for the door. When I opened it, I knew the question had been answered.

Jaxon

I had been trying to call Lor all morning. I couldn't understand why she was ignoring my calls. I was getting a little worried. Today was the day that we were supposed to get the results of the paternity test and I think we were both a little on edge.

I heard someone pull up outside. I went to the door and saw Lor's jeep. She got out and started toward me. Her eyes were all red and swollen. She had been crying, a lot. I ran to her. "Babe, what's wrong? Did you get the results?" She was sobbing. She put her arms around my waist and laid her head on my chest.

The crying was breaking my heart and it told me all I needed to hear. "We knew this was gonna happen, Lor. We knew it wasn't mine. It's okay. We are still going to be a family. We will handle of this together. Please stop crying." I put my hand on her chin and raised her head up to look at me.

She opened her eyes and met mine. "That was the hardest thing I've ever done."

She was killing me. I couldn't stand to see her hurting. "It's okay, babe."

She let out a little giggle, which was really weird because she still had tears streaming down her cheeks. "I had to tell Cade. I had to tell him...that the baby is yours. We're having a baby, Jaxon!" I was shocked. I couldn't speak. I stared at her. She put her hand on my cheek. "Did you hear me, baby? We're having a baby. We made a baby together. Jaxon, are you okay?"

I lost it. I had never been so happy in my life. I picked her up and pulled her into my chest. I swung us around in circles and prayed that this moment wasn't a dream.

Epilogue

Six Months later....

I loved days like today. Days spent with our family down by the pond. The kids were fishing. My and Declan's parents were there to help keep the kids in line. Jaxon and I were walking around the pond, holding hands, laughing, and enjoying each other.

It seemed like not too long ago, we didn't believe we would get to this point - the point where we were in love and about ready to have a baby together.

I never believed that I would find love again. After everything that happened with Cade and Stacy, I didn't think Jaxon and I would end up together. But it seemed like we were meant to be. Everything kinda brought us together. Destiny…maybe?

It was starting to get dark and my parents offered to take the kids home so Jaxon and I could spend some time together. The crickets were chirping their evening lullaby, and the fireflies were sparkling out across the pond. I couldn't think of a more romantic setting than this.

Jaxon spread an old blanket out on the bank. He sat down and easily pulled me onto his lap. "I am so fat. But you love me anyway, right?"

Jaxon laughed. "Baby, you aren't fat. You're having a baby. Our baby. My baby. That makes you the most beautiful woman in the world. Now, shut up and kiss me."

I did just that. We sat in each other's arms for a long time, just enjoying the beautiful evening.

All of a sudden, Jaxon started humming a very familiar Elvis song. I smiled as he started to sing *I Can't Help Falling In Love.*

While he was singing to me about how he couldn't help falling in love with me, I turned around in his arms. I had to see that sexy mouth while those words were escaping his lips.

He sang about how this was how we were supposed to be. Life had brought us together and no matter what we had done, it couldn't have been helped. We were made for each other, made to be together, and made to be the parents of this baby.

Jaxon sang about being a fool and moving too fast, but that he just couldn't help himself. His feelings were so strong, that it couldn't be avoided.

I placed soft kisses all along his jaw while he sang. He giggled when I made my way to his mouth. "How am I supposed to keep singing this sweet love song when you're attacking me with kisses."

I placed my hands on his shoulders and pressed him down into the blanket. "I guess you'll just have to stop singing then, won't ya?"

Very gently, but quickly, he turned me over on my back and started to kiss me. He placed light kisses on my cheeks, across my jaw, down my neck, and started to unbutton my shirt. I stopped him. "Um, no. Not right now. I want to go for a walk."

He looked up at me through those long dark eyelashes. "Excuse me? A walk? Now?"

I shook my head. "Yes, a walk. Now help me get my fat pregnant butt up off of this blanket."

He helped me up, and I went to my purse to get something out. I hid it in my pocket as we started walking around the pond. The moon was shining down on the pond, making it glisten. The stars were out. It was a beautiful, clear Missouri night. We were holding hands and slowly walking, not really heading anywhere, just enjoying the view.

When we got to the other side of the pond, I stopped. I turned toward Jaxon and he looked scared. "Everything okay, babe? Is it the baby?"

I hadn't realized it, but I guess was crying. "Jaxon, I never thought that I could love again. I never truly believed that I was meant to be anything more than a daughter, and a mother. I didn't even know I wanted you, until you showed up that day - my pierced, tattooed knight in shining armor."

He was smiling at me. He secretly loved it when I called him that. "You have taken your time with me. And I appreciate you so much for that. I love you Jaxon. Forever and always, I love you."

He leaned in and wiped the tears from my eyes. "I love you forever and always too, Loralei. There had always been something missing in my life. I just didn't know what it was, until I met you and the twins. We're having a baby together now. That's something I thought I would never be able to do. You have given me that, Lor. We are going to be the parents of three kids, crazy, huh?"

I really didn't think I could love him more than I already did, but that did it.

I dropped, slowly, I mean I was nine months pregnant, to the ground on one knee.

Jaxon dropped with me. "Babe, what's wrong?"

"Um, Jaxon, please stand up. I'm fine. Just give me a minute."

I reached into my pocket and pulled it out. I reached up and grabbed his hand. "Jaxon, I love you. I have a question to ask you. I was wondering...would you be interested in being my pierced, tattooed knight in shining armor for the rest of our lives?"

With those words, I pressed a shield charm into his hand. With the initials "J" and "L" engraved on it. "I thought that would be a good addition to my bracelet."

Jaxon pulled me to my feet. "Babe, don't you know by now. My answer to you is yes, it's always yes." He kissed me, a long, sweet, loving kiss that told me that everything was going to be okay. We were meant to be.

And that is how my destiny was changed forever.

Look for Cade's Story Coming Summer 2013

Destined to Succeed

Prologue

Cade – Six months ago

That was that. I wasn't the daddy. I was so damn sure that baby was mine. I was already picturing us on the ranch. Her ridin' horses and me teaching her how to be a real little cowgirl. Lor had shattered that dream when she knocked on the door that day.

I could tell she had been cryin'. Her eyes were all red and her cheeks were tear stained. I opened the door, and I just knew. I knew what she was about to tell me.

"Hon, it's okay. I can tell by the look on your face, what you're about to tell me. I'll be gettin' outta your hair, now." I started to turn and walk away. I couldn't help the tear that was streaming down my cheek. Damn, I wanted that baby to be mine. More than anything in this world. I knew I had lost her momma, but I was hopin'…well, it didn't matter what I was hopin'. It wasn't gonna happen now.

"Cade, I'm so sorry. I know how much you wanted it to be yours." Lor started to cry again.

"Hon, I know you're happy that it ain't mine, so quit your cryin' and go on home to asshat." I said with a chuckle. I was tryin' to tease her. To make her smile. And she did. She gave me a very small, sad smile. Then she turned and walked away. That was that.

Present

Goddamn, I was tired. It had been a hell of a day on the ranch. It was birthing season and we had the vet out all day. That was gonna cost a small fortune, but it was worth it when you saw those new calves and foals bein' brought into the world. I was sore. I was getting' too old for this shit. All I had been able to think about all day, was getting' home, takin' a shower, and crawling into bed.

When I walked around the front of my house, I saw Clay's truck parked out front. What the hell was he doin' at my place. He was screwin' up my plans.

I walked in the living room, hung my Stetson on the hat rack, and that's when I heard it. That fuckin' little bastard.

I flung the door to my room open. There he was. Screwing that little blonde hussy, Ana. What the fuck?

"Are you fuckin' kiddin' me, right now?" I hollered as I ran toward the bed.

"Get the fuck out man. Can't you see I'm a little busy?" He didn't even stop what he was doin' to say that. I grabbed him by the hair of the head and pulled him off of her.

"You. Get the hell out." Normally, I wouldn't have talked to a woman like that. But this chick was a pain in my ass. She was only screwin' Clay to get to me. She had tried everything in the world to hook up with me. It wasn't gonna happen. So, now she had moved onto him. I'm sure she was thinkin' about me the whole time. It was probably her idea to do it in my house, and my bed.

"Cade, baby." Ana said, biting her lip seductively. Then she curled her finger at me. "Join us?"

"You have got to be fuckin' kiddin' me…can you not take a hint. I will never screw you. You are not what I'm looking for." I was looking for a wife. Not some cheep ass floozy that just wanted to screw me to get my ranch.

"Ya'll have five minutes to get your shit and get the fuck out of my house. Tick-tock." I started toward the kitchen. I needed a beer. I grabbed a cold one out of the fridge and took a seat at the table.

All of a sudden I heard the front door slam and said a little thank you that they were gone. They weren't. I looked up and my cousin Cord was standing in the doorway.

"I need one of those too. Had a hell of a day," he said as he grabbed a beer out of the fridge and took a seat across from me at the table.

"You and your damn brother seem to think this is your house."

"Well, it kinda is, right? I mean you're like our brother. Mi casa, su casa?" He grinned and continued to suck down my beer.

"Why was your day so hard? Have a hard time pickin' out your tie?" I loved to give him a hard time. He was the only one in our family that had a job. Meaning, he didn't work on the ranch.

He was a lawyer. I always knew he would make somethin' of himself. Now, that brother of his was a whole other story.

"Asshole. I'm working on a big case. I'm going to have to go to Dallas next week. Why don't you come with me? It'd be good for you to get away from the ranch for a bit."

That actually sounded great. I hadn't had a vacation in years. This ranch meant everything to me. Since my parents had died, I had worked my ass off to make it the success it had become. But I trusted my farmhands. I knew they could handle it if I was gone for a few days.

"How long you gonna be gone?" I asked.

"Three days. Come on, it'll be like the old days. We used to have fun together, remember?"

"Yeah, that was before everyone in town knew you were a lawyer. That totally ruined your reputation." I laughed and threw my bottle cap at him.

Dallas would be fun. I needed to have some fun that didn't include visiting the local tavern and takin' home whatever girl I chose for the night. That shit was getting' real old, real quick. Loralei Harper made me realize I wanted a wife and a family. I wasn't gonna get that with one of those floozies down at the bar.

All of a sudden, I heard Clay screamin'. I ran out to the porch and saw what he was yelling about. I took off running toward the horse barn. What the hell was goin on? How did this happen? The farmhands were screamin' and runnin' out of the barn carrying the new babies we'd spent all day birthin'.

Clay, Cord, and I got to the barn about the time it happened. Flames were everywhere and then there was an explosion. I heard screamin' and cries of all of the animals that we couldn't get out. I tried to run in. I tried to save them. Cord and Clay pulled me back. I fell to my knees. Dear God, why, why? Were there people in there? Oh my God, where's Colt?

About the Author

Lisa M. Harley

I grew up in a small town in Missouri. Very similar to the fictional town I wrote about in Destined to Change. I moved to the big city right after I graduated. I work full-time and I am mom to a beautiful little girl.

I started writing in October 2012 when a Facebook group I am in had a prologue contest. I didn't win the contest, but everyone who read my prologue asked for more of my story. I decided I had to finish it and get these characters that were in my head out on paper. During the writing process it became clear that this was going to be more than one novel. It had to be a series. I have at least two more novels planned in the Destined Series. I also have an idea for a YA novel based on one of the characters in Destined to Change…hint, hint.

I am a really boring person, so this bio is really short. I love music and honestly couldn't have written this book without my Spotify playlist. I am kinda obsessed with frogs (not real ones) and office supplies are my downfall! I could spend my whole paycheck at the stationery store…boring, didn't I already say that? Lol

Also, I am slightly addicted to Facebook and Voxer. Please message me on either one…I would love to hear from all of you.

Contact Information:

Facebook: http://www.facebook.com/Destinedtochange

Twitter: http://twitter.com/Lharley77

Goodreads:

http://www.goodreads.com/book/show/17182066-destined-to-change

Spotify (Link to DTC playlist):

http://spotify.com/Destined to Change (Book 1 of the Destined Series)

Blogger: http://lisamharley.blogspot.com/

Printed in Great Britain
by Amazon.co.uk, Ltd.,
Marston Gate.